I0676201

COBALT SKIES

A MORE PERFECT UNION - BOOK TWO
PEGG THOMAS

Spinner of Yarns
PUBLISHING, LLC

S PINNER OF YARNS PUBLISHING

Sault Ste. Marie, Michigan

Copyright @2023 by Pegg Thomas
https://peggthomas.com/
Published in the United States of America
ISBN: 979-8-9850278-8-4
Cover Design using Midjourney.com
Cover Art Copyright by Spinner of Yarns Publishing

P RAISE FOR COBALT SKIES

Adventurous, poignant, and rich in historical detail, *Cobalt Skies* takes you across the Midwest with a cast of tough but lovable characters. Divided loyalties are tested during a tumultuous time of reconstruction and healing, but Hick and Cooter offer a perfect balance of wit and chivalry. If you enjoy a well-written tale of sacrifice, tenderness, and overcoming the odds, *Cobalt Skies* is for you.

~ Candice Sue Patterson
Author of *Saving Mrs. Roosevelt* and *The Keys to Gramercy Park*

Cobalt Skies brings together two lost souls seeking someplace where they can find peace, far from the memories of the war that tore apart the United States—and their hearts. You'll not want to miss Union veteran Sam "Hick" Hickman, Georgia native Mrs. Susannah Piper, and the odd collection of strays they attract along the journey. This engaging story will keep you turning pages long after bedtime so you can find out whether these polar opposites really will attract!

~ Jennifer Uhlarik
Author of *Sand Creek Serenade* and *Love's Fortress*

Pegg Thomas's novel *Colbalt Skies* is the first Christian western romance that grabbed my attention. The characters were courageous as they faced the rugged West during the after-years of the Civil War and the effects it had on their lives. With each turn of the page, the love that grew between Sam and Susannah warmed my heart and took my mind off the cold realities of the times we are living in. I read the book on a cold, rainy day, and it was a perfect pleasure to read.

~ Rita Gerlach
Author of *Wait Until Morning* and *The Holly and the Ivy*

Join Pegg's Newsletter

writing updates – sneak peeks – fiber arts updates – personal content
https://www.subscribepage.com/PeggThomas

This book is dedicated to the men and women who picked up the pieces of their lives after a terrible four-year war and worked to stitch a nation back together. A nation that would unite and fight again on distant shores to help others achieve freedom.

Writing is a solitary enterprise, and yet, it isn't. Without the love and support of my husband—my manager—my books would not be. He does so many little things that free up my time, make my load lighter, and sometimes just make me laugh. He's my encourager, supporter, and my best friend. And his words will forever spur me onward.

"That book ain't gonna write itself!"

CHAPTER 1

April 1867—near Kansas City, Missouri

IT WOULD TAKE MORE than an ornery bronc to stop Sam Hickman, but even he had to admit one of them could slow him down. And it had. Breath hissed between his teeth as he rubbed horse liniment into his aching hip. It was just aching, not broken, so he wouldn't be slowed down for long. A week or two. He winced when he rubbed directly on the bruise. Maybe three.

"Hello!"

Hick pulled up his britches with one hand and grabbed his Colt .45 off the top of his saddle with the other.

"You in there, Hick?"

Recognizing the voice, he relaxed and put the pistol back. "Come on in," he said as he secured his britches.

Big Bill Marlin opened the door of the empty stall where Hick bunked. As befitted his name, the owner of the Bar Arrow Ranch filled the opening. There weren't many men Hick had to look up to, but Big Bill was one.

"Heard you took a bad fall." The boss sniffed, his nose wrinkling at the pungent odor lingering in the stall. "Guess I heard rightly."

"You did."

"Do you want me to send for Doc Alderman?"

"Nope. I'll be fine in a few days."

Big Bill scratched his chin above the handkerchief tied around his throat. "I hate to say it, but I ain't got a few days."

Hick figured that was why the man had come. He had a contract with the army to supply horses—broke well enough for the cavalry to ride—and the pickup date was almost on top of them. A trio of ice storms had gotten them behind schedule.

"You're one of the best I've ever seen." The big man reached into his coat and drew out a wad of bills—a thin wad—and handed them to Hick. "Here's what I owe you with a little extra to see you through until your next job."

Not exactly fired, but a kick to Hick's pride all the same. He took the money and stuffed it into his shirt pocket. "Much obliged."

"Stay as long as you want. You're welcome at the bunkhouse for meals, too, same as always."

"I'll move on in the morning."

Big Bill shook his head. "Have it your way. Good luck to you." He touched the front of his hat and left.

The man had tried to move Hick into the bunkhouse a couple of times, not understanding his need to be alone. And Hick couldn't explain it. At least, he didn't want to. He felt most at peace in the stall next to Trooper, his horse. Most of the hands thought him unsociable. That was fine. It kept them out of his way.

Hick had spent four long years living cheek-by-jowl with other men.

His fingers moved to massage the old scar on his temple. He jerked them away when he realized it. Bad habit, that. The war was over, his wounds healed, and his life was his own again, to live as he pleased.

Responsible only for himself.

She'd never shot a man before, and Susannah Piper wasn't eager to pull the trigger on the heavy Colt Dragoon she clenched in both hands. But if one of those men rushed the soddy, she just might.

The squat soddy—little more than a cave in the dirt—meant nothing to her. Not with Abel gone. No, it hadn't meant anything to her even when Abel shared it. It had been a wintering place, nothing more. A much-needed stop on the journey to Oregon. The journey to their new life in a new land away from people who hated them for who they were.

Or more to the point, for who *she* was.

"Mrs. Piper!" The shout came from behind the soddy barn, where Peaches was stabled. "It's time you moved on, Mrs. Piper. Missouri has changed. We don't want your kind here."

Her kind.

Those men—at least three had ridden onto the property—had no idea who Susannah Mary Jessup Piper was. All they heard was her Southern accent, her thick Georgia drawl. And from that, they assumed she was a slaver and a traitorous rebel and probably a harlot to boot.

She was none of those things.

But she held the cocked pistol steady as she called out, "Get off my place. Leave me be."

"Ma'am, your husband said you'd move on come spring. He's gone, but spring is here. Time you honored his words."

Susannah and Abel had arrived in the fall and taken residence in one of the many abandoned, dilapidated homesteads in Jackson County. Back in 1863, after fierce fighting between Quantrill's Raiders and the Union Army, Brigadier General Thomas Ewing had issued Order Number Eleven, which exiled everyone in Bates, Jackson, Cass, and Vernon Counties from their homes. Susannah and Abel had chosen one of the deserted homesteads to winter in.

Susannah had every intention of moving on. Every intention of fulfilling Abel's dream to reach Oregon. She'd sold most of their belongings—including the wagon and team of horses—anything that couldn't be strapped to her mule or worn on her person. The coins were sewn into the lining of her oldest petticoat. But she planned to leave on her terms, not at her neighbors' demands.

She'd had enough of being treated like the enemy.

The war was over—had been for two long years—but she and Abel hadn't been able to get past it. He with his Union-blue britches and her with her Southern accent, they hadn't found a place that would accept them for who they were and not for where they'd come from. Abel had been sure Oregon would be that place.

She was left to find her way there by herself.

"Leave me be," she called, thankful that her voice was strong and smooth, not as weak and jittery as her belly.

"We'll ride off, Mrs. Piper, but we'll be back tomorrow, and the tomorrow after that, and the tomorrow after that until we've flushed you out. There's no place here for the likes of you."

Hoofbeats were followed by dust visible through the soddy's only window. Had they all left? Or was it a trap to draw her out?

Susannah glanced at her sack, saddlebag, leather satchel, and the makeshift saddle she'd cobbled together from an old pack saddle, a buffalo hide, and some rope. It wasn't pretty, but it would hold her and all her worldly possessions. She'd wait for an hour or so to make sure the men—her so-called neighbors—had gone, then she'd ready Peaches and ride out.

She should be able to make Kansas City by evening. She'd camp somewhere near there and enter the city in the morning. It shouldn't be too hard to escape notice until then.

She'd gotten very good at traveling unseen. Sneaking around wasn't a skill Susannah had been born with, or one she'd learned as a young girl growing up in Blackshear. No, she hadn't learned it until she'd helped Abel escape. So in a way, she could blame her newfound skill on William Tecumseh Sherman. If he hadn't been on the march, the Confederacy wouldn't have needed to move prisoners out of Andersonville and stow them in temporary prisons like the one near her home. Prisons without walls or fences. Prisons men could escape from. Union soldiers.

Like Abel.

No, traveling unseen wasn't a skill she'd learned as a youngster. But it was a skill she needed as a grown woman. Again.

Of all the bad luck. Hick let go of Trooper's front hoof and then picked up the rear one. At least the shoe on that one wasn't broken. But the front shoe was. He checked the other two, both badly worn but in one piece.

Hick mentally kicked himself for not asking the farrier at the Bar Arrow to put new shoes on Trooper. He would have, and Big Bill wouldn't have charged him for it. But his stubborn pride had gotten in the way. And Trooper was paying the price.

"Sorry, boy." He scratched the war horse's rump above the tail. "Should have thought more about you and less about me back at the ranch."

The horse turned his mostly white face to Hick, one blue eye and one brown eye blinking at him. They'd covered a lot of miles, ridden across too many battlefields, and faced death together more than once. The horse didn't deserve to go lame because Hick had been neglectful. He'd been sure the shoes would last as far as Kansas City.

He'd been wrong.

He led the horse to a grassy spot near the trees that grew along the river. It'd be a good place to camp. He let Trooper drink his fill, then stripped off his tack and gear. After fishing out his hatchet, he worked the broken shoe off the hoof, then hobbled the old horse so he wouldn't range too far.

The river was narrow there and deep, the water refreshingly clear. Hick filled both his canteens. Standing and straightening, he winced at the pain in his hip. Another night of rest would do it some good. But walking into town tomorrow?

Hick was a horseman, a cavalryman. Walking didn't set well with his disposition. But it was his own fault. He wouldn't compromise Trooper's feet for anything. Even his own. And his boots weren't in much better shape than the old horse's shoes.

With his coffeepot settled near the fire he'd built and a few thick slices of bacon sizzling in the pan, Hick relaxed against his saddle and watched the evening gather around him. The wind blew softly for a change, and the croaking of frogs and humming of insects grew louder as the darkness thickened. He may have dozed, but the scent of scorching bacon and boiling coffee roused him in a hurry. After setting the coffeepot aside to let the grounds settle, he slapped the bacon on his plate and leaned back against his saddle again.

His bum hip was going to force him to slow down, and slowing down left him time to think about where he was going. Since the war, he'd been drifting, working on this farm or that, making his way west until he reached the ranches. He knew horses, and he could make a good living breaking new stock, but at some point, he needed to think beyond that.

Thinking about the future was one of the hardest things for him to do when so many men had died in the war. Men who had no future to think on.

Why had Hick survived? Why him and not Denny? The pain struck as it always did when he thought of his brother. He rubbed the center of his chest. It should be Denny figuring out what he wanted to do with his life. He could picture his brother on a farm near their folks' place in Ohio. He'd have a pretty little wife and a trio of children by now. His future should have been all that and more.

But he'd followed Hick into the war.

He'd followed because Hick had talked of little else but honor and glory and service to the country. There may have been service to the country, but honor and glory he'd seen none of. War had been nothing like he'd imagined beneath the spreading oak trees on Pa's farm.

It had been...brutal.

Susannah dropped a handful of early wildflowers onto the mound at her feet. A crude cross made of sticks and rope held up by a circle of stones marked one end of the grave. Green sprouts pushed through the stark brown earth. New life taking over the old.

"'Bye, Abel. I wish it hadn't ended like this."

There were no tears. She'd shed enough of them weeks before. Theirs hadn't been a conventional marriage. It had been born of need, not love. But she *had* grown to love the gentle man she'd worked so hard and risked so much to save. Twice.

If only she'd been successful the second time.

But the season for those thoughts was long past. She must move forward. She must leave Missouri and its growing hatred of anything Southern behind. Oregon was her future. Abel had been sure they could rebuild their lives there. Maybe even start the family they'd both wanted, although she'd not conceived. He'd said that any folks willing to work hard could make a place for themselves in Oregon, which had never been part of the war.

"I don't know how we'll make it, Peaches."

The mule twitched an ear but didn't bother to raise her head.

"Oregon is a long, long way from here."

She glanced at the mule's overgrown, cracked hooves. Those must be addressed before they reached St. Joseph. No wagon master would take her if it looked like she'd neglected her animal. Abel would have taken care of those hooves, but Susannah lacked the knowledge. She'd have to find a farrier in Kansas City.

Susannah saddled the molly and tied on her bedroll, saddlebag, sack, and satchel, double-checking that everything was secure. There was no graceful way to mount, but she got her foot into the loop of rope that would serve as her stirrup and pulled herself up, hooking her knee over one horn of the converted pack saddle. It lacked any comfort of a sidesaddle, but the alternative was to ride astride like a man. On her makeshift contraption, that wouldn't be any more comfortable.

She turned Peaches toward the river and urged her on without looking back. Looking back hadn't done her any good in Georgia or Kentucky and it wouldn't do her any good in Missouri either.

Once she reached the river, she'd have some cover from the willows and scrubby trees that grew along its banks, enough to shield her from the boat traffic if she was careful. Enough to hide in if others were traveling by horse or wagon or even on foot.

She tapped the leather holster she'd fashioned for the front of the saddle, the hard length of the Colt Dragoon reassuring her that she could protect herself if she must.

How much she'd changed in two and a half years. From a doctor's daughter, working to help the sick and injured, to a woman on her own prepared to use a gun if need be.

Susannah turned her face to the sun. It was a new day. She had a new goal. And—Lord willing—she'd be in Kansas City the next afternoon. She'd buy a few provisions and make her way north to St. Joseph, where the wagon trains formed. From then on, she'd face each day as it came and survive as best she could.

Alone.

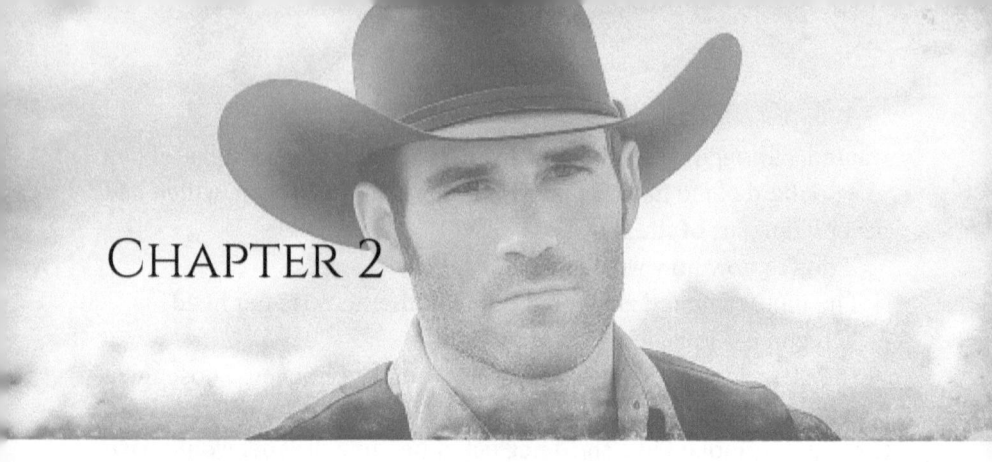

CHAPTER 2

T HE STENCH OF COAL fires, the rattle of wagon wheels, and the mass of humanity that careened down the dirt streets of Kansas City might not have spooked old Trooper, but Hick was ready to turn tail and run. He might have, if he hadn't been in the saddle. He'd walked most of the way to the city to save Trooper's feet, yet a man took his life in his hands if he thought he could walk down a street like the one in front of him.

Hick hadn't been in a big city since the end of the war. If he never entered another, that would sit just fine with him. He wouldn't be there at all if he didn't need to find a farrier. If anyone could find anything in the crush of traffic and people.

Trooper stopped abruptly as a dog raced in front of him, and Hick had to grab the saddle to stop himself from pitching over the horse's neck. A tow-headed boy chased after the dog and dodged between wagons. Someone ought to warn the kid's mother that she was about to lose a son.

Pain—as familiar as breathing—tightened his chest. He rubbed his palm over the ache and clicked to Trooper, starting the horse moving again.

As the crowd thinned, he caught sight of an uneven board sign with the name Harwood and a crude painting of a gray horseshoe swinging in the breeze on the far end of the street. He angled Trooper through the traffic and stopped at the hitching rail.

A thick man in a leather apron appeared in the open double doorway. "Help you, mister?"

"Need a new set of shoes."

"Got one inside and that one next"—he pointed to a black horse standing loose-hipped at the rail—"but you can tie your horse beside him. There's a saloon up the street and another around the corner while you wait."

"How long?"

The man squinted into the sun. "Be done by noon." Then he named his price and stuck out his hand. "Payment up front."

Hick pulled the bills from his shirt pocket and peeled off the amount, trying not to notice how little that left him to outfit himself for the trail ahead. Trooper was worth every penny and more.

He pulled his saddlebag from behind the bedroll and slung it over his shoulder, patted Trooper on the rump, and limped down the street toward a general store he'd passed. His hip still ached, and his feet did too. Trooper wasn't the only one who needed fresh footwear. They'd both have to be re-shod to reach the mountains.

Hick wasn't sure just when he'd decided to go to the mountains, but the urge was strong to see them. Not for the beauty, although he'd heard them described that way many times, but for the solitude. It was said they were higher and wider and less populated than the mountains he'd ridden through during the war. He'd need to outfit himself to live there.

The door hinges squeaked as he entered, and a little bell dancing above his head made him duck.

"Sorry about that." The man behind the long counter grinned at Hick. "One of these days, I need to fix it so you tall fellers don't knock your heads on it."

"Yup." Hick straightened his hat.

"What can I help you with?" the man asked.

"Heading to the mountains."

"Hunting gold?"

Gold? No. That was a fool's errand. Some men might find it, sure, but most wouldn't. Nope, it was horses that interested Hick. Horses raised on a high range with wide chests, sound feet, and strong legs. Horses the army would pay handsomely for.

"Nope. Plan to settle out there."

The man let out a low hum. "You're a brave one, what with the Indians all in an uproar."

The past two years had kept the army busy, moving from battling rebels to battling the plains Indians. Hick wasn't looking for any battle, however. He'd had his fill of fighting. If the Indians would leave him alone, he'd be happy to do the same with them. Maybe his attitude was too simplistic, but he was willing to take his chances.

The shopkeeper made a few suggestions, and soon Hick's saddlebag was stuffed. The new boots pinched his toes, but they'd stretch with wear. Hick paid his bill, pocketing the handful of coins that remained of his last pay. He'd have to find some work along the way west—after his hip healed.

He picked up his old boots, the bottoms of which were as worn as Trooper's shoes, and headed outside. The crowd of people and animals was even more dense. He walked around a team of draft horses and dodged a woman riding a mule before crossing the street.

An old man sat on a wooden bench in front of a barber shop, wrapped in a blanket despite the warm sun. His cheeks were weathered, his hair thin and stringy, hanging from under a tattered hat. Thick rags wrapped his boots, or maybe just his feet, it was hard to tell. Hick set his old boots down beside the man.

The old man lifted his head, eyes cloudy and watery. He nodded.

Hick touched the brim of his hat and moved on.

Two women left a diner as he passed, the scent of frying onions swirling from the door. Hick's stomach growled. It wasn't quite noon, so he backed up and entered the diner. It was small and tidy with checkered cloths on round tables. He swiped off his hat and hung it on the rack near the door.

"Sit wherever you like." A perky waitress breezed past him with a tray of empty plates. "I'll be right with you."

He selected a chair that would keep his back to the wall, where he could watch the door.

"What can I get for you?" The waitress returned almost before Hick's backside hit the chair. "Special is calves' liver and onions." She leaned closer. "Truth is, nobody makes it better than our cook."

"I'll take that." Anything to fill his belly that he didn't have to cook himself was good.

"Coffee? Black?"

"Yes, ma'am."

She whisked away with an energy that made Hick feel old and tired.

He wasn't old, was he? His mind ticked back to when he'd signed up for the war. He'd been eighteen so that made him... he shot a glance at the calendar on the wall. He was twenty-four years old. He'd be twenty-five come July. But the four years he'd served in the cavalry with the First Ohio, Company C, had aged him.

He'd seen too much.

Lost too much.

He adjusted his aching hip on the hard chair. Falling off broncs hadn't done him any favors since leaving the army.

Sometime during his walk that morning, a plan had come together in his head. A plan that would take him to the mountains he longed to see. If he could gather a few good horses, seed stock to start his own ranch, he'd take his time and break the youngsters out proper. No more leaping on the back of a wild horse and holding on for dear life.

Hick knew how to handle horses. Pa had taught him and Denny... Pain lashed through him, and he pushed the thought away as the perky waitress slid a loaded plate in front of him.

He dug into the food like a man on a mission. Which he was.

Get his belly full, pick up Trooper, and get out of town.

Food was going to be Susannah's biggest concern, that and her mule's hooves. As much as she'd have liked to avoid Kansas City, she needed to address both of those needs. She'd only been to the city once with Abel, before he'd become too ill to travel. She slowed Peaches as a tall man carrying an old pair of boots walked in front of them, barely glancing at her.

Susannah guided Peaches to the hitching rail and dismounted, the tall man still in her range of vision when passing traffic didn't interfere. She couldn't say what it was about him that drew her attention. Other than a pronounced limp, he blended in with most of the crowd moving along the street. His worn clothing could use a washtub. His cheeks were stubbled with several days' growth. His hat rested on a shaggy thatch of light brown hair that needed trimming. It all pointed to someone traveling through, not a local citizen.

He stopped beside an old fellow huddled on a bench and set down the boots. Neither spoke, and the tall man limped away. The old one bent and unwrapped his feet, which were bare even of socks, then slipped on the boots. A grin broke over his face, and he sat up straighter.

An unexpected pressure built at the back of Susannah's throat. When had she last witnessed an act of kindness? She couldn't remember. But it was pretty clear the tall man and the old one weren't together.

Perhaps kindness did still exist.

She untied her satchel and entered the general store. The clerk at the counter was busy with what looked like a man and wife, so she occupied herself looking at the displays. In her pocket, she jingled the handful of coins she hadn't sewn into her petticoat, which was stashed in her satchel. The coins in her pocket wouldn't get her much, but enough to make it to St. Joseph. She could fully supply her needs with her hidden coins when she found a wagon train that would take her to Oregon.

"Help you, ma'am?" the clerk asked.

"I need some supplies." She ignored the frown that settled between his brows at her Southern drawl and plunged on. "Enough to see me to St. Joseph."

"Just you, ma'am?"

"Yes." The way his gaze raked from her hat to her shoes made her want to squirm. Or slap him. But she stood tall and plastered a haughty expression on her face. She was no soiled dove to be gawked at in such a fashion.

Even if she was traveling alone.

He hummed a minute, then started offering her options.

She dug the coins from her pocket and set them on the counter. "Whatever this will cover will be fine."

He poked at the coins, counting them and muttering to himself before he grabbed items from the impressive expanse of shelving behind him and placed them on the counter in front of her. It was more than she'd hoped. He wrapped everything in brown paper and tied it with a thick cord. She'd have to squeeze to get it all in her sack.

"Thank you." She hefted the bundle and headed back to the street.

Once her purchases were stowed in the sack secured to her saddle, she mounted Peaches and rode down the street. A sign with a horseshoe on it caught her attention. Tied out front was a white-faced bay with a thick bedroll tied behind its saddle.

Susannah pulled Peaches to a stop and glanced into the farrier's shop. A bear of a man worked a forge inside, his hammer sending sparks into the air. When he turned and saw her, he put the tools aside and approached.

"Help you, ma'am?"

"Peaches needs her hooves trimmed." She dismounted.

His eyebrows rose at her accent, but he bent and examined the mule's feet, then straightened. "You want shoes on her?"

"No, thank you, she's never been shod." She patted the molly's neck. "She's got good, hard hooves."

He grunted, quoted her a price, and thrust out a hand.

She'd have to dig out a few of her hoarded coins, but it couldn't be helped. "A moment, sir." She turned her back and worked her hand into her satchel until her fingers reached the old petticoat. The worn fabric gave way to her fingernails, and she withdrew three of the coins which she dropped into his palm.

He took Peaches by the bridle and led her into the building.

Susannah had nowhere else to go, so she sank onto a bench outside the farrier's door as the tall man who'd given away the boots approached. His hazel eyes scanned the street without ever seeming to land on any one person or fixture. His limp seemed more pronounced than it had earlier, but the shiny new boots might have something to do with that. New footwear always took some breaking in.

He didn't spare her a glance, just slapped his saddlebag on the bay and then checked its hooves, lifting each foot in turn. Whatever he saw must have satisfied him, because he untied the animal and mounted, but not very gracefully. And then he rode away.

What a strange man.

She hadn't expected a greeting, exactly, but he'd stopped within six feet of where she sat and hadn't so much as made eye contact with her. He'd at least touched his hat to the shoeless old man. A small act of kindness toward her—even just a nudge of his hat or dip of his chin—would have gone a long way to restoring her faith in humanity.

Peaches issued a long, drawn-out bray from inside the building. Susannah rose and went to the doorway. At the second bray, she entered and ran her hand down the mule's face. "Hush, girl. You'll be far better off when he's done."

"You should have had her in here weeks ago, ma'am." The farrier wielded a wicked-looking rasp, long thin shavings peeling off Peaches's hoof with each pass. "Not good to neglect an animal's feet."

As if she didn't know that, but she wasn't about to explain her situation to a stranger. "I will take more care in the future."

He grunted, dropped the hoof, and moved to the other side.

Peaches scrunched her face in the beginning of another bray, but Susannah hushed her, rubbing the velvety nose. "Almost done."

The farrier was good at what he did, Susannah could see that. With sure cuts from the nippers and even strokes of the rasp, Peaches was standing properly on all four feet, all cracks and chips gone.

"Thank you, sir."

He eyed her up and down, but not in the same way as the general store man. More in a way that said he was surprised to be thanked. Probably the men simply untied their animals and rode away, as the tall man had. Well, she could muster her own small act of kindness.

"I have never seen her hooves look better."

She tugged on the bridle and led Peaches to the street, mounted, and started in the same direction the tall man had gone. Perhaps he was on his way to St. Joseph too.

For a moment, even in the crowded street, the weight of being truly alone pressed against her.

If only Abel had lived.

The road was dry and busy from Kansas City to St. Joseph. On a good day with an early start, Hick would have completed the journey. But the stopover for supplies and horseshoes had wasted almost half a day. By the time the sun was working its way across the western sky, Hick's hip was telling him he'd been in the saddle long enough. He started looking for a good place to camp for the night.

He'd passed buggies and wagons and other riders throughout the afternoon, but with the approach of evening, the road was empty ahead of him. He swiveled to glance behind, drawing in a quick breath at the pain that lanced his hip. Someone was riding far back there, but nobody was close.

While the road didn't follow the river exactly, it was easy to spot by the thick growth of willows and brush that flourished along its banks. He nudged Trooper in that direction. The old horse needed a drink, and Hick could fill his canteens. The shelter of the trees would break the wind as well. His tarp would be the only other protection he'd have against the elements.

He turned Trooper in a circle and scanned the area one more time before heading into the thicket he'd chosen for his camp. Nobody else was in sight. Years of training kept him vigilant even after the war. One couldn't be too careful. The war was over, but the old hurts and angers weren't. Things might have been different had President Lincoln lived—but he hadn't. President Johnson hadn't done much to bring the country back together.

Hick didn't spend much time worrying about politics, but he'd heard enough around the ranches where he'd worked. Men just naturally liked to grouse about the things they couldn't change.

Dismounting was going to hurt, but there was nothing for it. With gritted teeth, he levered himself to the ground, clinging to the saddle to stay upright until his hip would hold him. Trooper stood as patient as ever, turning his face as if to ask what the trouble was.

"That young bronc busted me up some." Hick stroked Trooper's white face. "He'd be a good one if someone could take the time and train him right." A good horse was worth more than gold in Hick's book. A horse like Trooper.

With the ease of long practice, he stripped the tack off Trooper and buckled the hobbles to his front legs. The old horse could eat and drink and move around, but not very far. Then Hick tied his tarp to a handy tree branch, where it would stop the wind, and got a fire built behind it. Just a small fire. He'd eat the cold food he'd bought, but he'd need a bit of coffee to wash it down.

An hour later, on his back with his saddle for a pillow, the stars visible through the budding tree branches, and Trooper cropping the new spring shoots nearby, Hick relaxed. It wasn't just a muscle thing—although those relaxed as well. It was a whole-being relax. It was as if the pressures of life had disappeared, at least for the moment. Hick pulled his blanket a little higher against the cool air.

"This is what I was born for, Trooper. Life doesn't get any better than this."

The bay snorted, for all the world as if he'd understood and disagreed, and then returned to grazing.

The war horse was right, of course. Hick had grown up in a large family surrounded by farms owned by extended family. As a youngster, he'd never been alone. He'd thrived on the companionship and competition of his brothers and cousins.

Before the war.

He closed his eyes and flipped onto his side, good hip to the hard ground. The muscles across his shoulders tensed, and he bent his legs to draw his feet up under the blanket. That was all it took, one fleeting thought of the war, and his relaxation was over.

CHAPTER 3

S USANNAH WAS CLOSE ENOUGH to the tall man to know where he was, yet downwind far enough that his bay wouldn't catch the scent of Peaches. She'd moved into the cover of the trees when he'd angled toward them earlier. It was better to remain unseen if she could. After allowing the mule to drink at the river, she tethered it to a sturdy tree and let her curiosity get the better of her judgment.

She crept closer to the tall man's camp.

He obviously knew what he was doing. A small fire burned in front of the tarp, the canvas slanted to keep in much of the heat, and the aroma of coffee made the camp... homey. Inviting. Better than her hastily dumped saddle with its bedroll and gear.

The bay jerked up its head and glanced in her direction.

She scooted back toward her own set-up, such as it was.

If her only impression of the man had been that act of kindness she'd witnessed, she might have drawn up enough nerve to approach him. After all, he was heading toward St. Joseph. No reason they couldn't travel together.

No reason other than she was a woman alone, and he was a man she didn't know. A man who'd ignored her in town. He couldn't have missed seeing her on that bench, so it'd been his intention to ignore her.

That was what kept her from approaching him.

Peaches dozed under the tree she was tethered to. Susannah untied the animal and led her to the river for another drink before settling down for the night. The water was quiet, the boat traffic anchored and waiting for daylight. Even the most experienced river captain wouldn't sail the Missouri River's twists and turns and sandbars in the dark.

But Peaches had barely dipped her muzzle to drink when she tossed her head, flinging water in Susannah's face. The unmistakable sound of an oar slapping water reached them. Before she could cup the mule's muzzle to silence her, Peaches released a raucous bray.

Susannah could get away unseen, but not with the molly. And since she couldn't walk all the way to Oregon, she wasn't about to leave the animal behind. As surefooted as a mule was, it was too large to crash through all the brush at the river's edge without making noise—a lot of noise. Nevertheless, Susannah pulled on the lead rope and urged the molly on.

"What's that?" A gruff voice came from the darkness.

"What do you think, you fool?" Another, deeper voice answered. "It were a mule. Ain't you never heard one before?"

"Not in the river."

"Ain't in the river, don't you hear it? Pull up to the bank."

Panic seized Susannah. Nobody would be moving on the river in the dark unless they were up to no good. She tugged harder on Peaches's rope, but even over the sounds of the mule's crashing came that of men in pursuit. There was no way she could grab her belongings and saddle the mule before they caught up with her. She'd have to leave it all behind. She stopped and climbed onto Peaches bareback, legs astride, then waited, trembling, while the men came into view. Maybe she could draw them away from her meager belongings. It was the only chance she had to not lose everything, and she was taking it.

"There he is," one of the men shouted.

"That ain't no *he*." The bigger man ran toward her, pushing branches out of his way. "That's a woman."

Susannah tugged Peaches around by the rope on her halter and planted her heels in the mule's ribs.

Peaches jumped forward.

Susannah gripped a handful of scruffy mane and managed to keep her seat. The men behind her yelled at her to stop, but her only thought was to lead them far away from her pile of supplies and the coins sewn in her clothing. Supplies and coins she desperately needed to make it to Oregon.

Then a gunshot rang out.

The braying of a mule jerked Hick awake. He grabbed his Colt .45 and sat up. In the moonlight, Trooper stood with his ears perked, facing downriver. A fragment of an image niggled at Hick. The quick glance behind him, the outline of a rider. Had the rider been on a mule? He could have been. Missouri was full of mules.

How close was the animal? There wasn't much on earth louder than a mule, and on a still night near water, sound could carry a long distance. Trooper wasn't bothered by the sound, just interested. If danger were close, the war horse would be snorting and tossing its head.

Hick climbed to his feet, leaning heavily on the tree that held his tarp until his hip accepted his full weight. He holstered his pistol and pulled the rifle from his scabbard, then moved to Trooper's side and removed the horse's hobbles. The drumbeats of hooves reached them and then...

A pistol shot.

Rifle snapped to his shoulder, Hick braced his feet and waited for whatever animal was charging his way, crashing through the brush.

The nearly white nose of a dusty-gray mule appeared. The animal slowed to a walk, probably at the sight of Trooper. The war horse snorted and reared, letting the mule know who was in charge.

"She's slowin' down!" Came a male voice from behind.

She?

Bent over the neck of the mule, one arm wrapped around its skinny neck, the hatless rider lifted her face to Hick. A face creased in fear and framed with a mane of dark hair.

Hick grabbed the mule's rope and steadied the animal, but had no time for a closer look at the woman on its back as two men came into view. One of them clutching a pistol. They stopped, glanced at each other, and then looked down the barrel of Hick's Spencer.

The smaller man without the gun pointed to the woman on the mule. "She's ours. She run away from us, but she's ours."

"You always shoot at what's yours?" Hick snugged his finger on the rifle's trigger. He'd seen enough of people who thought they could own another human being. He'd looked through his sights at more than he could count.

"Hey, mister, we got no trouble with you, and we ain't lookin' for any." The smaller man shifted a step away from the other.

"Stay right where you are." Hick didn't need them splitting up. "If I need to, I'll drop the big guy with the gun and have a slug in you before you can run ten feet. Understood?"

"That ain't very friendly." The bigger man's voice was almost a snarl, but he lowered his pistol.

"Never said it was."

"Just send the woman back over here, and we'll be out of your hair, mister." The shorter one took another step away from his partner.

Hick pulled the trigger, aiming just to the man's left to scare him back into place, then aimed back at the big man before he could raise his pistol.

"Ma'am?" Hick asked, "you want to go with these two?"

"No, sir. I don't know them." Her voice was tight, and her accent was Southern. Deep Southern. Hick hadn't heard the like since riding across Georgia. "They banked their boat near my camp and started chasing me."

"Seems the lady doesn't relish your company." Hick kept his rifle on them. "Best you return to that boat and move on."

"My gear, my satchel." The woman whispered. "Don't let them take all I have."

She was worried about her stuff? Hick was facing down the men who'd been chasing her, who'd fired at her, and she was worried about her *stuff*? Frustration blew through him like a spring thunderstorm.

"You, big man, drop the pistol." Something must have changed in his voice, because the other man obeyed. "Turn around and march back to your boat." They continued to stare at him for a few heartbeats. "Now!"

The big man started to grab for his pistol, and Hick shot. The metallic *ping* that followed said he'd hit the gun. In the dark. He couldn't have done that again if he'd tried, but the two he was facing didn't know it.

"I said move."

They did. Hick grabbed the mule's rope and followed, keeping his rifle waist high and steady in one hand, finger still on the trigger. Hoofbeats told him Trooper followed.

"Thank you." The woman's voice was still tight and low.

"Where is your camp?"

"It should be straight ahead. I rode directly to yours."

Had she known he was there?

The men picked up speed, and Hick had to stretch his hip to keep up. Every step brought a fresh stab of pain. Every step riled his anger another notch. When the men started running, near the bank of the river, he slowed and let them go. In a moment, the slap of oars against water reached him. Good riddance.

"They're gone, ma'am. Where's your camp?"

She pointed, and he walked the mule in that direction, Trooper tagging along behind. Hick almost stepped on the small bundle in the dark. She'd picked a good place to camp.

"Found it, ma'am." He turned to her as she started to slip from the mule. Slip, not dismount. He caught her with one arm and lowered her to the ground along with his rifle. "Ma'am?"

She didn't respond.

Something warm and sticky met his hand as he removed his arm from around her shoulders.

The pistol shot.

She'd been hit.

Hick turned her onto her side. She moaned, but didn't come around. He couldn't see much in the dark, but he felt a tear high on the shoulder of her coat. Its dark color hid the blood. He'd need light to see how bad it was.

The only light nearby was his fire. He started to lift her, then stopped and checked out her gear. He wasn't in any shape to carry her back to his camp, but he could saddle the mule and hoist her onto its back. It'd be a lot easier to hold her on the animal if it was saddled.

The saddle was as strange a contraption as he'd ever seen, and it took him a few minutes to figure out how to secure it to the mule. Rather than be helpful, the mule tried to bite him. Twice. But he got it done, then he tied on her bedroll. He grabbed her canvas sack and tied it to the saddle, avoiding another bite. She'd set great store by her stuff, wanting it back even with a bullet in her.

It took him two tries to get the woman into the saddle. The mule shied away from him the first time, so he brought Trooper up beside it and tried again. When the mule started to move, the war horse pinned its ears and showed its teeth. That was all it took for the ornery mule to comply.

He walked as fast as he could back to the fire, one hand holding the woman on the mule, the other keeping his rifle ready. He didn't expect the men would return, but stranger things had happened.

At the fire, he laid her as close as he could, then added more wood to feed the flames for better light. She roused a bit when he sat her up to remove her coat.

"What?" Her voice was breathy, confused... Southern.

"You've been shot, ma'am. I need to see the wound."

Her head lolled to the side, and he got the coat off. He had to move her again so the light would show on her shoulder. The wound was high, and her light-colored blouse was drenched in blood. The bullet had passed right through the top of her shoulder, plowing a furrow. It likely never touched a bone. She'd been lucky.

Just an inch over and it would have gone through her slender neck.

He hoped she'd continue to be lucky. He pulled his clean shirt from his saddlebag, folded it into a thick wad, and pressed it against the wound to stop the bleeding. Hick had seen men bleed out and wounds less serious turn infected. Good men had died. Way too many good men had died.

He'd do everything he knew to see that this woman didn't.

Fire burned a path across Susannah's shoulder and brought her back to consciousness. She gasped, arching against the assault.

"I'm sorry, ma'am, but it has got to be done."

She opened her eyes. A man's face swam before her in the darkness. The tall man. Her memory returned in a rush. The men from the boat, the shot, the scorching pain in her shoulder, the tall man with a rifle.

"My satchel? My provisions?" Her voice was thin and weak. She swallowed and tried again. "I must fetch—"

"They're here."

Relief almost eclipsed the pain. Almost.

The cool breeze sent a chill over her skin. Her skin? She patted her arms and chest, bare of any covering above her corset. "My clothes."

"I'm sorry, ma'am, but I had to know the extent of your wound. I stopped the bleeding, washed it out, and treated it with whiskey."

The strange man had undressed her.

"I had to cut your blouse and your, um, underclothing, ma'am, and I'm sorry for that too."

Her chemise? He'd cut her chemise? She sagged against the hard ground. At least she had needles and thread packed. She could patch the garment.

He pressed his hand against her shoulder, and she winced.

"Seems all I'm doing is apologizing, but I need to wrap the wound now. I used my clean shirt to make a bandage."

As her thoughts cleared, her training kicked in. "Is the bullet still in?"

"Nope, ma'am. It creased you good, but didn't stay."

That was a blessing. She flexed her shoulder, gritting her teeth. "Nothing is broken or dislocated."

"Doesn't appear to be."

"You washed it with whiskey?" She tried not to shudder at the lingering burn.

"Yup, ma'am. I did."

"And the bleeding, is it stopping?"

"It appears to be, ma'am."

He seemed to know what he was doing. "Are you a doctor?"

"Nope, ma'am, but I've patched my share of wounds."

There was something tired and worn in the way he said it. "You were in the war, then?" She'd heard stories while attending the prisoners at the makeshift prison in Blackshear, stories of men attending the wounded on the battlefields. Men with no training other than repetition and necessity.

He nodded, lips pressed into a firm line.

It comforted her to know he'd some training, however he'd received it. But before she could ask another question, her eyelids refused to obey her and drifted closed. She slipped into the darkness, strangely comforted that the tall man watched over her.

Sleep was out of the question. Hick sat with his back against the tree, his rifle on one side, Colt .45 on the other. Those two men were long gone, which was lucky for them. If Hick had known the woman had been shot, he might have returned the favor. He would for sure have put the fear of God in them. But there could be others out there. There was likely more to the situation than he knew. After all, she was a woman alone.

It was best to keep watch.

The night was quiet other than the drone of night insects and the deep-throated frogs along the river.

And the mule.

He'd tied the animal where it could reach some grass, but the long-eared molly was more interested in Trooper. The war horse ignored her, but as he moved from one grazing spot to the next, the mule would make a little squeal and run to the end of its tether.

At least it wasn't braying. That had been raucous enough to wake the dead, and the woman needed sleep. The wound wasn't fatal, as long as it didn't get infected, but she'd lost a good deal of blood. Bouncing around on the top of that mule hadn't helped her any, but she'd shown a lot of pluck to do what she'd done.

Hick had to respect that.

Come morning, he'd offer to see her to her family. He had no idea what a woman was doing on the road alone at night, but if she'd been one of his sisters, he'd want someone to see her safely home. It shouldn't be too far. For all her concern about her possessions, the canvas sack couldn't hold enough provisions for a long trip.

He adjusted his hip on the ground, then gave up. There was no way to sit that didn't hurt. Half a day in the saddle had him more sore than he'd expected. The thought of riding on in the morning didn't appeal, but there was nothing for it. He'd have to get the woman back to her people.

She must have a husband somewhere. She looked old enough to be married. Even in the moonlight, it was easy to see she was pretty. Her dark hair had escaped its ribbon and waved around her face. Relaxed in sleep, her face was smooth, her chin slightly pointed. She was a little thing, but strong. When he'd poured the whiskey on her wound, he'd needed both hands to hold her down.

Best he didn't remember the feel of her skin against his rough fingers. Best he remember that she probably had a husband somewhere. Or a father. Or a whole passel of brothers.

But if she did, why was she on the road at night... alone?

CHAPTER 4

D AWN FINALLY BROKE ACROSS the horizon. Hick had managed to doze off and on, but still had to rub the grit from his eyes. He moved as quietly as he could to rekindle the fire, then hobbled to the river to fetch water for coffee. It wasn't likely to make his hip hurt any less, but coffee was the only way to start the day, as far as he was concerned.

He paused to give Trooper a good scratch, then cast a glance at the mule. At some point, the animal had settled down and lay stretched out on the ground, one long ear poked up and swiveled his way. He'd have to lead it to the river for a drink.

But coffee first.

Hick had learned to be frugal during the war. One never knew when supplies would be available to replenish what was used, but as he stifled yet another yawn, he poured an extra measure of ground beans into his pot. He needed it. He set the pot near enough to the fire to heat and then glanced at the woman.

The most vivid blue eyes he'd ever seen stared back at him. They weren't pale blue like Ma and his sisters', but a dark, striking color. And they were watching him with a palpable sense of wariness.

"Morning, ma'am."

She shifted, grimaced, and managed to sit up, pulling her blanket around her. "Good morning." She blinked and looked around, then gathered her blanket as if to rise.

"Whoa there, ma'am." Hick set aside the bag of coffee and stood. "Let me help you."

"I can stand."

"You lost a lot of blood, ma'am. Best you let me help."

She cocked her head, sizing him up. What did she see? Hick wiped his hands on his britches, then straightened his hat. When was the last time he'd put on a clean shirt? Or taken a bath? Or shaved? He scratched at the whiskers peppering his jaw. No wonder her lips ticked down into a slight frown.

Then she nodded.

He stepped close and steadied her while she got to her feet. She clutched his arm when she wobbled, but let go once she steadied, grasping the tree trunk.

"What's your name, ma'am?" That seemed a safe place to start.

"Susannah Piper." She adjusted the blanket. "Mrs. Susannah Piper."

Well, he'd figured there had to be a husband somewhere.

"I'm Sam Hickman, but people call me Hick." He touched the brim of his hat. "I reckon your husband will be worried about you, ma'am."

"He's dead." The words were stark and blunt with no fresh pain in her face. Her husband had been dead a while.

"Then maybe I could see you back to your family? Maybe your pa?"

"He's dead too, and before you ask, so are my brothers, as far as I know."

As far as she knew? That wasn't uncommon since the war. So many men had died, buried near the battlefield where they fell, or the camp where they'd sickened and died of disease, and too often without proper notice sent to the families. Especially in the South, and her accent was as Southern as a body could get.

"Where is home for you, ma'am?"

Her blue eyes met his again, and in their depths was a mingling of sorrow and something else. Something... strong. That was the only word he could put to it.

"Oregon."

He rocked back on his heels.

"No, I haven't been there yet, but that's where I'm heading."

Hick scratched the back of his neck. "How do you plan to make the trip, if you don't mind my asking?"

She tilted her chin to the north. "They say wagon trains are leaving St. Joseph almost daily. I plan to join one of them."

"By yourself?" The disbelief in his voice earned him a frown. "What I mean, ma'am, is that the wagon masters won't take a single woman on a train." Especially not one as young and lovely as the woman standing in front of him. Everyone knew that. That was just begging for trouble in a wagon train filled with single men striking out on their own to seek their fortunes in the West.

No wagon master worth his salt would allow it.

If the world hadn't been threatening to spin around her, and if the pain in her shoulder hadn't locked her teeth together, Susannah would have given the man a piece of her mind. She had plenty of experience being alone. What could he possibly know about it?

But the world did tilt, her shoulder feeling like it'd been kicked by Peaches, and she needed the privacy of a bush in the worst way.

"If you will excuse me a moment." She let go of the tree and wrapped the blanket tighter around her shoulders. "I will take a walk to the river."

She took a step, wobbled, and he grasped her elbow to steady her.

"Better let me help you, ma'am."

"No, sir. What I need requires privacy, I assure you."

Understanding reddened his cheeks above his beard. If it could be called a beard. It was more like he'd neglected to shave. In fact, there was nothing tidy about his appearance. But then, she was wearing a blanket with her hair falling around her shoulders, so who was she to condemn him on his grooming?

"I'll see to your mule, take her to the river farther downstream." He took a step back but kept his eyes on her. "You sure you'll be all right?"

"If there is one thing I can assure you of, Mr. Hickman, it's that I can take care of myself. I've had a lot of practice." Which was true. After Mama died, Daddy had followed all three brothers into the war. That had been early in the fall of 1861. Three and half years later, she'd met Abel. Another three years later, she was on her own again.

Peaches came to her feet, shook off the dirt and dead grass that clung to her coat, and worked up to a long, loud bray. All the people she'd loved had left or died—or both—but at least Susannah had the mule.

Mr. Hickman gave her one more glance, as if to assure himself that she wouldn't fall over, then went to attend Peaches.

Susannah walked in the opposite direction, finding a concealing bush first, then making her way to the water. Kneeling to wash her face and arms while keeping the blanket from slipping took all her strength. By the time she was done, her muscles were quivering, but the water had revived her some too. How she was going to get into the saddle, much less stay there, was a mystery.

But she had to.

Mr. Hickman had tethered Peaches, but his horse was gone when Susannah returned. A moment of panic hit, but she squelched it. After all, he was under no obligation to her. Then his tarp rustled in the breeze. He wouldn't have left without that. He'd be back.

She found her bedroll, minus the blanket wrapped around her, and dug out her spare clothing. On shaking legs, she retreated to the bushes again and managed to change her clothes mostly one-armed. The bullet had struck her left shoulder, and she was right-handed, so it could have been worse. Thank goodness she'd long ago discarded her dresses that had buttoned down the back. She bundled the clothes she'd removed. Aside from repairing her chemise and blouse and jacket, she'd need to wash out the blood.

There was a lot of blood, which accounted for her weakness. Had she been a patient, Susannah would have prescribed rest and a rich bone broth, but she didn't have the luxury of either.

Mr. Hickman's back was to her as she approached the camp. He squatted near the fire, whistling a tune she didn't recognize. When she drew closer, he turned, his hand hovering over the pistol at his hip. A cautious man.

"Mrs. Piper"—he relaxed his hand—"I hope you're hungry."

His hair was wet, he wore a different shirt, and he'd shaved, a small smear of blood marring one corner of his chin. The change was startling. He was younger than she'd first assumed. Much younger.

The scent of sizzling bacon joined the aroma of coffee, and her stomach growled. "I am."

"But first"—he stood and dusted off his knees—"I should take a look at your wound. It may need another dose of whiskey."

Susannah had checked the wound while washing. It hadn't felt hot, and she'd repositioned the bandage, utilizing its clean side. While what he said made sense, the thought of baring her skin to him in broad daylight was too much.

"I checked it at the river. It's painful, but not hot, the discharge is normal, and the redness is not more than what's to be expected under the circumstances."

"You sound like you know what you're doing."

"My daddy was a doctor." She blinked back an unexpected surge of loss. "He trained me as a nurse. I assisted him for several years before the war and carried on after he signed up."

Mr. Hickman gestured to the fire. "Then you know better than me, ma'am. Breakfast is ready." He glanced back at her. "Thing is, I only have one plate and cup."

"I have one of each in my sack." She fetched them, then handed him the plate before sitting down. Falling down, almost. He shot her a pointed look, obviously a sharp-eyed man who didn't miss much.

He handed her the plate filled with bacon, then reached over and poured coffee into her cup. She'd love a bit of sugar to go in it, but even black, it was welcome.

She waited while he filled his own and got seated. "Thank you, Mr. Hickman, for what you've done. And for the food. I am much obliged."

He stopped with a crispy slab of bacon halfway to his mouth and eyed her over the meat before returning it to his plate. "You're welcome, ma'am."

Even as her mouth watered at the smell of bacon—something she hadn't tasted in a long time—she was grateful. Grateful this man had rescued her. Grateful to be on the road to Oregon.

Grateful to be alive.

She tore off a piece and chewed the overcooked meat. As good as it tasted, it was still all she could do to finish it. The pain, the weakness, and the uncertainty of what would happen next filled both her mind and her stomach. She needed to eat and get back on Peaches.

But all she wanted to do was sleep.

Hick lingered over the fire, getting warm again after his plunge in the Missouri River. Spring might be awakening the land around him, but the river was fed by snow melting far north of them. He was chilled to the bone. He took a final gulp of coffee, swished the last bit around in his cup to stir up the grounds, then emptied it into the fire where it hissed for a moment.

The sun was well up into the sky. He should be in the saddle and heading north.

Mrs. Piper rustled behind him, but he didn't turn her way. What was he going to do with her? He couldn't just saddle Trooper and ride off, leaving a woman on her own, injured and unprotected. His folks had taught him better than that.

So had the war.

He'd seen enough people left along the roadsides to fend for themselves. Women. Children. Black slaves set free with no means to support themselves. Soldiers without arms or legs or eyes. They were as much casualties of the war as those who had fallen on the battlefields.

But he'd rode past them all, tried his best not to see them. He'd stayed in formation, riding with his regiment, heading for another battle that would displace even more people. And while he'd wished they could have done something for those people, it had been a vague wish, a sort of longing that people would stop destroying other people. That he and his regiment would stop destroying people and property. But he hadn't been in a position to take responsibility for what was happening. He'd simply followed orders. It was easier that way. He'd learned that early in the war.

And then, they'd promoted him.

He never wanted to be responsible for another person ever again.

"Mr. Hickman?"

His name was a question. That couldn't be good.

"Ma'am?"

"If you would be so good as to saddle Peaches, I believe I am ready to be on my way."

Peaches? The mule's name was Peaches? Only a woman would name an animal something like that.

He stood, took a deep breath against the pain in his hip, and faced her. She reclined against a tree, her face pale as one of Ma's sheets flapping on the line, but she'd gathered her belongings. Her bedroll was tied to her saddlebag, a sack and a satchel rested on top of it. Her eyes were clear, her chin lifted in determination, but her voice lacked force. In short, she was in no condition to travel.

Neither was he.

"I plan to camp here for the day, ma'am. You're welcome to stay and rest." He raised his hands when her eyebrows drew down. "You have my word that I will behave as a gentleman."

"Why are you staying here? Why aren't you riding on?"

Hick rubbed his hip. "I came off a bronc on the last ranch I worked. My hip needs time to heal. Nobody is going to hire me to break horses until it does."

"Are you sure it isn't broken?"

"Yup, ma'am. Just a bad bruise."

"You may have bruised the bone, which will take a while to heal." Expressions flitted across her face too fast to follow, but they ended with a firm nod. "I thank you for the offer to share your fire, Mr. Hickman."

"Most folks just call me Hick, ma'am."

"So you said, Mr. Hickman. But I am not most folks."

Nope. He could see that. Hick hadn't been around that many women—other than his two older sisters and his ma—but this one had spunk. There was a story there, sitting against the tree. A story about how a Southern woman—by her speech, an educated Southern woman—had come to be in western Missouri heading for Oregon.

Alone.

The easiest way to get tangled in that story was to ask, and Hick wasn't foolish enough to do that.

They'd rest for a day—maybe even two—and then set out for St. Joseph. He'd see her safely to the city, and then they could part ways. He'd ride on for Omaha. From there, he'd head west to the mountains. It was said wild horses roamed those foothills, free for the taking. A start to his horse ranch. Far away from battlefields and cities and... people.

Avoiding people was the best way to ensure he didn't disappoint anyone ever again.

CHAPTER 5

S UNLIGHT FILTERED THROUGH THE budding branches over Susannah, lighting the inside of her eyelids. She came awake with a start. She'd been leaning against the tree. How long had she napped? She rubbed her eyes and glanced up. The sun hung almost directly over-head. As if in response, her stomach growled.

"Welcome back, ma'am." Mr. Hickman crouched next to his gear. "Are you hungry? I have some jerky and hardtack in my saddlebag."

"I am." She pushed her hair back from her face. She needed to find a ribbon in her satchel. "But I prefer pancakes."

He stared at her a moment, then rubbed his jaw. "Ma'am, I don't have the makings for pancakes."

"I do." She rose. The nap had restored her. At least, the world didn't spin. She fished a ribbon from her satchel and slowly, painfully tied her hair back, then pulled the ingredients for pancakes from her sack along with her skillet and a bowl.

Mr. Hickman readied the fire, spreading the glowing coals evenly.

Susannah added a spoonful of lard to the skillet and set it on the coals, then mixed the batter. She didn't have an egg or milk, but she was used to eating pancakes made with water. Someday, she'd have a cow again and a whole flock of chickens. Oregon must have plenty of both. Abel had talked about farming out there, growing crops bigger and thicker than anything they'd seen in Georgia or Kentucky.

She poured the batter into the hot skillet and the aroma filled the camp, setting her stomach grumbling again. With a practiced toss, she flipped the pancake, then rose and pulled a can of peaches from her sack. "Mr. Hickman, if you would open this and hand me your plate?"

He punctured the tin then held out his plate. It didn't take long for him to finish the pancake, drizzled with syrup from the canned peaches. She slid another onto his plate before making one for herself. Neither spoke until the pancakes were gone and they'd eaten the last bite of peaches.

The combination of a full stomach and her loss of blood made her eyelids heavy. She rose to wash the dishes, but staggered.

Mr. Hickman grabbed her by the elbow and steadied her. "I'll wash up, ma'am. You should rest again. You've gone all white."

She felt pale enough to see right through her. "Thank you. I believe that would be a good idea."

Susannah retreated to her tree, but this time, she unrolled her bedding and stretched onto it. She intended to watch the tall man while he worked, but her body had other plans.

The scent of coffee tickled her awake later, as the sun touched the tops of the trees to the west. She'd slept the entire afternoon. The bay horse cropped grass nearby. Peaches had been moved and drowsed in the sun at the edge of the tree line, ears relaxed, bottom lip sagging.

There was no sign of Mr. Hickman.

She took advantage of the privacy to retreat into the bushes, then made her way to the river to wash the sleep from her face and rinse out her bloodied garments. She set the chemise aside. It was ruined beyond repair, and there was no sense in wasting soap. She could fashion a new wound dressing with the clean parts that remained.

The river was busy, four boats passing as she scrubbed the cloth with sand from the riverbank. If it weren't so costly, she'd have taken one of the boats to St. Joseph. Heaven knew what Peaches would have thought of that. But boats and trains were beyond Susannah's hoard of coins. She and Peaches would have to make it to Oregon by their own power.

With the worst of the stains removed, she pulled out a single bar of lye soap and worked a lather into the fabric. It was the best she could do under the circumstances. The garments could dry overnight, and perhaps tomorrow night she'd have time to mend them, seated around a fire in St. Joseph with the rest of those waiting for the wagon train to start west.

She returned to camp and was spreading her clothing on the bushes to dry when a whistled tune reached her. Mr. Hickman came from the river as well, but farther downstream. The whistle was probably a courtesy to alert her of his presence. There was a kind and thoughtful side to the man, even if he was short on words. He stopped when he saw her.

"Good to see you up and about, ma'am."

"I'm afraid I slept most of the day away, but at least I got my clothing laundered. I washed your shirt, the one you'd bandaged me with. It'll be ready to pack away in the morning."

He limped farther into camp. "I believe I will spend another day here." He shrugged. "My hip isn't anxious to climb back in the saddle."

Wasn't it? Or was he being kind again—to her? Her thoughts swirled around that idea for a moment, but the grimace as he knelt to feed the fire said his pain was real. A bone bruise could be a nasty thing, often taking more time to heal than a clean break.

If she were honest, the extra day would be good for her as well. Even after sleeping most of the day, she was exhausted from washing the clothes. But she would make them dinner before she collapsed again.

"If you would share some of that jerky you mentioned, I have corn-meal and currants. I could make a pot of mush for our supper."

"That sounds fine, ma'am."

"I'm sure you'd prefer a steak or even stew."

"I normally eat jerky and hardtack when I travel, so hot mush is more than fine." He flashed her a grin, the first she'd seen. He was quite handsome, his face neatly shaved. So different from Abel's thick beard. "Be nice not to have to chew so hard."

Susannah fetched what she needed from her sack, almost ducking her face into the canvas to cover for the flustered reaction she'd had to his grin. A friendly grin, nothing more, but how long had it been since anyone had offered such to her?

He hadn't lied to her. Hick's hip ached worse than the day that bronc had pitched him heels over elbows. But it was a healing kind of ache. He'd had enough experience to know the difference, and to know he could have moved on.

Dawn's rays broke free of the horizon without a cloud in the sky. It should be a good day. Maybe he'd hunt something for their supper. Something Mrs. Piper could turn into a broth to strengthen her. She was a good cook. She'd proved that.

He hadn't learned much else about her. Hard to learn about a woman who slept all the time. But she needed it. He had enough experience to know that as well. Too much experience, even with wounds that never bled.

The war—no matter how hard he rode away from it—never left him alone. And when he wasn't busy working or riding, it closed in on him. He didn't suffer the night terrors that he'd witnessed in others, or the shakes that some men got, but guilt rode heavy on his shoulders and weighed him down. The bone-deep guilt of what he'd done. Not just Denny, although it was most often about him. There'd been other men who'd died in Hick's arms. Fellow cavalrymen, his brothers-in-arms, and even once a Confederate soldier, a mere boy in a man's uniform, who had fallen to Hick's sword. A boy who should have been home in his ma's kitchen—

"Mr. Hickman?"

Mrs. Piper's voice pulled him from the spell of his guilt. He closed his eyes and pinched the bridge of his nose before turning away from the fire toward her. She was seated with her back against the tree, blankets wrapped around her in the early morning chill.

"Ma'am?"

"I believe I am fit to ride this morning. I feel remarkably better than yesterday."

Hick rose and grabbed another stick to feed the fire. "I'm not, ma'am. Another day will do me good."

"It is imperative that I make it to St. Joseph. The wagon trains leave in the spring to make it through the mountains before the heavy snows." There was a tinge of desperation in her voice. "Abel and I arrived too late last year. I can't miss them again."

"One more day won't stop you from getting on a wagon train." If a wagon master would sign her on, which he doubted, but it was no concern of his. "Me and Trooper are going to rest here one more day. What you and your mule do, that's up to you."

She shifted without rising, but he could almost feel her annoyance from across the open space between them. Funny how women could do that. Ma had always been able to—

"Then I suppose Peaches and I will stay one more day." She rose and folded her blankets. "Do you have more bacon? I could cook that with biscuits."

"Yes, ma'am." Hick pulled the small slab of bacon from his saddlebag and handed it to her. "I'll see to your mule."

"Her name is Peaches."

"So you said." But he wasn't going to call the animal by that fool name. What if someone heard him? Then he snorted to himself. Who'd hear out here? But *Peaches*? They'd been good on the pancakes, but it was no fitting name for a mule. A mule that took a snap at him as he untied her tether.

After breakfast, the bacon having been cooked to perfection instead of scorched and the biscuits as tender as any he'd ever bitten into, Hick shouldered his saddle.

"I'll take Trooper out and see if I can't hunt something up for supper."

Mrs. Piper's hands landed on her hips. That was never a good sign on any woman.

"If we are here to rest for another day"—she fairly glared at him—"why would you ride off to hunt?"

"Because, ma'am, you would do well with some broth to build your blood back up." He turned his back on her and strode to Trooper. The old bay lifted his muzzle, spring grass dangling from his lips as if to say he hadn't finished his breakfast yet. "Don't you start." Hick slung the blanket and saddle onto Trooper's back, then reached under and drew up the girth. "Bad enough the lady is complaining about my actions."

He mounted and rode away without looking back. Maybe he should have grabbed his saddlebag and bedroll and just kept going. He didn't need anyone telling him what to do and when to do it.

He'd had his fill of that during the war.

Susannah fumed at being delayed as she bit off the thread, finishing the repair on her jacket. He could have ridden on today. His leaving to hunt proved that.

But the time allowed her to mend her blouse as well as the jacket. Mr. Hickman's shirt was folded and set on his bedroll. She'd even mended a small tear on one elbow. She had nothing else to occupy her hands until he returned with whatever he might bring to cook. If he brought anything at all.

She should be halfway to St. Joseph by now. It was a perfect day to travel, not a cloud in the sky, with a light breeze instead of the usual windy gusts off the prairie. There was nothing keeping her from saddling Peaches and riding away. She didn't owe Mr. Hickman anything. He'd rescued her, and she was grateful, but that didn't give him the right to make decisions for her.

And yet, she waited for his return. She'd built up a head of indignant steam during the wait. Which he didn't deserve. He'd treated her with respect and kindness.

But if the wagon trains left without her, her options would be reduced to two unpalatable choices. She would have to marry again—and soon—or turn to the oldest profession for a woman. That, she would never do. Perhaps she could gain employment as a nurse, but it wouldn't be easy, not only because of her Georgia drawl, but because money was still scarce following the war.

There was a slim chance she might find work as a schoolteacher. She was better educated than most, thanks to Daddy, but finding a position before she ran out of money would take a minor miracle. Without a single reference, a hefty miracle. With her Southern accent, an impossible miracle.

Peaches chuffed and worked herself up to a full bray, her nose pointed to the east.

Susannah fumbled among her belongings and pulled out the Colt Dragoon. It was loaded, so she cocked the heavy piece, aimed it at the sound of something moving through the bushes, and waited.

Then a whistle reached her. She lowered the pistol but didn't let go until a familiar white horse face pushed into view.

"Whoa, Mrs. Piper, it's me." Mr. Hickman raised a hand, his eyes on her pistol.

She eased down the hammer and set it aside. "I wasn't sure."

"You were right to be careful." He nodded toward Peaches. "She's a good guard for you." Was that a note of respect in his voice? She'd gotten the impression that he wasn't fond of mules. Or maybe just of her mule.

He held a pair of prairie chickens by their feet. "How about these for supper?"

"I wish I had a pot to stew them in." The birds would be tough this time of year, coming off a lean winter.

Mr. Hickman dismounted and handed her the birds. "You can use my coffeepot, ma'am."

She'd already surmised the man treasured his coffee, so the offer was generous. "Thank you. I'll see what I can do with them if you'll tend the fire."

It wasn't long before she had the birds plucked, cleaned, and cut up, and the pot set on the fire. Then she sat back and waited for them to cook.

"You must be a good shot to have killed those birds with your pistol." She glanced at the tall man relaxed on the other side of the fire. "Daddy always hunted birds with a musket loaded with birdshot."

"Prairie chickens aren't like other birds. You can always find a few that will hunker down in the grass and not fly."

"Well, I appreciate the fresh meat, however you managed to bring it back."

They settled in silence, the twitter of birds in the branches and the burble from the river making it a peaceful silence, not an uncomfortable one.

"Mrs. Piper?"

The tension in his voice drew her attention. "Yes?"

"You do know it's not likely a wagon master will let you travel on his train, don't you?"

She stripped slivers of bark off a stick and fed it to the embers. "I know it will not be easy to get one to agree."

"Easy? Ma'am, it'll be more than halfway to impossible."

"And yet, I have little choice." She met his hazel eyes for a long moment. "It's the only way I can reach Oregon."

He looked away, rubbing his jaw. After a few minutes, he turned back to her. "It's not likely to happen, ma'am." His voice was low and steady. "No self-respecting wagon master is going to sign on a single woman. It's just begging for disaster on the trail."

Anger flared through Susannah. Not because of what he'd said, but because he was right, and because it was wrong. "Mr. Hickman, this country has survived a great war—your own President Lincoln said as much. Do you not think that one wagon train could survive a single woman riding along?"

In the tense silence that followed, she lifted the lid on the pot and poked the pieces of prairie chicken around in the simmering water with her peeled stick.

He said nothing for so long, she thought he wouldn't answer. When his words came, it was as if he had to pull each one loose. As if he didn't want to ask the question at all.

"What's a woman like you doing out here by yourself, ma'am?"

"A woman like me?" She didn't try to keep the indignation from her voice. "What sort of a woman do you think me to be, Mr. Hickman?"

He raised both palms toward her. "I mean, a woman from the South, ma'am."

"And what do you know of Southern women? Do you assume we're all lazy and ignorant and beat our slaves before bed? Or perhaps you assume we have the morals of an alley cat?" Her voice rose with each point.

"I do not, ma'am." His voice held anger in reply. "If I thought that, you'd know it by now."

She settled down, breathed deeply for a moment. "I am sorry, Mr. Hickman, I'd no right to accuse you of that." She met his eyes again. "But I have met more than one man with those assumptions of 'my kind' of woman."

And it hurt that he might have thought of her like that, even for a moment.

What was he supposed to think? Hick glanced away from the blazing blue eyes across the fire. He'd known better than to ask. He should have kept his mouth shut. He should keep it shut now, for sure. But something prompted him to plunge on against his better judgment.

"You didn't answer the question, ma'am. What brought you out here?"

"Nothing a Union soldier could understand, I'm sure." She tossed the words at him like a brick, smacking him in the face, the heavy Southern drawl rasping against his skin.

"What could you possibly know about Union soldiers?" The words were forced from between his teeth as he glared at her.

"I watched your kind ride into my town. I saw the destruction in lives, homes, and property. I fed the children left fatherless and tended to the widows." Her voice didn't rise, but each word grew sharper than the last. "I experienced the despair, the loss, and the death."

"Do you think death and destruction was one-sided in that war?" He practically bellowed the words. Trooper lifted his head, ears swiveling and alert to danger.

She lifted her uninjured shoulder, then let it drop. "I suppose you saw your share of the atrocities—"

"Ma'am, you have no idea." He stood. "You know nothing about what it was like to ride into war. Don't make assumptions based on your own ignorance." He pointed at her. "You know nothing about being a Union soldier. Don't assume you do."

Her eyes were clear, and her voice steady when she answered, "I'm not as ignorant as you think I am. I married a Union soldier."

CHAPTER 6

P EACHES PLODDED ALONG BEHIND the bay, long ears bobbing in rhythm, her steps jarring the wound on Susannah's shoulder. The pain was bearable, the wound healing nicely. And at least they were on the road again.

Mr. Hickman had made his coffee and then tended to the animals while Susannah had cooked breakfast. They'd spoken no more words than necessary, the tension of the previous evening still thick between them.

It wouldn't matter much longer. She'd find a wagon train that would accept her and bid the tall man goodbye, thanking him for his assistance. That would be the end of their acquaintance. Until then, the silence suited her just fine.

But as they rode toward St. Joseph and the buildings came into view in the distance, she broke the stillness of the afternoon.

"Will you be joining a wagon train west?"

He jerked a glance at her, as if he'd forgotten she rode behind him. "Nope, but I'll see you safely to the wagons."

She knew very little about the man other than he'd been in the war, that he had a streak of kindness, and that he had a temper if provoked. He'd said nothing about himself or his plans. And, of course, those things shouldn't matter to her. She urged Peaches up beside the horse.

"Where will you go?"

He squinted into the distance. "North to Omaha."

And that was it. No details. No reasons. Why did she feel as if she needed those all of a sudden? It hadn't mattered the day before or the day before that.

"Do you have family there?"

This time he frowned. Not at her directly, but at her question. "Nope."

The buildings grew larger as they neared the town. Soon she and Mr. Hickman would part. She'd have to find where the wagon trains formed up, and then purchase the rest of her supplies. Depending on what they required, she may need to purchase another mule. For her alone, she didn't need a wagon. She might purchase an oiled tarp like Mr. Hickman had though. It would be a nice addition to her bedroll.

But in spite of herself, she wanted to know a little more about the man beside her first. She pulled Peaches to a halt.

Mr. Hickman stopped his horse a few steps farther on, then twisted to look back at her. He'd shaved again. Hazel eyes watched her, giving away nothing of his thoughts.

She moved Peaches up beside him. "We are about to part company, Mr. Hickman. I would like to know something about you before we do."

"Why?"

Why? That was a good question. "I prefer not to part with harsh words between us. You came to my assistance when you were not obligated to."

"You're welcome, ma'am." He faced forward and clicked to his horse. The bay continued toward town.

Susannah sighed, then thumped her heels against the mule's ribs. Peaches sauntered forward, seeming to prefer the man and horse leave them behind.

Perhaps Susannah should wish for the same. But she didn't.

She wasn't a fool. She knew the risks she'd take to join a wagon train. Knew that not all men were the caliber of Mr. Hickman. She was comfortable with him.

But he'd made it very clear that he wasn't interested in her.

She thumped Peaches a little harder and rode the jarring trot until they caught up with the silent man and his horse. They entered the town side by side.

St. Joseph was different than Kansas City, and yet the same. The noise, the dust, and the crush of humanity. She had no idea where to start looking for the wagon trains, but Mr. Hickman stopped beside an old man smoking a pipe and leaning against the support of a porch in front of a saddlery.

"Sir, where are the wagon trains gathering?" he asked.

The old man removed the pipe and poked its stem down the street and to the left. "Be over there past the town proper. Can't miss 'em." He looked them up and down. "You and the missus heading to California or Oregon?"

Mr. Hickman touched the brim of his hat. "Much obliged." He clicked to the bay and started down the street.

The old man replaced his pipe and mumbled around the stem in his teeth, "Ain't very talkative."

"No." Susannah got Peaches moving. "He certainly isn't."

It took a ridiculous length of time to work their way down the street around wagons, buggies, carts, drays, and even a stagecoach. But then more wagons came into view, large wagons fitted with sheets of white canvas stretched over hoops, row after row of them.

A shiver of excitement—or was it dread?—danced across Susannah's shoulders. She was at the point of no return. After she signed on with a wagon train, she had to see it through. She'd heard there would be a few army forts along the way, but no towns.

Once she and Peaches left St. Joseph, there would be no turning back.

As always—at least since the war—being in town made Hick itchy. The sooner he got Mrs. Piper to the wagons, the sooner he could continue on his way. Alone. There was enough daylight left to ride another three hours north before setting up camp for the night.

If the wagon train would sign her on, she'd be someone else's responsibility. It was a big if, but she seemed the type of woman who could pull it off. If anyone could.

He hadn't minded her company too much, and she was a whole lot better cook than he was. He'd enjoyed eating biscuits that weren't burned, and he'd never tasted a better prairie chicken than the ones she'd boiled and then fried. She'd even found some spring greens to cook the night before. It'd been a long time since he'd eaten fresh greens.

But something had prompted her to start asking questions, and questions led to things Hick didn't want. Telling someone his business meant letting someone into his life. He didn't want that.

Especially not a woman.

Women needed to be cared for, watched over, protected, and provided for. He'd learned his lesson with Denny—he wasn't fit to watch over anyone. He closed his eyes for a moment and willed away the memories, then urged Trooper toward the line of covered wagons.

A man dressed in a combination of buckskin and flannel seemed to be the one in charge. Hick stopped Trooper nearby and waited for the man to stop arguing with a couple about the weight of their wagon. Mrs. Piper and her mule halted alongside him.

Hick could almost smell the anxiety coming off her. At least she understood what she was facing.

The argument ended with the man's threat to cut the couple out of the wagon train if they didn't comply, then he turned to Hick. "Looking to join the train?"

"Not me." He poked his thumb at Mrs. Piper. "But the lady is."

The man ran a gloved hand across his mouth and sized her up and down. "Where's your husband, ma'am?"

"Dead." She didn't hesitate, didn't work up to it, she just laid it out plain.

The man shook his head. "Can't help you." He started to turn away.

"Wait." She slipped from the mule, and only because he was watching closely did Hick see her lips tighten in pain. Her shoulder needed a lot more time to heal. "I can offer my services to the wagon train, mister..."

"It's Billings, ma'am, the wagon master here, and we don't need no *services* by lonely females on this train." He started to turn away again.

"Mr. Billings"—she grabbed his sleeve—"I'm a trained nurse."

That stopped him. He eyed her up and down again with a bit more respect, then shook his head. "It don't make no nevermind, ma'am. I can't take a lone female across the prairie."

"But I must—"

"Susannah Jessup? Is that you?" A lanky man strode their way, boots pounding the earth. His accent matched that of Mrs. Piper, but why did he call her Jessup? "You have a lot of nerve showing your face here." He pointed to the ground as he stopped barely a foot from her, towering over her.

Hick dismounted.

"What's this all about?" the wagon master asked.

"If you're letting this woman on the train, I'm off it, that's what."

"Billy Williams, I'm glad to see you made it through the war." Her words were smooth and gracious, but her face had lost its color, and her bottom lip trembled on the last word.

"No thanks to you." The man's words were laced with something stronger than anger... hatred? He turned to the wagon master. "This woman is a traitor. She sold out to the..." He glanced around at the crowd they were drawing. "She sold out the whole town back home." He pivoted and marched back toward the wagons.

The wagon master took Mrs. Piper's elbow and walked her back beside the mule. "You best move on, ma'am. I can't take a lone female, and I sure can't lose my best scout over one." He helped her mount.

"There are other wagon trains, are there not?" she asked.

He shook his head. "Not that will sign you on. Not now." He jerked his head toward the retreating scout. "He'll tell them all the same story before the sun sets." He pivoted and followed the scout.

Hick mounted Trooper. He'd known there was a story behind the woman. But a traitor?

A traitor to whom?

With hands that shook, Susannah lifted the reins. Peaches picked up on her mood, and the placid mule danced sideways, bumping into Mr. Hickman's horse.

"I'm sorry." She firmed her grip and breathed deeply to gather herself.

Mr. Hickman didn't move. He glanced at the people milling around the wagons for a long minute, then turned his attention to her. "A traitor?" Even as he asked that short question, Susannah got the feeling that he didn't really want the answer. Which was good, because she didn't wish to discuss it.

"Billy was my brother Philip's best friend. We've known each other all our lives." She adjusted her skirt over the saddle. "I haven't seen him since he marched out of Blackshear with the rest of the young men."

He still didn't move, and his horse dropped one hip, resting.

Susannah decided to wait him out, but as she did, she couldn't help noticing Billy Williams going from man to man, pointing her out to each one. Poisoning the whole population of the wagon train against her.

"Looks like the wagon master was right, ma'am." Mr. Hickman had no doubt seen the same. "What will you do?"

She bit back the urge to snap at him. He'd refused to tell her anything of his plans, but he wanted to know hers? As if she had any. Her one hope to get somewhere she'd find acceptance had been dashed to pieces by Billy.

How had he known? He'd been with the army when she'd done it. He must have gone back to Blackshear. While she was fairly certain no one had seen her that night, her disappearance would have led to questions. Speculations. Accusations.

And they'd have been correct.

"Ma'am?"

"I don't know."

He shifted on his saddle, the leather creaking, the horse straightening and giving a shake of its head, the bit jingling. The man looked her over, not missing any detail, for sure.

Susannah willed herself not to fidget.

"How are you situated, ma'am? Can you afford a decent boarding house?"

Could she? Yes, for a time. But what would happen when the money ran out? Could she get a decent job? What if there were other ex-Confederate soldiers from Blackshear coming to St. Joseph to make their way west? Would she be cast out again?

Was there anywhere in the country other than Oregon that would take a Southerner who had turned her back on the Confederacy? Memories were long and hearts were hard.

"For a little while, I could." She wouldn't lie to him. He might be close-mouthed, but he'd been kind to her.

"St. Joseph moves a lot of Southerners west, many to California but some to Oregon." He rubbed the back of his neck. "I'm guessing there won't be as many departing from Omaha. But that's no guarantee they won't meet you in Oregon."

Where Mr. Hickman was going. Did that mean...?

"We can put a few more hours between here and there by nightfall." He turned his bay and clicked, the horse stepping out.

Even before Susannah had recovered from the shock of his of-fer—because that was what it was, however off-handed—Peaches followed.

She turned in the saddle and looked over the wagons one last time. Billy stood by the one at the end, his arms crossed, a scowl on his face, as if he needed to make sure she left. How could he hate her so much? What she'd done, she'd done out of human kindness, not as a strike against the Confederacy. But she must be the only one who saw it that way.

Abel had, of course, but he was gone. In the end, she'd lost him too.

She was following another man she didn't know into another part of the country where she'd never been. The similarities weren't lost on her. Was history repeating itself?

She hoped not. And she was fairly certain that the stiff-backed man riding ahead of her would never make her the offer Abel had. She didn't wish for it. Not again.

Oregon was still out there, like a beacon of hope. There had to be more than one way to get there. And if so, Susannah Mary Jessup Piper was going to find it.

CHAPTER 7

AS SOON AS THEY'D cleared the town streets, Hick put Trooper into a lope. He didn't look back, figuring the mule would follow. Mrs. Piper had already proved she could ride, and Hick wanted to get as far away from those lines of wagons as possible before darkness fell.

Missouri was still reeling from the fallout of the war. The state had changed leadership since the surrender and was run by anti-slavery politicians who were as radical in their own way as their slavery-supporting predecessors had been radical in theirs. A little moderation would have gone a long way to healing the breach, but it was the way of things to swing from one extreme to the other. Hick understood that. But the result was a state filled with uncertainty and distrust.

Still, Hick hadn't seen the level of outright hatred shown by Billy What's-his-name since the battlefield. He wouldn't put it past the man to come hunting Mrs. Piper, but doubted he'd venture too far from St. Joseph. They could put fifteen miles behind them if they pushed the animals. Old Trooper would make it, and the mule was young and healthy.

After a mile or so, he slowed the horse to a trot, gritting his teeth against the jarring in his hip. Mrs. Piper's shoulder would be feeling it too, but her safety would have to come before her comfort.

And his.

Traffic on the road had thinned to the occasional rider or wagon, and Mrs. Piper brought her mule up beside him.

"What awaits in Omaha, Mr. Hickman?" She rode the mule's trot well, barely bouncing in her ridiculous saddle. "I know you didn't prefer to talk about it before, but now that I am accompanying you, I should like to know what to expect."

"They say the rails have been stretched clear across Nebraska." A new state in the Union he'd sacrificed so much to keep intact—to make better. "Figured I'd find a job, earn a little stake, and then head farther west."

"To Oregon?"

Oregon again. What was her fascination with that state? He'd heard half of it was bone dry and the other half soggy.

"Nope, ma'am. To the mountains."

"What's in the mountains?"

Nothing and no one, which sounded like heaven to Hick. He slowed Trooper to a walk and let the horse breathe.

"Good horse country and wild horses free for the taking."

"What about the Indians?"

"No more than you'd have crossed paths with on the wagon train." He shot her a glance. She seemed composed, relaxed in the saddle. The color had returned to her cheeks. "The army is out there too, ma'am, protecting the citizens."

"Yes, I suppose it is. And I suppose there are towns wherever the railroad has reached."

There were, but not the kind of towns she'd want to be in. Hick had heard stories. Two of the men working on the Bar Arrow had worked on the railroad for a season. The stories they told weren't fit for a lady's ears.

And traitor or not, Mrs. Piper was a lady. But he better find out what the traitor part meant. "Mrs. Piper, what did that man mean when he called you a traitor?"

She turned her face away from him, and for a while, he thought she wouldn't answer, but eventually she straightened and stared ahead. "I married a Yankee."

A traitor to the South. He could hardly fault her for that. The entire South had been traitors to the Union, so her being a traitor to traitors... that balanced things out and sounded reasonable to him. There must be more to the story, however. He waited, but her lips remained closed, compressed in a firm line. Fair enough. He hadn't exactly talked her ears off either. He clicked to Trooper and settled the horse into a mile-eating trot.

Hick knew all he needed to know. After all, he'd be parting company with her at Omaha.

He didn't ask any more questions, and Susannah released a silent sigh of relief. Of course, Mr. Hickman was a Yankee himself, like Abel. The way he sat his horse, the way his eyes roved their surroundings, even the way he packed his saddlebags proved he'd spent time in the army. He wouldn't view her as a traitor.

Although she hadn't told him the whole of it.

All that, combined with the kindness he'd shown, made her feel safe with him. How much different her trip would have been had she needed to use her skills at remaining hidden. If she'd had to slip from one patch of cover to the next and lie in wait while traffic passed by on the road or the river. Even with the extra two days of rest they'd taken, she'd reached St. Joseph in about the same amount of time she'd allotted. They'd continue to make good time to Omaha, riding side by side in the open.

"How many days will it take us to reach Omaha?"

"I'm not sure. Maybe five, maybe six."

Suzannah mentally tallied up the food in her sack. She'd planned to restock in St. Joseph, but under the circumstances, she'd been happy to ride away without stopping.

"Will there be towns along the way? I will need to purchase food."

He shrugged. "We're following the river, so there should be some settlements, at least."

Even a settlement would have a trading post selling flour and coffee and salted or dried meat.

Her shoulder ached—it more than ached. With each pound of a hoof, it answered with a painful throb of its own. But there was nothing to be done about it. Pain was part of healing. How often had she heard Daddy say the same to his patients?

Let the pain keep you still so your body can heal. Even pain has its purpose.

The pain that followed the memory was in her heart, not her shoulder. The war had taken so much from her, but losing Daddy had been the last straw. Perhaps it was what had pushed her over the edge that night. If she could go back...

She'd do the same.

Daddy had instilled it in her to help those who were sick and hurting, defenseless and needy.

She looked at the strong profile of the man beside her. One who'd given his boots to an old fellow with rags around his feet. The same one who was taking her to Omaha, away from Billy Williams and his condemning words. It was instilled in Mr. Hickman, too, the urge to help those in need.

Did he even realize it?

Susannah had been under no illusions that her own people would accept what she'd done, but at first, she'd thought the Yankees would. She'd even thought they might respect her for it. Abel's family had squashed any such hopes. And then the people of Missouri had buried them.

But Mr. Hickman hadn't turned her away, and by that, he'd planted another seed of hope. Hope that she could find a place to start over. A place to belong. A place to once again call home with people who wouldn't forever see her as a traitor to their cause.

The sun was casting long shadows over the water by the time Hick searched for a place to camp for the night. They'd covered close to fifteen miles by his reckoning, but since they were following the river, those miles had twisted and turned in a few places. They were closer to St. Joseph as the crow flew. But Billy What's-his-name wasn't a crow.

He was, however, a scout. He might know the lay of the land.

The ground tilted up to the small rise overlooking the river. Hick stopped and looked around. The horizon darkened behind them and to the west, away from the river. Could be rain in those clouds. A trio of deer moved into view, too far away to shoot for supper. A gunshot would draw unwanted attention anyway.

Mrs. Piper didn't move or say anything while he finished his surveillance. She looked about ready to fall out of her saddle.

Hick moved Trooper off the crest of the rise to a thicket of willow and brambles on the other side. The thicket would help hide their smoke and offer some protection from the rain. It was still on somewhat higher ground, so the rain would wash down to the river. He dismounted, gripping the saddle while he eased his weight onto his hip. It was improving. Slowly.

He moved to the mule. "Let me help you down, Mrs. Piper. You look done in."

"Thank you." Even her smile was tired.

He raised his arms, and she more or less slid into them. She weighed next to nothing, so he scooped her up and deposited her at the base of a tree. "You sit there. I'll see to Trooper and your mule."

It didn't take him long to strip the tack from both animals and lead them to the river for a drink. Then he hobbled Trooper and tethered the mule, who nipped at him in the process. Ungrateful beast.

When he got back to the tree, Mrs. Piper was sound asleep. She didn't rouse while he started the fire and set his coffeepot to brewing. They'd eat a cold dinner of hardtack and jerky, but it would go down better with hot coffee.

He squatted by the fire and studied her. He'd been pushing questions aside ever since she'd been called a traitor, but they returned. Jessup must have been her name before she married, since she'd admitted that she'd grown up living near that scout from the wagon train. She couldn't have been old enough to marry before the war, although some of those Southern women married young.

But how had she managed to marry a Union soldier while her family was obviously fighting for the Confederates? Where had her family loyalties been?

Ma had been at odds with Pa over Hick and Denny joining the war. It'd been the first time he'd ever heard his parents argue. Loudly. As far as he knew, they'd stayed on opposite sides of that fence. He and Denny had left, with only Pa waving goodbye. Ma had glared. She'd not said a word or lifted a hand.

Hick rubbed his chest.

"Are you feeling poorly?"

The words snapped him back to the present.

"I'm fine, ma'am. How are you feeling?"

She sat up straighter against the tree. "I'm not the one rubbing my chest."

Hick dropped his gloved hand to the handle of the coffeepot and gave the contents a little swish.

Mrs. Piper rose and joined him at the fire. "I could make another batch of pancakes."

That sounded a heap better than what he'd rustle up.

"Are you up to it? There is plenty of hardtack and jerky."

"I think we can do better than that." She set about fixing their supper.

A rumble of thunder reached them.

"I'll rig a shelter." Hick unrolled his oiled tarp and rope. By the time Mrs. Piper was loading his plate with a pancake, he'd finished. He ate two while she cooked one for herself, barely finishing before fat raindrops plopped around them.

Hick gathered the rest of their belongings under the tarp's protection.

"I'm sorry, ma'am, but we'll have to share this tonight if we want to stay dry." The tarp was large enough that they weren't crushed together, but it was still close quarters with a woman.

A beautiful woman.

She settled with her plate on her lap and looked around. "I prefer to be dry." Then she turned her attention to her dinner.

When she was done, she set her plate aside. "Mr. Hickman, we don't know much about each other, but I would like your assurance that I can trust you."

"What?" He wasn't stupid, he knew what she was referring to. No man could be around such a pretty woman and not have certain thoughts. But they'd been together for days, and he hadn't made any move to—

"I feel that I can, but I'd like to hear it from you nonetheless." She tilted her head, dark curls escaping in the damp air to frame her face. "I perceive that you are, above all, a man of your word. My husband was such a man. I knew from the start that I could trust him, but I asked him to assure me of his intentions as well."

"What did he say?" Hick wasn't sure why he asked that, but it popped out before he could think about it. Forcing his attention away from those bluer-than-blue eyes, he opened his canteen and took a swallow of its tepid water.

"He said he would marry me."

Hick choked.

Susannah had often been accused of being too blunt, and Mr. Hickman's reaction proved it true. She waited for him to stop coughing and sputtering, then added, "I do not expect nor desire the same from you. I wish you to confirm that you are willing to act as my protector—only as my protector—until I can find passage to Oregon."

He wiped his mouth with the back of his hand, his face not hard to read even as darkness settled around them. She'd shocked him. "Ma'am, if I had paper and ink, I'd sign a document assuring you that I have no interest in any"—he waved a hand between them—"other understanding between us."

"Then I may safely stay with you until I secure passage to Oregon?" It was a lot to ask, she knew it was, but what other option did she have?

He drew back and watched her for a long moment. "I'll see you safely to Omaha, ma'am. Beyond that, I'm not willing to commit."

It was a fair answer, if less than she'd hoped.

It wouldn't get her to Oregon, but it was a step in the right direction.

CHAPTER 8

T HE RAIN HAD STOPPED overnight, but Hick's back was wet as he saddled Trooper. He'd slept at the very edge of the tarp shelter for fear of Mrs. Piper misconstruing his movements. Their conversation had rattled him and robbed him of sleep. Not just that she was bold enough to ask the questions, but that she wanted to stay with him until she found passage to Oregon—however long that might take.

He'd spent two years avoiding responsibility for any person other than one Sam Hickman. He'd learned his lesson. He wasn't about to get himself tied to Mrs. Piper—not in any way.

Mrs. Piper was saddling her mule. She appeared to have slept well. She was certainly more alert, more focused, than she'd been the night before. Her questions hadn't robbed *her* of sleep. Nope, she was obviously refreshed and ready to meet the day.

In contrast, Hick's shirt was cold and damp, and his jaw cracked while trying to stifle a yawn. He was working his way up to a good grouch, and he knew it. He stopped and breathed in deeply through his nose. The scent of bacon and biscuits lingered in the air. He should stop his internal mutterings and enjoy his full belly.

His bedroll and saddlebag in place, Hick slid his rifle into its scabbard and mounted Trooper. He waited while Mrs. Piper climbed aboard the mule, then nodded upriver. "Ready, ma'am?"

"I am." She urged the molly forward.

Hick tapped Trooper with his heels and followed the mule until they cleared the thicket, then passed by and took the lead. They were coming into some open country, and he didn't want his vision hindered by someone in front of him.

Not someone like Mrs. Piper, anyway. Before her questions the previous evening, he hadn't noticed the way her coat hugged her shoulders or the way her skirt flared from her waist and flowed over her knee bent around the saddle's horn. Hadn't noticed the rich darkness of her hair.

Better to have all that behind him.

They rode across mostly flat, open land through the morning without a word spoken. The only sounds were the river when they rode close to it and the ever-present wind. Twice Hick had sighted deer, but neither time had presented a good shot. Fresh meat would be a nice change, but for just the two of them, it would be better to flush a rabbit or more prairie chickens.

They topped a low rise as the sun reached its peak, and something caught Hick's eye. He stopped Trooper and motioned for Mrs. Piper to stay back. That she did somewhat surprised him, but he ignored her as he scanned the shallow bowl of land before them. A hawk soared high overhead, motionless wings skimming the air currents. Last year's brown grasses bent in the wind. A small buckskin horse cropped grass across the bowl, a saddle on its back. Tall willows grew alongside the river.

From one of them, a man twisted in the wind.

Hick had seen a couple of hangings in his life, but never a man hung upside down.

He tapped Trooper with his left foot and moved the horse sideways into some concealing brush while he watched.

The mule was noisily cropping foliage behind him.

The hawk made another lazy circle overhead.

Mrs. Piper remained silent.

Hick watched, waiting for something else to move.

Or someone.

Because that man hadn't hung himself in the tree.

They should give this place a wide berth and ride on. Whatever had happened below was none of their concern. And burying a dead man wasn't high on his list of things to do on the way to Omaha.

He was on the verge of lifting the reins and moving when the small horse scented them and raised its head.

What if it was Hick down there, swinging from that tree? What if it was Trooper standing guard? He'd want someone to cut his body down, bury him, and maybe mumble something Christian over his grave. But mostly, he'd want someone to take care of Trooper.

He waited another handful of minutes, and still nothing sinister moved. With a weary sigh, he nudged Trooper out of the brush and over the rim of the bowl. Hoofbeats followed, and then a slight gasp as Mrs. Piper no doubt saw the man hanging in the tree.

He should have warned her about that.

The mule trotted up beside Trooper.

"What happened here?"

"No idea, ma'am."

Her face was drawn, the mule's reins clenched in her fist.

"Whoever did this has moved on."

Those intense blue eyes met his. "What are you going to do?"

"Bury the man and see to his horse."

She gave a short nod and stayed close to his side.

As they drew closer, the horse squealed and spun in a tight circle, then bucked and stopped, facing them. Its head was high, nostrils wide. Everything about it said mustang. A good horse, one that was staying near its owner. If it was broke well enough, it might be a better mount for Mrs. Piper than the mule.

Best tend to the man first and deal with the horse after.

Hick dismounted and dropped the reins. Trooper would stand ground-tied for as long as it'd take for the burying.

Mrs. Piper stayed on her mule, her head swiveling to take in their surroundings.

He was pretty sure they were alone.

But it never hurt to have someone keeping watch.

It wasn't the first dead man Susannah had ever seen. Far from it. She'd attended a number of deathbed visits with Daddy before the war. During the war, she'd seen even more. Not just soldiers who'd returned too wounded to serve anymore, many of them dying at home, but there'd also been the women and children left behind. With too little food and too much disease, so many had succumbed to death despite her efforts.

Dying is as much a part of life as living is, Susannah girl.

Daddy hadn't believed in shielding her from the harsh realities of life, maybe because of Mama's struggles in that way. But for whatever reason, Susannah was thankful for his forethought. Had she been raised in a more genteel way, cosseted and shielded, she might have crumbled years before.

Like Mama had.

Sticks snapped beneath the willow as Mr. Hickman walked around the man. He reached up and grabbed something stuck on a branch, a frown building between his brows.

"What is it?" she asked.

"Fishing line." He shrugged. "Maybe it fell out of his pocket."

"Can you cut him down?"

Mr. Hickman studied the situation. "There's no rope."

"No rope?" She leaned closer. The man's leg was caught where a limb split into two and a third branch had been broken off. The man's boot was hooked over that broken branch.

Mr. Hickman pushed on the man's leg, probably to get a better look.

The hanging man groaned.

Mr. Hickman jumped backward, tripped over a branch on the ground, and landed on his rear with his gun drawn and aimed at the one hanging from the tree.

Susannah slipped from Peaches and rushed to the poor fellow's side. "Hello? Can you hear me?"

Another groan, but no flicker of an eyelid.

She knelt beside him. Half-dried blood matted one side of his hair, but he was breathing evenly. Fingers pressed against his neck found a steady pulse. She looked up at Mr. Hickman, who still held his pistol, but it was aimed at the ground.

"He's alive."

Hick holstered his Colt .45. Of course he was alive. Dead men didn't groan.

"He's breathing, and his pulse is strong," Mrs. Piper stood and studied the man's leg caught in the tree. "His head is injured. We need to get him down without letting it smack into anything, including the ground."

Hick pulled a coil of rope from his saddle. He made a loop and slipped it over the man's dangling arms, then tightened it around his chest below his armpits. He tossed the other end over a thick branch, pulled it tightly enough to move the man's body to the side, and tied it off.

"That will work," Mrs. Piper said. "Good thinking."

Her praise shouldn't have brought a warm flush to his neck that it did. Hick moved to get a look at the stuck leg. He braced his feet and grabbed a firm hold just above the knee. "Best stand back, ma'am." Then he shoved up.

The little fellow came to with a howl like a scalded coyote. His body stiffened, both arms flung outward, and he gave a mighty kick with his free leg, connecting solidly with Hick's shoulder.

Hick stumbled sideways, fancy stepping to keep on his feet. Pain exploded in his hip as he came to a stop with his back to the tree.

The mustang squealed and charged toward its rider. Trooper flung his head up and pinned his ears in a menacing look that stopped the smaller horse. The mule chuffed a few breaths, ending in a bray.

Behind Hick, rope creaked, the tree limb groaned, and the little man yelled fit to birth a baby. Working himself to stand straight, Hick's breath caught against the pain, but he got turned around.

The fellow hung suspended by his armpits, his backside a foot off the ground and his legs—one minus its boot—stretched before him. If the glower on his face meant anything, it wouldn't profit Hick to stand around waiting for a thank-you.

Susannah rushed to the stranger's side. "Can you stand?"

He gave his head a little shake, then peered up at her. Why, he was barely more than a boy. His hair was overly long and the same color as Missouri River mud. His eyes were maybe a half shade darker and widely spaced, which she'd always thought of as a sign of intelligence. He was thin to the point of emaciated, but when he grinned at her, there was a lively spark in his eyes.

"Reckon so, ma'am, iffen ya was to lend me an arm to lean on."

A rude snort came from Mr. Hickman's way, but Susannah ignored it. She braced her hands on his ribs under the supporting rope. "Slow and easy now, just bring your feet under you. They are likely to be numb from hanging that way."

"Yes, ma'am, they do feel a mite off."

But he stood, and she steadied him when he swayed. He started picking at the knot in the rope, but she pushed his hands away. "Your fingers are swollen. Let me untie that for you."

His only answer was another grin.

"Here, let me." Mr. Hickman took over the knot, and it fell away. Then he eyed the boy up and down. "How'd you get stuck in that tree?"

"Let me make sure he doesn't have any other injuries first, Mr. Hickman, and then he can answer your questions." Susannah led the boy to a large rock and urged him to sit. She pulled her sack from behind her saddle and unstrapped her canteen. She dampened a square of her ruined chemise and cleaned off the wound on his head.

"Thank ya, ma'am, for doctorin' me like this. I'm much obliged." He flinched when she cleaned the open wound.

"Hold still." She added more water to the cloth. "It's no bother."

Mr. Hickman came up beside her. "Since the two of you can talk, he can answer my questions now."

"One moment." She took the boy's chin in her hands and tilted it up, then lifted each eyelid and peered closely. "Yes. He should be clear-headed enough to answer. There's no sign of a concussion."

The boy glanced at Mr. Hickman. "She some kinda female doctor?"

"As close as you'll find."

His confidence in her skills surprised Susannah, but she appreciated it.

"Sure beats ol' Doc Baxter. Smells a mite nicer too."

Susannah turned her face away to hide the twitch of her lips. He was a cheeky young man, but the harmless sort.

"What's your name, son?" Hick asked.

"They call me Cooter." He rubbed his head and winced. "My proper handle is Jeremiah Malachi Woods." He grinned again. "I never seemed to grow into all of that, so folks been callin' me Cooter since I were a pup."

Pup seemed an apt word. Cooter was small and slight with a big grin. He struck Hick as a fellow more willing to please than most folks.

Mrs. Piper said, "Well, Mr. Woods—"

"Oh, no, ma'am." The boy raised both hands as if to ward Mrs. Piper off. "I answer to Cooter and only that. Mr. Woods was my grandpappy. I expect I'll be just Cooter my whole life."

"Very well, Cooter"—she handed him her canteen—"you should drink something. Just a few swallows for now. It'll help you regain your equilibrium."

Cooter eyed the canteen, then took it from her like it was a live eel. "My what, ma'am?"

She smiled and patted his shoulder. "Your balance and general feeling of wellness."

He swallowed the water and handed the canteen back.

Mrs. Piper set it aside and drew a small packet from her sack. "And now I should stitch that gash on your head."

The young man sprang from the rock like a startled frog. "Oh, no, ma'am. I'll be just fine without no stitchin'."

"It's short but deep. It will heal better and faster if I close the wound, and you won't start it bleeding again."

"Better listen to her,

" Hick said. "The lady knows what she's doing."

"But I—"

"Son." Hick lowered his voice and leaned forward. "Don't make me have to hold you down."

Cooter's Adam's apple bobbed a couple of times, then he sank back onto the rock.

Mrs. Piper threaded her needle, standing in back of the boy and out of his range of vision. She was good.

"Mr. Hickman, I'm going to need your bottle of whiskey."

He fetched it from his saddlebag and handed it to her.

"Cooter"—she leaned around until she was eye level with the boy—"this will sting, but it must be done to help prevent infection. You understand?"

The young man's Adam's Apple bobbed again, and his eyes looked fit to fall out of his head. Hick was ready to hold him down, but Mrs. Piper didn't wait for that. She grabbed hold of Cooter's head and poured whiskey over the wound.

To the boy's credit, he watched his language. His speech might say hillbilly, but someone had raised him with good manners. He wouldn't feel the needle much with the sting from the whiskey still at work, but Hick figured he could use a distraction.

"How'd you come to be hanging in that tree?" Hick asked.

"Well, now, that there is a story." The young man settled in like a natural-born storyteller and barely grimaced when the first stitch went in.

CHAPTER 9

S USANNAH WAS VERY GOOD at suturing. Daddy had often had her do the stitching because her fingers were both nimble and quick. Even with her shoulder hurting and arm a little stiff, she could close the gash.

"I was more than some hungry when I got here,"—Cooter pointed at the ground—"and it bein' about noon, I thought to catch a fish."

"That explains the fishing line." Mr. Hickman pulled it from his pocket.

"Glory be! I thought I'd lost it sure. It bein' my last string, I was afeared I'd go hungerin' for a spell."

Susannah had to keep her lips pressed together as Cooter's story unfolded. She pushed the needle through again, but Cooter was so absorbed in his story, he barely flinched.

"How did fishing land you in that tree?" The disbelief was thick in Mr. Hickman's voice.

"I durn near landed me a big one in that river." Cooter pointed his thumb over his shoulder. "It took my bait and leaped into the air. I ain't goin' to say it were large, but I wouldn't of been surprised to see Jonah pop outta its mouth, neither."

Susannah bit her lip to keep from laughing and pushed the needle through for the final stitch.

"I planted my boot heels in the mud of that river bank, reared back fit to fall on my backside, and gave a mighty jerk on that line. Well, mister, I'm tellin' it gospel now, that fish jumped so high I was alookin' at his belly. Then he up and flipped like to which I ain't never seen a fish do afore. And wouldn't ya know it"—he smacked his hands together—"he sprung offen that hook like a cork shot from a jug."

The boy's shoulders sagged. "I hit the ground when the line went slack, and durn if it didn't sail clean over my head and land its hook into this here tree."

Mr. Hickman ran his glove down his face, likely to hide a smile. "That explained the fishing line. And it being your last piece, you just naturally had to fetch it down."

Cooter grunted as Susannah tied off the last stitch. "Guess I still had me some of that river mud stuck on my boots."

And that explained the fall. No doubt about it, this Cooter was what they'd call back home a *character*. But he seemed a harmless sort, and his chatter lightened her mood.

"I surely am glad ya come along with the missus when ya did."

Mr. Hickman coughed. "It's not like that."

"It's not like what?"

Susannah cleaned her needle and scissors with a bit of whiskey, then returned them to her packet. "What he means is, we aren't married."

The young man's demeanor grew somber.

She hurried on when Mr. Hickman remained silent. "My name is Mrs. Piper, and he is Mr. Hickman. He's escorting me north to Omaha."

"And ya ain't hitched?"

She met his eyes squarely. "We are not."

"This is as good a place as any to take a break." Mr. Hickman said. "I'll see to Trooper and your mule."

He limped off as fast as he could and left her to explain things.

The coward.

Hick stripped the saddle and gear off Trooper, then did the same for Mrs. Piper's mule. The ornery thing nipped at him again. He eyed the mustang, but the animal moved away from him. It wasn't hobbled or tethered, so he had no way to catch it.

A sharp whistle pierced the air. The mustang tossed up its head, snorted, and then trotted to Cooter like a well-trained dog. That was a handy trick.

Hick glanced at Trooper, but the war horse was a little long in the tooth to be learning something new. Hick walked over to the mustang once it reached Cooter. It was a small but well-built horse, its buckskin hide shone with good health, and it could probably go all day and half the night if it had to. Just the type of mustang he hoped to catch near the mountains.

Cooter stripped it of its saddle and gear. The feisty animal flung its heels higher than its head and then bolted off at a full gallop.

"He'll come back?"

"Once he's worked them kinks out, or iffen I whistle."

"Good horse you got there. Handy, that whistle."

Cooter grinned. "First thing I taught Rumpus once we come to an understandin'."

"Rumpus?" Odd name, but *odd* fit with what Hick'd seen of Cooter so far.

"Our first ride didn't go so good." As if that explained everything.

They watched the horses for a moment. While Rumpus galloped around the meadow, Trooper dropped to his knees and then over into a vigorous roll.

Cooter glanced at Mrs. Piper and then at Hick. "I don't hold with men and women traveling together who ain't married. It ain't fittin'."

What right had he to question anything? "What are you, a preacher?"

"I ain't, but my grandpappy was. He raised me to do right. This"—he gestured from the woman, who was pulling foodstuff out of her sack, to Hick and back—"ain't right."

Hick pushed his hat back from his forehead and rubbed the ache forming there. He hadn't asked for Mrs. Piper to join him, and now this young upstart had the nerve to accuse him of something that wasn't happening. That wouldn't happen.

"There is no *this* between me and Mrs. Piper."

Doubt wrote itself loud and plain across the young man's features.

"She's a widow woman who was traveling alone. A couple of fellows jumped her, one shot her and ran her and the mule into my camp a few nights back."

Cooter gaped at him for a moment. "Shot her?"

"Yup."

The young man stared at Mrs. Piper for a long moment. "She don't seem to be hurtin' none."

"High in the left shoulder. The bullet grazed her deep. And being a doctor's daughter, she knew how to patch it up herself." He looked to where she bent over a fledgling fire. If that was coffee she was putting together, he'd be eternally grateful. He could use a midday cup after the almost sleepless night. "She's tougher than she looks."

Cooter scratched his chin. "And ya ain't...?"

Hick shook his head. "Nothing like that. I told her I'd see her safe as far as Omaha."

"Huh. Well, I'm sorry I misthought the situation." Cooter pressed his lips together and gave a firm nod. "Understandin' how things is, I reckon I can ride along with ya to Omaha. Give her a bit more respectability when we get to town, me being a chaperone and all."

Hick sputtered, but the young man was already striding toward Mrs. Piper.

Ride with them? It was bad enough traveling with one person he didn't want. Was he to be saddled with two?

Mr. Hickman had dropped his saddlebag near her saddle, so Susannah figured he wouldn't mind if she pulled out his coffeepot. Seeing the way he'd appreciated the hot drink the several mornings they'd been together, it might sweeten his disposition—even without sugar. It was clear he wasn't charmed by Cooter.

Not like she was. There was something about the young man that reminded her of John, her youngest brother. He'd been the charmer of the bunch and Mama's favorite. Not that she hadn't loved all her children—she had. But there'd been a special place in her mother's heart for John. When he'd died at First Manassas in July of 1861, Mama had started to slip. No matter what Daddy dosed her with or how hard he and Susannah had tried to talk her past the grief, they'd watched helplessly as Mama had wasted away.

"Mrs. Piper?"

Cooter's voice brought her back to the fire and the coffeepot still in her hand.

"Yes?"

"Ma'am." He pulled his hat off and twisted it between his hands. "I'm right sorry for thinkin' there was somethin' between ya and Mr. Hickman. He done set me straight on that."

Susannah busied herself filling the coffeepot from her canteen, trying to ignore the heat on her cheeks. "It was a natural assumption."

"Well, ma'am, so nobody else goes and thinks that way, I told Mr. Hickman that I'd ride alongside ya to Omaha."

Susannah looked up, swallowing a lump in her throat. The boy—young man—was obviously serious. When was the last time someone had cared how other people thought of her? Abel had, of course, but he hadn't been able to change anyone's opinion. Cooter probably wouldn't either, but it meant something that he wanted to try.

"Thank you."

He held out his hand. "Can I refill that canteen for ya?"

"Sure." She handed it over and watched him walk to the river, showing no ill effects from his accident.

"Looks like we got a tagalong." Mr. Hickman's voice carried a level of disgust that angered her, but she bit back any retort. After all, she needed him. And, deep inside, she sensed that his disgust—like his silence—hid something else. Something deeper.

She rose and faced him. "I appreciate the reason he's coming with us."

The tall man snorted, then caught her eye and had the grace to glance away. "You're right, ma'am. I can see how this might look. If him riding along makes it easier on you, then naturally, he's welcome."

But he wasn't. Not really. Everything in his demeanor shouted otherwise. And yet, he was allowing it.

For her.

For the second time in as many minutes, she fought with the knot that tried to form in her throat. A knot formed of unshed tears and the tendrils of a growing hope.

"I took the liberty of setting up your coffeepot."

"Thank you, ma'am."

"I was careful to not disturb anything else in your saddlebag."

"Well, ma'am, there's nothing in there to worry over. I travel light. Just a couple of shirts and socks and whatever food I have left."

"Speaking of food, I can put together something for our noon meal." She glanced at the river. "It might be best if we stayed here until tomorrow. If Cooter's head isn't pounding, it soon will be. The rest would do him good."

"Weren't you the one in a hurry to get moving?" He raised an eyebrow at her.

"To meet the wagon train, yes, but you were right about that." That she wasn't on it still made her blood boil. "It's not fair that women aren't allowed to join without a husband."

"Maybe not, ma'am. But it's the way things are."

Susannah had grown up the complacent sibling in her family. The only girl, she'd filled all the roles expected of her. Helping Mama around the house, working in the garden, even becoming a nurse to assist Daddy. She hadn't learned to kick against the goads until she'd helped Abel escape. But even in her deepest despair, she never regretted that decision.

"I don't know how much food you have, ma'am, but I don't have nearly enough to keep three people fed all the way to Omaha. Cooter doesn't appear to be carrying any provisions. It's best we keep moving."

She hadn't thought of that. "I have a little flour, a half sack of cornmeal, a tin of lard, a tin of baking powder, and two more cans of peaches." Which wouldn't go far to feed three people for very many days.

"I've got enough bacon for one more morning, some hardtack, jerky, tinned beef, and a small sack of beans."

She smiled. "Well, between us, I'd say we could get by."

Cooter approached, swinging her canteen. "Iffen ya give me an hour or so, I could catch some fish for supper."

"We've seen the way you catch fish." Hick strode to his saddlebag.

"That little thing"—Cooter pointed to the tree he'd been hanging in—"were just a pile of misfortunes." He puffed out his chest. "I'll have ya know that I've caught more than my share of fish in my life, and that's a fact."

Fish sounded awfully good to Susannah, but from the stiff set of Mr. Hickman's shoulders, they weren't going to enjoy it anytime soon.

"We'll have hardtack and jerky with that coffee." Mr. Hickman handed the food to them. "Then we saddle and ride on."

They each filled a cup, and Susannah chewed on her jerky while a piece of hardtack soaked in the coffee. Trying to chew it without soaking was a good way to break a tooth. The men did the same.

Peaches and the horses grazed nearby. It was an almost idyllic scene. Susannah relaxed and enjoyed the warm sunshine on her shoulders. The left one hurt, but there was no sign of infection, and the pain was bearable. She'd been lucky.

Lucky that Mr. Hickman had been nearby.

Mr. Hickman was determined to get them to Omaha as soon as possible. Was it really because he thought they'd run short of food?

Or was he anxious to be rid of her?

CHAPTER 10

AFTER HE SADDLED THE mule for Mrs. Piper, Hick hefted his saddle to his shoulder and limped to Trooper. The horse turned its face toward him, one brown eye and one blue eye staring as if to say another hour of grazing would be preferable to hauling his carcass down the trail. Hick took a moment and gave the horse a vigorous scratching above the tail.

"I like seein' a man who treats his horse good." Cooter led the saddled mustang closer.

"Me and Trooper been together a long time." Hick rubbed the small scar on his temple.

"Was ya in the war?"

"I was." But it was a closed subject.

"That where ya picked up the scar yer a-rubbin' on?"

Hick dropped his hand but didn't look at Cooter. Maybe the boy would take the hint and not ask about the war. He'd been avoiding that subject for two years, and he sure wasn't going to start jabbering about it now.

"I wasn't," Cooter said.

Hick paused, then gave the cinch one last tightening pull. Most men wouldn't offer that bit of history. There were those who didn't look kindly on men who'd refused to fight, both North and South. Hick was torn between agreeing with them and being eternally grateful that Ma had managed to keep his two youngest brothers out of the war.

Cooter swung into his saddle with the ease of one born to it.

Hick followed suit, his hip protesting when he tried to make the swing as smooth as Cooter's.

Mrs. Piper was already seated on her mule.

Hick reined Trooper around and pointed him north, then clicked his tongue. The old horse stepped out at a brisk walk.

The mustang paced beside him, getting close enough for Trooper to pin his ears before it backed off a couple of steps.

Hick patted the old war horse's neck. Maybe if Hick could pin his ears at Cooter, the fellow would take the hint and move off on his own. But that wouldn't be fair to Mrs. Piper.

"The war didn't hit me right," Cooter said.

The voice jarred Hick, annoyed him. He'd grown used to traveling in silence. Mrs. Piper was quiet, and he appreciated that about her.

"Grandpappy had up and died that winter afore the war, so I was free to go, but I was a mite young and small for my age."

Didn't look like he'd grown much.

"When I seen that Pony Express poster in town, and Mr. Sawyer read it to me, I knowed that was what I oughta do."

Must have been some poster.

"What'd it say?" Mrs. Piper rode her mule up on the other side of Cooter.

"Might misremember it some, but along the lines of 'skinny orphans what ain't over eighteen who can sit a horse good.' It went on as how they'd pay twenty-five dollars a week. Why, I rode straight off to the nearest Pony Express station and made my mark on the paper."

Twenty-five dollars a week. No wonder Cooter could afford the Spencer rifle in his scabbard. Hick gritted his teeth. He'd signed on with the First Ohio Cavalry for thirteen dollars a month. He hadn't been able to afford his Spencer until after the war.

"It were dangerous work. More than a few of them fellas I signed on with is buried along the trail. We didn't get shot at like them soldier boys, what with people lined up and shootin' all organized like. Nope. It were bandits hidin' behind rocks and Injuns after yer hair. And iffen ya got yerself hurt, there weren't no wagon followin' with doctors and such neither." He twisted in his saddle to look at Hick. "Reckon ya saw yer share of them."

Hick grunted. He hadn't thought about the dangers of the Pony Express. He'd been too busy chasing Johnny Rebs.

They rode north along the river for a couple of hours, Cooter rambling on and Mrs. Piper occasionally responding, but Hick quit listening.

The Missouri twisted and turned like a snake on the end of a stick. If he knew Nebraska at all, he'd cut across country and likely save a day or more of travel. But he didn't, so they were better off keeping the river in sight.

The last thing he wanted was to get lost and wander around Nebraska with a widow and a loud-mouthed kid..

They passed a few homesteads, sod buildings that squatted against the landscape, but didn't approach any. Men worked in the fields behind oxen or mules, and once they passed a woman taking laundry off a rope. She'd shielded her eyes to see them better. It must be lonely for a woman on the prairie so far from a town.

They passed what looked like a trading post, but Mrs. Piper was still looking over her shoulder frequently. Hick probably was too, if he thought about it. More distance between that angry Southerner at the wagon train and them would be a good thing, so Hick decided not to stop. He didn't want to run into any more trouble than he'd already collected.

It was nearing evening when Hick realized the other two had stopped talking.

Cooter was slumped in his saddle, head bobbing against his chest. Mrs. Piper rode next to him. She probably thought she could steady him if he started to slip off. If she tried, she'd no doubt set her shoulder to bleeding again.

They needed to stop for the night.

Ahead was a rocky rise with the usual willow thickets near the river. He headed Trooper in that direction. The rocks would give a nice break from the wind.

Hick's stomach grumbled. He looked forward to whatever Mrs. Piper could make out of their meager larder. Whatever it was, it would be better than what he could do.

That was one advantage to having her along, but it irked him to admit it. He didn't want any advantages to being with other people. Maybe he'd watch her more closely and figure out how she made things so tasty.

That would help once he was on his own again.

They stopped near a short cliff of rocks, and Susannah dismounted, happy to have her feet on the ground again. Peaches was a good mule with a steady gait, but the makeshift saddle was less than ideal for hours spent atop it.

Cooter had awakened and slid off his horse. "Iffen ya don't mind, I believe I'll try my hand at fishin' again. Got me a powerful hungerin' for fish, I do." He adjusted his hat. "And I got my reputation to think of. Cain't have folks thinkin' poorly of my fishin' skills."

"We have enough food to share," Susannah said.

The young man held up a hand. "I don't need charity, ma'am. I pull my own weight." With that, he whisked the gear off his horse and started for the river.

Mr. Hickman was unsaddling his horse when she asked, "Do you think he'll actually catch some fish?"

He shrugged. "Stranger things have happened."

The man could at least appear interested. She turned her back to him and stripped Peaches, tethering her near a grassy patch. Perhaps she should invest in a set of hobbles when they reached Omaha. They worked well for the bay horse and gave it more room to graze. She was pretty sure Cooter's whistle trick wouldn't impress the very independent molly.

While Mr. Hickman gathered sticks and started a fire, Susannah pulled out the ingredients for corn cakes. They'd go well with fish or jerky, whichever they ended up eating for supper.

And then what?

While she kept her hands busy, Susannah's thoughts wandered to what she'd been avoiding since leaving St. Joseph.

How was she going to get to Oregon?

Would she ever get to Oregon?

And if she didn't, what would become of her?

She was staring into the distance, a fingernail between her teeth, when Mr. Hickman voiced her thoughts.

"What do you plan to do, ma'am?"

She lowered her hand but didn't face him. "I wish I knew."

"Why is Oregon so important to you?"

"Abel said it was the one place where a Southern woman and a Yankee man could live in peace." She turned to him then. "That's all I want, Mr. Hickman. I want to live in peace. I want to get along with my neighbors. I want to help people. I want..." She sucked in a shaky breath. "I want a life where I can be useful and respected again."

"Is that what the war took from you, ma'am?"

It was that and so much more, but she couldn't bring Daddy back, or her brothers, or Abel or Mama. All she could do was find a place for herself. It was a large country, and Oregon was clear on the other side of it.

"I don't expect you could understand, Mr. Hickman." She gave the corn batter a vicious stir. "As you pointed out to me, there are things you cannot understand if you haven't been through them."

She and Abel hadn't been able to win over his family, for Pete's sake, or their Missouri neighbors. She had no reason to think Mr. Hickman would ever understand. It shouldn't hurt, but it did.

The very human need to be understood and accepted shouldn't be so hard to achieve.

An uncomfortable feeling worked its way across Hick's shoulders and slithered down his back. The similarities between Mrs. Piper and himself—similarities he'd have scoffed at a day or two ago—smacked him in the face.

They were both running from the effects of the war.

And they probably weren't the only ones. Those people waiting in St. Joseph to cross the prairie, how many of them were running as well?

"Will these do?" Cooter's voice cut the silence that had surrounded the camp. He marched in with his hand held high and three silvery fish hanging from a bent willow twig. He'd actually done it.

Hick's mouth watered at the sight.

Mrs. Piper exclaimed over the fish, praised Cooter's prowess with a hook, and within minutes, had corn cakes cooking in the skillet, and the fish rigged on sticks and roasting.

But Hick couldn't allow himself to relax and enjoy the night. In spite of himself, he'd begun to feel responsible for the two people squatting near the fire. Two people who needed his protection.

CHAPTER 11

TWO DAYS LATER, HICK pulled Trooper to a halt at the top of the last rise in a chain of low hills that fanned out from the river. Below them sprawled a city so new he could almost smell the sawdust and mortar used to put it together. On a hill to their left sat two large brick buildings overlooking the city like night-watch cowboys guarding the herd.

Mrs. Piper brought her mule next to Trooper, and Cooter stopped on the other side of her.

He stood in his stirrups, scanning the buildings below. "You reckon that's Omaha City?"

"Yup." It was too large to be anything else.

The little man settled back in his saddle and nodded toward the two buildings to their left. "What you suppose them are?"

The evening sun glinted off the glass windows of the longer one with a square tower thrusting out of its center like most government buildings liked to have. The other building was square and strong as if the builders were declaring it there to stay.

Hick rubbed his jaw, gloves rasping on his unshaven face. "Marks of progress, I'd say."

Cooter leaned over and spit. "Grandpappy used to say that progress was like huntin' coons."

"How's that?" Mrs. Piper asked.

"Takes an awful lot of bumpin' around in the dark before ya get a shot at somethin' worthwhile."

That sounded about right.

Hick touched his heels to Trooper's sides, and they ambled down the hill before skirting the riverbank into town. The acrid scent of coal smoke hung in the air. Wasn't much else to burn for cooking or heating in these parts. Several dingy steamboats tied to docks attested to the delivery of coal so far into the prairie.

They turned by a wooden sign labeled Farnham Street. They passed a few seedy-looking saloons and an equally seedy-looking inn plus more than a few huts and shanties crammed in against them.

The mule stayed next to Trooper, and Cooter stayed close on Mrs. Piper's other side as women came out of the shanties and huts to watch them pass. Several made less-than-subtle offers that matched their garish clothing.

Mrs. Piper kept her chin raised and her eyes straight forward. She wasn't a woman to be shocked or cowed by such behavior. But then, as the daughter of a doctor, she'd likely seen worse than the wares displayed by the women along the street.

They rode on. Brick buildings and board buildings lined both sides of the street for the next three blocks. Stores, shops, offices, and even a theater comprised that section of town. Down the side streets, the spires of several churches came into view. A good dozen buildings rose three or more stories. And even before noon, the tinny music of saloons floated in the air. The horses stepped across a rivulet of open sewage that ran alongside the boardwalk in front of the businesses. Omaha wasn't a true city yet, but it was on its way.

On the far side, Hick spied a feed-and-seed store. There were three places to get the sort of information he wanted in any town. Places where locals congregated and job postings were talked over. He hadn't seen a barbershop, and he wasn't about to leave Mrs. Piper on her own while he entered a saloon, so the feed-and-seed store would do.

He dismounted at the hitching rail, tied Trooper, then helped Mrs. Piper down. Cooter had his mustang tied and was in the store before Hick and Mrs. Piper entered.

It was like any such store, it smelled of dust, grain, and earthy minerals. Hick would have purchased a bag of oats for Trooper, but he didn't have the money. He approached a burly man wearing a leather apron behind the long counter.

"Morning." The man wiped his hands on a rag. "What can I do for you?"

"I'm looking for work."

The fellow eyed him up and down. "Ranch work, I suppose."

"I've experience there, but I'll take whatever I can turn my hand to."

"Can you read?"

"Yup."

"You look strong enough. I could use a man here for a while. Nothing permanent, I'm afraid, but I'm shorthanded for a week or so."

Hick glanced around the store. Bagging feed and seed and loading wagons shouldn't tax his hip too much. "I'm interested."

"Name's Baker, Nat Baker." The man stuck out his hand and they shook.

"Sam Hickman, folks call me Hick."

"Can you start right away?" Baker named a fair wage.

"I need to set up camp first, but I can be back after lunch."

"That'll work."

"Where's the best place to camp nearby?"

Baker pointed south. "There are several good spots on Forest Hill. Get your missus and your gear settled, and I'll see you back here." Baker strode off to wait on a customer.

"You didn't correct him," Mrs. Piper said as they stepped away from the counter.

Hick caught Cooter's attention from across the room and nodded toward the door. "Best we set up camp so I can get back and start work."

Cooter joined them as they stepped outside. "Ya hired on?"

"I did."

They mounted, and Mrs. Piper nudged her mule close. "Why didn't you correct him?"

"I don't plan to be here very long, so there was no reason to." He glanced at her. "I'm moving on as soon as I've got some money in my pocket, ma'am."

The past two days had worn on him like a hair shirt. He was ready to move on. Alone. Best she knew that so she could make her own plans.

Plans that wouldn't include him.

They'd camped too far out to walk to town without arriving at least somewhat disheveled, which wouldn't do, so Susannah hefted the saddle on Peaches. Lunch over and Mr. Hickman gone to start his job, it would be a fine time to see what Omaha had to offer her in the way of a job or passage to Oregon.

Mr. Hickman had said he'd move on soon. *He'd* move on—not *they'd* move on. She needed to find a way to support herself. Omaha was much larger than she'd thought it would be, and that gave her some confidence that she'd be successful in obtaining respectable employment.

"Where ya off to, ma'am?" Cooter returned from the river with their canteens freshly filled and dripping at his side.

"Into town." She climbed into the saddle. "I need to find passage to Oregon, and if I can't, then a job to support myself."

Cooter set the canteens near the remnants of the fire and scratched his head. "Reckon maybe I should see iffen I can scare up a job too?"

"A man needs to be able to support himself." She smiled at him. "I know you're a hard worker, or you wouldn't have lasted with the Pony Express."

He grinned back. "That's purely a fact, ma'am."

"You decide what's best for you, but I need to go to town."

"Want me to escort ya there?"

No, she didn't, but how to say it tactfully? "It might be better if I went alone. It will pose fewer questions, I think."

"Questions?"

She sighed. "Questions about how I arrived and with whom."

He frowned for a moment, but then said, "Oh. I think I follow ya, ma'am. Might not look right, approachin' a business with someone like me hangin' around behind ya."

"Yes, precisely. But that's not to say you couldn't follow a few minutes behind to look over the town on your own."

Cooter removed his hat and knocked the trail dust from its shabby felt. "I guess maybe I oughta change into my clean shirt and spruce up a mite first."

She hid a smile behind her hand, then turned Peaches toward town, saying over her shoulder, "That sounds like a good idea."

Approaching Omaha from the southwest this time, where the buildings seemed a bit more reputable, Susannah urged Peaches onto a wide and busy avenue with Thirteenth Street on its sign. She rode past a bakery, a tobacconist, and a shoe and hat store. Then another sign caught her eye. It was small but neatly painted, and it hung straight, nailed to a post.

James H. Peabody, M.D.

A wave of loss gripped Susannah's throat. Daddy's sign had been larger, but not much. It had swayed in the breeze from chains that supported it, its gentle creaking a comfort on a hot Georgia afternoon.

With the constant wind of the prairie, a solidly nailed sign was more prudent.

She slipped from Peaches and tied the mule, then brushed the worst of the wrinkles from her skirt and faced the red-painted door beneath the sign. Being a nurse wouldn't get her to Oregon, but it might allow her to eat and put a roof over her head. She drew in a steadying breath, then pushed open the door and stepped into an empty room.

The smells of camphor and alcohol struck as a small bell jingled overhead. She swallowed against the knot in her throat as memories of Daddy flooded her.

A bearded gentleman entered through an open doorway, wiping his hands on a piece of toweling. "How may I assist you, ma'am?"

"Are you Dr. Peabody?"

"I am."

Susannah presented her hand, which he took. "I am Mrs. Susannah Piper. My daddy was a doctor, sir, and I am well-trained as a nurse." She reclaimed her hand. "I am seeking employment as such until I secure passage to Oregon."

"A nurse?" His voice was low, his deep-set eyes well-spaced. "From the South?"

"Yes, sir." She could do nothing about the way she sounded. "Georgia. My daddy ran his practice there until the war."

"And now?"

"He died." The flicker of pain in the other man's eyes helped her to continue. "He was working in a field hospital and succumbed to dysentery."

"He was probably overworked to the point where his body could not fight off the infection. I am sorry, ma'am. We learned much during the war, but not quickly enough."

He'd said *we* as if he'd been there. It didn't surprise her. Few doctors wouldn't have served where their need was the greatest.

"I'm sure you are correct, sir. But it leaves me in the position of needing to care for myself. You see, my husband survived a prisoner of war camp, but in the end, it had taken too large a toll on his health. He passed away last fall."

Dr. Peabody rubbed a hand across his eyes. "I visited several of those camps. The conditions were intolerable." He cocked his head. "Which one was your husband in?"

"Andersonville, sir."

He straightened, then leaned forward. "Your husband was a Union soldier?"

"He was." She almost didn't continue, but if she hoped to work with this man, it would do her no good to hide the whole truth. "But Daddy and my three brothers all fought for—and died for—the Confederacy."

"Mrs..."

"Piper."

"Mrs. Piper, it would appear you are an extraordinary woman."

"I expect, sir, if you knew more Southern women, you'd find I'm not as uncommon as you suspect." At least, she hoped she wasn't the only one who defied the misconception so often thrown in her face since she'd left her native land. She wasn't lazy, slovenly, of loose morals, or in favor of slavery. Mostly she was just...

Tired.

"Perhaps you're right." He motioned to the empty chairs in the room. "As you can see, my practice is far from busy at the moment. I'm fairly new here. I'm not sure I have enough work for a nurse." He held up a finger. "But a colleague of mine, Dr. Conkling, has newly been appointed our health officer here in Omaha. He may have such a need. If you would give me a moment—"

The door behind Susannah burst open, and a young girl stumbled into the room. "Doc, we need you at the boarding house. Ma says one of the boarders is took sick real bad."

"Tell your ma I'll be there directly, Patsy."

The girl nodded, whirled, and raced away, leaving the door open.

Dr. Peabody shut it and turned to Susannah. "Mrs. Finan, the girl's mother, may be the most level-headed woman in town. If she's pan-icked enough to send her daughter racing over here"—he looked to the other doorway and then back at her—"perhaps you should accompany me, and we'll see how we get on. Wait here while I fetch my bag."

"Of course, doctor." While she'd never wish an illness on anyone, Susannah was thankful for the timing. Even if she couldn't work for Dr. Peabody, if she showed herself well, he might give her a good reference for Dr. Conkling.

Neither option would get her to Oregon, but either would provide her with a means to support herself until she found a way west.

Hick shouldered another sack of seed corn and limped to the customer's wagon. He tossed the sack on top of the stack. One of the horses hitched to the wagon tossed its head. It was one of a matched team of Percherons. He hadn't seen many such teams west of Ohio. The customer had money to own them. Which also explained the wagon filled with seed corn, wheat, and feed oats. Hick pulled the bill of sale from his pocket and checked off the items. Everything loaded except for hog rings. He'd have to ask someone where to find those.

"I'm stronger than I look, iffen that's worrisome." The voice reached him, and Hick turned. Cooter, hat in his hands, spoke with Baker at the counter. "And I ain't too proud to push a broom or shovel up after horses."

Hick approached them to ask about the hog rings.

Cooter grinned at him. "Hey, Hick."

"You two know each other?" Baker looked from Cooter to Hick and back.

"Yes, sir. Me and Hick been travelin' together for a spell."

That was one way to put it, but when Baker shot Hick a glance, he nodded to confirm it.

"Brooms and shovels are in the back, young man. Guess the place could use a bit of cleaning up. Not sure I'll have work for you every day, though."

"Thank ya, mister. I'll just be gettin' to work then." Cooter crammed his hat on his head, walked to the back of the store where Baker had pointed, and disappeared behind a curtain.

"He a good worker?" Baker asked.

"He rode for the Pony Express."

The shop owner whistled between his teeth. "He doesn't look old enough, but then, I guess they started them young."

"Where can I find the hog rings?" Hick asked.

Baker pointed to a display of half-barrels against the far wall. "Over there. Paper sacks are on the end."

Hick found what he needed to fill the order, then returned to the wagon. He handed the sack to the driver waiting on the wagon's bench. "Here you go. All set."

"Thank you." The man gathered the reins and released the brake. "See you next week."

A weekly trip to town for supplies. How long had it been since Hick had done that? Pa and Ma had looked forward to those outings. He and his brothers and sisters had piled into the wagon, the youngest on Ma's lap, and enjoyed the afternoon. It usually ended with a stick of candy, which kept them all quiet on the ride home.

Home. Of all the things he missed, it was that feeling that sometimes caught in his throat. The feeling of home.

He looked around the street at the forming town. It wasn't bustling like Kansas City or even St. Joseph, but one day it would be. From where he stood, three new buildings were under construction, the ring of hammers and rasp of saws adding to the noise of the street.

But somewhere to the west were mountains, and before the mountains were foothills populated with wild horses. It was quiet there. That would be his new home.

Cooter rounded the building pushing a barrow, the long handle of a shovel leaning against his shoulder. He grinned and parked the barrow where the wagon had been. "Between the two of us workin', we'll have a good stake soon." He slid the shovel under a pile of manure and tossed it in the barrow. "Wherever we go next, we'll be fixed for it."

We?

Rather than respond, Hick returned to the counter and ripped the bottom sales slip from the spindle to load the next wagon.

We.

Strangely enough, the idea didn't rub against his nerves as much as it had. Cooter was a chatterbox, but he'd proved he could fish. Hick might need a man like him to help round up the mustangs. If Rumpus was any indication, Cooter knew something about training horses.

Maybe having the young man tag along wasn't a bad idea. After all, Cooter was a man, not a boy, and not someone Hick needed to protect and provide for.

Nothing at all like Mrs. Piper.

CHAPTER 12

D R. PEABODY LED THE way down the street, his black leather bag in one hand. Men touched their hats, and women nodded as he passed, several murmuring greetings of, "Good afternoon, Doc."

Susannah hurried to keep up with the man's long strides. He didn't let the people's greetings slow him down, just touched his hat in return. A man on a mission, as a doctor ought to be.

Two blocks down and one to the right, they stopped at a three-story building with a porch the length of its front. Dr. Peabody rapped on the door, and it was opened by the same girl who had burst into his office.

"Come in, Doc. Ma's upstairs with Mr. Bury. Follow me." She scampered away with the doctor behind.

Susannah closed the door, then hurried to catch up.

The doctor walked into a room on the second floor, and Susannah followed. The sour smell of sickness filled the space. A man lay on the bed, his color almost the same as the sheets. An older woman rose from a chair when they entered.

"Thank you for coming so soon, Doctor." She gestured at the man and backed out of the doctor's way. "Mr. Bury didn't come down for breakfast this morning, and when I hadn't seen him at lunch, I came to check on him. I'm afraid he's in a bad way."

The doctor bent over the patient. "Mr. Bury, can you hear me?"

The man's eyelids flickered. He licked his lips and nodded.

"When did you begin to feel poorly?"

"Sometime after dark." The words were thin, reedy.

Susannah stepped toward the woman. "Warm water is needed, rags to clean up the mess, a fresh slop bucket, and keep the other tenants away from this room."

"Who are you?" she asked.

"I'm Mrs. Piper, a nurse."

With a nod and one last glance at the bed, wrinkles building between her brows, the woman left the room.

"Thank you, Nurse." The doctor turned to her and dropped his voice. "Have you any experience with cholera?"

"Too much, I fear."

"Clean the man as best you can and change the bedding. I'll instruct Mrs. Finan to burn it, as well as the man's clothing." He went to the door. "I'll have her bring you alcohol to clean with, then I must inform Dr. Conkling. Be sure and clean your hands with the alcohol when you're finished. That is imperative. It's one thing we learned on the battlefield that works." He tapped his fingers on the door frame for a moment, as if gathering himself for what was to come. "You'll be all right on your own until I can return?"

"Yes, Doctor."

"Fine." He gave a crisp nod and left.

Cholera. The word spiked fear through Susannah.

People in Omaha were going to die.

The sun sank below the horizon as darkness gathered around the campfire. Hick poked at the flames with a stick, his stomach grumbling.

Where was Mrs. Piper?

Cooter stood a few feet away, scanning the distance between the camp and town. He wouldn't be able to see the buildings before long. Full dark would be upon them.

A coyote yipped to the south.

Where the devil was Mrs. Piper?

Cooter took off his hat and banged it against his leg. "I cain't see no more." He came and crouched by the fire. "Wish I'd a went fishin' this afternoon instead of workin'. Fish woulda filled my belly."

Hick reached into his saddlebag and pulled out the last of the jerky. He handed Cooter half.

"Should we save back some for Mrs. Piper?" Cooter asked.

"She's got supplies in her saddlebag." Hick ripped off a chew of jerky.

Silence lingered over the camp while they ate, the sounds of night insects growing in the darkness.

"She shoulda been back by now, don't ya think?" Cooter asked.

Hick shrugged. After all, she might not come back. Maybe she'd found her way to Oregon. That would be a good thing. But part of him chafed at not knowing.

"You sure she didn't say where she was going?" he asked Cooter.

"Just to town to look for work or a way to Oregon. I done offered to go along, but she didn't want me there maybe raisin' questions she'd rather not answer."

Mrs. Piper was a smart woman. She'd land on her feet somewhere. Likely with a roof over her head and something better than jerky to chew on. But it still rubbed Hick wrong—the not knowing.

"Mebbe so we should ride back and look around," Cooter said.

"Look where?" Hick pointed in the darkness toward the town. "We wouldn't know where to start."

"We could ask around."

"I believe that's what she'd most want to avoid." He glanced at the younger man. "Don't you?"

"Yeah." Cooter slumped against his saddle. "I don't like not knowin' what's become of her. She's a fine woman." He sat up straight. "Ya don't suppose something bad happened to her, do ya?"

He hadn't... until then.

Hick pushed to his feet, stifling a low groan as his hip protested. "I'll saddle Trooper and ride down there." He pointed a finger at Cooter. "You stay here in case she shows up."

The young man nodded.

In minutes, Hick was riding into the darkness. After a woman he never wanted to be responsible for. One he ought to be relieved to be rid of.

A woman who might need his help.

"I need to let my people know where I am." Susannah shrugged into her shawl against the cool of the evening, glad she'd left all her belongings tied behind the saddle. "Thank you for seeing that Peaches was cared for."

"Thank you, Mrs. Piper, for all you did today." Dr. Peabody held the mule's reins while she mounted.

"I'll go straight to the boarding house in the morning."

"I'll be there to relieve Dr. Conkling, so I will see you then."

She settled her skirts, then gathered the reins. "Do you think it will be bad?"

"Mr. Bury told me he'd recently come from Memphis. Dr. Conkling has had a telegram confirming that the disease is raging there." He patted Peaches on the shoulder. "We must do our best to contain it to the boarding house."

"I will see you in the morning."

He stepped back, and she urged Peaches onto the quiet street. The stores were all closed, but piano music drifted down a side street from a saloon. There was only one other rider in the street, coming toward her on a white-faced horse.

Mr. Hickman.

Was he looking for her? And why did that question cause a little hitch to her breath?

She urged Peaches into a trot, and he stopped his horse as they neared, then he turned the bay to trot beside her.

"Mr. Hickman." She smiled at him. "It's very late. Are you just leaving work?"

"I was looking for you, ma'am."

Her stomach tightened, probably from not having eaten anything since breakfast. "I found a job, and I just finished."

He shot her a glance that she couldn't read in the darkness. "Doing what, ma'am?" His voice had taken on an edge.

"Working as a nurse, sir." She almost spat the next words. "What did you think?"

He had the grace to look away for a moment. Honestly. Did all men assume the worst of Southern women? She'd thought better of Mr. Hickman. Or maybe just hoped for better.

"When you didn't come back to camp, and it grew dark..."

"You just naturally assumed I'd come to town to turn prostitute, is that it?"

"Nope, ma'am." The edge was back, but more defensive this time. "But I thought you may have run into trouble."

She sighed. He'd been concerned. "I did run into trouble." She slowed Peaches to a walk as they left the street at the edge of town. "Cholera."

That jerked his head in her direction.

"Dr. Peabody says it's the first case he's seen. With a little luck and a lot of work, he hopes to contain it to the boarding house where it broke out."

"Cholera."

Of course, Mr. Hickman would know the dangers of that. It had been one of the more ravishing diseases to run through the camps early in the war before the cause was better understood. So many soldiers had died of it.

"We must use your coffeepot to boil all our drinking water, and while you're working, if possible, drink ale. It's safer. We should buy more whiskey for disinfecting should we need it."

"I'll do that."

"And Mr. Hickman?"

"Ma'am?"

"Thank you for coming to check on me."

He was the only person she knew who would have.

She'd found work as a nurse. Hick should have figured that out. She'd been right to get testy with him. They finished the ride to camp in silence, but it wasn't a strained silence. It was more of a comfortable silence.

That bothered Hick.

Earlier in the day, he'd considered taking Cooter along to the mountains. Tonight he was comfortable with Mrs. Piper. But in his heart, he knew he'd do better on his own. Away from people. Away from entanglements. Away from responsibilities he wasn't fit to hold.

"Ya found her." Cooter stepped from behind his mustang, his grin visible in the fire's light. "I knowed ya would."

"He did." Mrs. Piper dismounted. "But I must leave again at first light." She paused. "Have you men eaten?"

"Yes, ma'am. Me and Hick finished the last of the jerky. It weren't a patch on yer cookin', but it did the trick."

Hick took the mule's reins. "I'll see to the mule. You fix yourself something to eat."

She looked up at him, her dark hair making her face even paler in the moonlight. "Thank you, Mr. Hickman."

Something knotted in his chest as he stripped the molly of her tack, led her to a grassy spot, and tethered her to a sturdy bush. The animal must have been hungry because it didn't even bother to nip at him.

Mrs. Piper was eating peaches out of a can when he returned to the fire.

"There is cholera in the town," she said. "You'll both need to be extra careful. One doesn't contract the disease from the sick, but from contamination, especially of water." She glanced at Cooter and pointed to the canteens. "We'll need to boil all of the water from now on before drinking or cooking with it, or even washing. And fill the canteens upstream of town."

"Will the horses—and yer mule—need it boiled too?" Cooter asked.

"I've never heard of an animal suffering from cholera." Mrs. Piper glanced toward the animals. "I'm sure they'll be fine."

"It be a nasty disease, for sure," Cooter said. "I remember it killed a whole passel of folks back in Kentucky afore the war. Whole families up and died away."

"We didn't understand the way it spread back then. If anything good came out of the war, it was the advances in medical knowledge." She lowered her head for a moment, then met Hick's eyes. "The war changed us all. It's only right that something changed for the better."

Had the war changed him? Hick thought about her words as she finished her meager supper and then unpacked her bedroll to settle for the night. Or had the war just pointed out his flaws?

That was a question he'd never know the answer to.

Cooter bedded down across the fire from Mrs. Piper. Hick fed a few more sticks to the flames, then made his own bed a short distance away. The heat was welcome, as April nights on the prairie could be cold, but he preferred not to be too close. He wanted his eyes accustomed to the darkness should he need them. That was a trick he'd picked up during the war.

The war might not have changed him, but he'd learned things. Many of those things he wished he could forget. He lay on his back and rubbed his chest. The familiar pain of missing Denny always accompanied memories of the war. It was time to turn his thoughts to something else. Another trick he'd learned.

All three of them were working. They wouldn't see a payday until week's end, of course, but when they did, Mrs. Piper could move into town and find a boarding house. It was one thing for him and Cooter to sleep under the stars, but she was a lady.

He flicked a glance at her dark shape under her blankets near the fire.

She didn't belong out there. He had no doubt that she was strong enough, but she deserved better after all the war had stripped from her. She ought to be in a fine parlor somewhere, sipping tea next to a brick fireplace, a soft bed waiting for her.

Hick shifted on the hard ground, pushing that last notion away.

Once they had pay coming in, even if he and Cooter had to chip in, they'd see her set up in a respectable boarding house. She might never make it to Oregon, but she could build a new life in a young city like Omaha.

And then Hick could forget about her. Though, as her image swam in his vision, those striking blue eyes aimed his way, it worried him that forgetting her might not be so easy.

CHAPTER 13

P EACHES TROTTED ALONG THE road as the sun broke free of the
horizon. Susannah shielded her eyes against the brightness as she
urged the mule onto the boarding house's street. She tied the animal
to the hitching rail, then knocked on the door. A small flock of hens
pecked at bugs in the dirt beside the porch while she waited. After a
few minutes of nothing but silence from the other side, she knocked
again.

The same girl she'd seen the day before opened the door, her hair
a knotted mess over one shoulder.

"May I come in?"

The girl shook her head. "Doc said not to let anyone in."

"I'm not anyone. I'm the nurse. Remember me from yesterday?" The
girl squinted at her. "I was with Dr. Peabody in his office, and I arrived
here with him."

There was no comprehension on the young face. Her eyes were
glazed, and sweat slicked her face. Susannah pushed into the room
and pressed her palm to the girl's brow. Fever. Susannah's stomach
lurched, the pancakes she'd made for breakfast heavy in her middle.

"Is the doctor upstairs?" Dr. Conkling had planned to remain until
Dr. Peabody arrived.

The girl shook her head, weaving on her feet.

Susannah supported her lest the girl topple over. "Where is your
mother?"

"I'm here." The older woman came into the room.

"Dr. Conkling?" Susannah asked.

"He left before midnight." The woman dabbed at her cheeks. "Poor
Mr. Bury didn't make it."

Dead.

And the girl Susannah supported was no doubt the disease's next victim.

"Your daughter isn't well, ma'am."

The woman gasped, hurrying forward to take her daughter from Susannah.

"You should put her to bed right away. I'll ride for Dr. Peabody."

"Thank you, Nurse."

Susannah returned to Peaches and headed to the doctor's office, hoping he resided in the rooms above, or else she'd have to waste time asking someone for directions. She arrived and pounded on the red door. It took a few minutes, but the door opened. Dr. Peabody, wearing a dressing gown, took a step back and allowed her in.

"Doctor, I've just come from the boarding house."

"I'm sorry about that. I had no way to contact you when the patient passed away."

"The girl is ill."

"Patsy?" Concern sharpened his features. "What are her symptoms?"

"Fever and dizziness were all I observed before instructing Mrs. Finan to put her to bed and coming for you."

"Well done." He glanced past her. "Put your mule in my stable around back. I'll join you back here once I've dressed."

She'd barely returned to the door when the doctor, fully dressed and carrying his medical bag, opened it.

"I had planned to make the boarding house my first stop this morning." He shot a glance at her. "I should have risen earlier, I see, if I wanted to stay ahead of you."

"I had trouble sleeping, thinking about the implications."

"As did I." He smothered a yawn and lengthened his stride. "I suppose that proves us both conscientious in our calling."

Susannah hiked her skirt a bit higher and trotted to keep up.

Dr. Peabody didn't bother knocking, just opened the door and held it for Susannah. Once inside, he started up the stairs. She followed, trusting he knew where he was going. They bypassed the second floor and continued up to the third. From there, they simply followed the sound of retching.

Patsy leaned over a bucket on one side of a bed, supported by Mrs. Finan. On the other side, a younger girl appeared as pale as her sister. Dr. Peabody examined Patsy while Susannah approached the sister.

"Hello, I'm Nurse Piper. What's your name?"

"Bitty." The voice was small and weak.

"Are you feeling poorly?"

The little girl nodded.

"Well, let's see what we can do to help you feel better, shall we?"

Another nod, but before it was over, the girl began to retch. Susannah's heart sank.

"How are you feeling, Mrs. Finan?" Dr. Peabody asked.

"Not at my best, doctor."

"And the boys?"

Boys? How many children were there?

"They are about their chores and seemed fine this morning."

"Mr. Finan?"

"He's due back tonight. He took the boat down to St. Joseph five days ago."

"Was that before Mr. Bury arrived?"

The older woman pressed fingers to her forehead, then nodded. "Yes, I believe it was."

Dr. Peabody exchanged glances with Susannah. Mr. Finan hadn't taken the disease aboard the boat to St. Joseph. That was a blessing. But how many in the boarding house would become ill?

How many would die?

Cholera.

The word swirled around the feed-and-seed store like an ominous mist. Hick heaved another sack of seed onto a customer's wagon, then dusted off his gloved hands. The man Mrs. Piper had been nursing was dead. Everyone seemed to know it.

Word was, those in the boarding house had fled like rats off a sinking ship, and the family who owned the place had come down with the disease.

Mrs. Piper was in the middle of it.

He wiped the back of his wrist across his forehead, then readjusted his hat and glanced in the direction of the boarding house. He could admit to himself that it made him uneasy, her being there with all that illness.

"Ya thinkin' about Mrs. Piper?" Cooter asked, leaning on his shovel.

The wagon rolled away from the loading dock, and Hick headed for the next bill of sale. He stopped and looked back at Cooter. "She'll be all right. She's a nurse, after all."

The young man nodded, then set to with his shovel, cleaning the area before the next team and wagon pulled up.

Hick ripped off a bill of sale and scanned it for the next order.

"Hick." Baker motioned him to the far end of the counter. "I suppose you heard of the cholera."

"Can't help but hear of it. Seems to be the only thing folks are talking about."

"It's not good for business. I'm afraid people will stay away from town once word spreads." The shop owner worried a rag between his hands.

"Farmers need to plant, and they can't do that without seed."

"You're right. Of course, you're right." The poor rag was wrung almost in two. "But if things slack off, I won't be able to keep you on. Just so you understand."

Hick touched his hat brim. "You say when, and I'll push on."

After a nod, Baker hurried to assist a customer.

More than likely, people would swarm over the feed-and-seed store to get what they could before things got out of control. Hick knew farmers. There wasn't much that would keep them out of their fields in the spring.

Not even the threat of cholera.

Noon came, and Baker turned the sign on the door so it read closed. "One hour, fellas. Be back and ready to go then."

Hick and Cooter ambled outside and looked around. There was a bakery down the street, and Baker had told him of several diners within a short walk. But when he reached into his pocket, his fingers hit very few coins. Not enough for two meals. Maybe enough for bread at the bakery.

"Cooter, you got any money?"

The younger man looked away and shook his head.

Hick sighed. Bread it was. He headed in that direction, Cooter following. They lucked out finding day-old bread that looked like it might be a few days old, but it was affordable, so Hick bought two loaves. He handed one to Cooter.

"You might want to save half for tomorrow. I'm out of money until we get paid."

Cooter tore the end off his loaf and bit into it, mumbling around the mouthful, "When ya reckon that'll be?"

"Baker said tomorrow night, it being Saturday."

Cooter shoved another chunk of bread in his mouth, then paused. "Hick?" The word came out muffled.

"What?"

"Maybe we should take some bread to Mrs. Piper, do ya think?"

He didn't answer, just turned onto the boarding house's street. He knew where it was from all the talk at the store that morning. The mule wasn't tied out front, but it made sense that someone would have put the animal up for the day. Hick knocked on the door and waited.

Cooter had stuffed the rest of his loaf back into the paper it'd been wrapped in. He stared at it. The boy must be half-starved. As skinny as he was, he needed every bite.

Hick knocked again, harder.

A half-grown boy opened it. "We can't take any boarders right now." He started to close the door, but Hick stuck his boot in the way.

"We're here to see Mrs. Piper."

No recognition flickered in the boy's eyes.

"The nurse?"

"Oh." He looked behind him, then back. "You best wait outside, but I'll let her know you're here." Then he closed the door as Hick backed up.

"I'm right glad we didn't need to go inside," Cooter said.

Hick was too, but he kept his peace. The door opened again shortly. Mrs. Piper's dress was covered with a long white apron, and she looked every inch the nurse.

"Oh. I wondered who'd be looking for me."

"We brung ya some bread"—Cooter held out his loaf—"for lunch."

"That was very thoughtful, but I'll be eating here for the next few days. In fact..." She stepped onto the porch and closed the door behind her. "I'll be staying here for the foreseeable future. The owner is away, his wife and daughters are ill, and the boys aren't old enough to manage on their own."

"We heard the boarders left," Hick said.

"Which is a hardship for the business, but a blessing in a way, so long as they didn't carry the disease off with them." Mrs. Piper opened the door again. "I'm not sure when I'll be back at camp."

Hick rubbed his jaw. "Might be best to plan on staying in town, ma'am."

Her eyes snapped to his, understanding in their depths. "Yes. I believe you're right." She stepped inside, but turned back to him. "Mr. Hickman, don't ride on without saying goodbye."

"We wouldn't do that, ma'am." He touched his hat brim and started back to the store.

Cooter fell into step beside him, already filling his mouth with more bread. Behind them, the door to the boarding house closed.

It sounded very... final.

Susannah had to force herself to shut the door, to not watch Mr. Hickman and Cooter walk away. He said he'd not leave without saying goodbye, and she had no reason to think him less than a man of his word. On the contrary, she had every reason to believe he was honorable.

Perhaps that was what made it so hard to turn back to the business of nursing the sick.

She entered the kitchen, a large room and well organized. She'd had no problem finding an apron and everything she needed to make a restorative broth. The cold cellar was full, as were the pantry shelves.

With no boarders to feed, Mrs. Finan surely wouldn't mind feeding Susannah from her stores in exchange for her nursing.

After adding a few more chunks of coal to the stove, Susannah stirred the broth and replaced the pot's lid. One of the boys came into the kitchen, the half-grown one she'd met at the door that morning. Had it only been a few hours ago? She'd not had time to sort them out by name.

"I'm awfully hungry." He eyed the pot.

She'd have to feed them too since there was no one else, but she didn't mind. There was precious little she could do for those sick in bed. At least she could feed those who weren't.

"Find your brothers, and I'll fix you a meal."

"They're upstairs. Neither one was feeling too good."

Oh, no. "Then help yourself to the bread and cheese. I'll see to your brothers." She started for the door, but paused. "Wash your hands first, with soap, all the way to your elbows, you hear?"

"Yes, ma'am."

"If you don't, you might get as sick as Mr. Bury."

She left him with his eyes nearly bulging, but at least she was certain he'd do as she'd said.

The two other boys, younger than the one she'd left below, were stretched out on a bed. Both fevered. Susannah had snagged two pots on her way up and put one beside each boy. She fetched a pitcher, filled with water she'd boiled that morning, and bathed their faces, then washed their hands.

The sound of retching had her heading down the hall. Mrs. Finan moaned from her room, so Susannah hurried past to the girls' room. The littlest one was over a bucket, mess running out both ends. The poor dear.

By the time Susannah had her cleaned and in fresh clothing, the other sister started. Susannah hurried from one patient to another until her stomach cramped painfully. She stopped and pressed a hand to her middle, then sighed. Not sickness—hunger. That she could address.

She glanced out the window. It must be the middle of the afternoon. Dr. Peabody had said he'd be back after noon. She had a sinking feeling that some of the boarders had taken the illness with them.

After another painful cramp, she headed for the kitchen. She scrubbed her hands and arms, wiping them with whiskey and drying them off. She ladled a helping of broth, blowing on a spoonful before tasting. It was heavenly—or maybe she was just that hungry. The boy had left the cheese and bread on the table, so she helped herself to both. She couldn't nurse the others if she neglected herself.

She was ladling the cooling broth into cups when the boy returned.

"I'm glad you're back," she said. "Wash like I told you, and then I need you to offer your brothers sips of broth."

"I don't know how to nurse nobody."

"I'll show you, don't worry." She pointed to the bucket of boiled water. "Wash now. Use plenty of that lye soap."

She put the cups on a tray and carried them upstairs, where she showed him how to support the boys and hold the cup for them. They were terribly weak.

Where was the doctor?

The door opened and shut downstairs, then footsteps. She left the boy to follow her instructions and awaited the doctor in the hallway. But it wasn't Dr. Peabody, it was Dr. Conkling.

"I got here as quickly as I could, Mrs. Piper." He removed his hat and mopped his face with a handkerchief. "As feared, the disease is spreading. Dr. Peabody is seeing to several other cases."

"I'm sorry to hear it, but not surprised. Two of the boys have it too, as well as the girls and Mrs. Finan."

"I wish I could get you some help, but the fact is, people are too frightened to offer their assistance."

"I'll do my best, sir. Now, let me show you the patients."

The doctor approved of what she'd done as well as her plans to stay in the boarding house to care for the family. He encouraged her to rest when she could but gave her a wry smile that said none of them would sleep much in the days ahead.

Others would slip into sleep and never awaken.

But not her. She'd survived too much already. She wasn't about to let cholera be the end of Susannah Mary Jessup Piper.

Chapter 14

BAKER HAD KEPT THE feed-and-seed open on Sunday—a rare occurrence but a prudent one. It had allowed the area farmers to get their seed and get out of town. Hick stood at the loading dock and glanced up and down the empty street near noon on Tuesday.

It was eerie after the hustle and bustle of the past three days.

The disease was spreading, and people were understandably frightened. Hick might have been frightened himself, but the war had made him somewhat immune to death. He'd seen more than his share of it, and when his time came, he'd accept it. He was at peace with his Maker. He wasn't a model citizen or a pillar of society—far from it—but he knew enough of the Bible to trust in its promises. And in the end, what more could a man hope for?

Cooter pushed a broom across the loading dock, sweeping nothing but a skiff of dust he'd missed earlier that morning.

"Hick, Cooter." Baker approached them. "I'm sorry, but I'm going to have to let you men go." He held an envelope out to each of them. "I can keep things running until the sickness ends with my regular help, and hopefully by then my other man will be back."

"Thank you." Hick accepted his pay. "We'll be moving on."

"You're fine workers." Baker wiped his hands down his leather apron. "I included a reference with your pay. You never know when you might need it."

"Appreciate it." Hick touched the brim of his hat and walked into the street, Cooter at his heels.

"So that's it, huh? Is we movin' on?"

Hick turned onto the boarding house's street. "Yup."

"We goin' to say goodbye to Mrs. Piper?"

"Yup." He'd promised he would, and he also wanted to be sure she was all right, that she hadn't succumbed to the cholera. It didn't seem likely that a nurse would, her knowing how it was spread and all, but it could happen.

Cooter let loose a gusty sigh. "I don't mind sayin' it, I'm goin' to miss her. And I don't mean just her cookin'."

Hick wasn't about to voice it, but he'd miss her cooking too. If he were honest with himself, he'd miss her in other ways as well, but he had no right to, so he pushed the thought away.

Smoke curled into the sky from behind the boarding house. There'd been many fires lit for burning clothing and bedding of the ill all across town in an attempt to stop the disease. Hick rapped on the door. The same boy as before opened it. There were dark circles under his eyes, and his hair hadn't seen a brush or comb in a while.

"Is Nurse Piper still here?" Hick asked.

"She is. I'll fetch her, but you best wait outside." He closed the door.

Hick leaned against the porch railing.

Cooter stuck his hands in his pockets and rocked from toes to heels, making the porch boards creak.

The creaking had about plucked Hick's last nerve when Mrs. Piper opened the door. She was wearing a white apron smudged with what looked like soot, her hair was braided and hanging over one shoulder, and the smudges under her eyes were worse than the boy's.

Hick straightened and pulled off his hat. "Mrs. Piper, ma'am, we came to tell you we're pushing on."

"So soon?" Surprise lifted her voice on the last word.

"There's no more work for us"—Hick shrugged—"what with the cholera keeping people shut in their homes."

"Of course." She scanned the vacant street. "I hadn't realized..."

She probably hadn't set foot outside the house in three days.

"Well, I am sorry to see you go, Mr. Hickman, and you as well, Cooter." She offered a smile that was as tired as it was genuine. "Mrs. Finan has survived the disease, and Mr. Finan has returned, but"—sadness clouded her eyes—"they've lost two sons and one daughter. I'll be staying and helping them through the funerals tomorrow at least."

"And then, ma'am?" asked Cooter.

The tired smile returned. "Dr. Conkling offered me a position with his practice."

"What about Oregon, ma'am?" Hick wasn't sure why he asked. She'd be better off staying in Omaha than traveling across country by herself.

"Perhaps I can save enough to purchase a train ticket next spring. By then, the doctors tell me, the tracks will stretch halfway to Oregon. Perhaps I can find a family heading that way who would take me on as a maid."

Hick was perversely glad her dream hadn't ended. Glad for her.

"Will you two travel on together?" she asked.

"Yes, ma'am." Cooter grinned. "I reckon without ya along to feed us, Hick'll be needin' my fishin' skills to keep meat on his bones."

Hick snorted. Cooter made it sound as if he'd done the rescuing and not Hick. But the younger man had grown on him, he couldn't deny that. He slapped his hat back on his head.

"Time we moved on, ma'am. Best of luck to you."

"And to you. Both of you."

Was that a sheen of tears in her eyes as he turned away? Hick refused to look back. She was in many ways a remarkable woman. She'd do well in a place like Omaha—and maybe Oregon someday.

But the foothills of the mountains were no place for a lady.

"Nurse?"

Susannah closed the boarding house door and leaned against it for a moment, letting the feeling of being left behind pass.

"Nurse? Oh. There you are." Mr. Finan entered the front room, a can in one hand, a brush in the other, and whitewash splatters up and down the front of his clothing. He was in bad need of a bath and a shave, but hope shone from his bloodshot eyes. "Mrs. Finan is hungry. That's good news, isn't it?"

"It's very good news." They needed some. Dr. Conkling had been by earlier that morning and fumigated the house with sulfur, ordering Mr. Finan to whitewash the rooms while Susannah burned everything that had touched the victims.

Her heart squeezed at the loss of the two little boys and the youngest girl. Life could be cruel sometimes. No one who'd survived the war hadn't learned that lesson.

"I'll fix her a tray and take it to her," Susannah said. "I've finished burning the bedding, clothing, and rugs from the boys' and girls' rooms, your room, and Mr. Bury's." They'd moved Mrs. Finan and Patsy to a small room off the kitchen.

His shoulders sagged as he glanced toward the stairs. The man had lost so much.

"I expect within a few weeks the house will be full of boarders again." It was hard to let go of traveling to Oregon, but there was no hope for it until the following spring. "I'll be needing a room myself."

He faced her again. "You're staying?"

"For a while, at least."

"My dear Mrs. Piper." He cleared his throat and wiped the back of one hand across his mouth before continuing. "We owe you more than can be repaid—ever. You have a home with us for as long as you desire. I could not take a penny from you for it."

"Well, we'll see about that when the time comes." She patted his arm as she walked past on the way to the kitchen. Susannah would pay her own way, of course.

The pot of broth was still warm, so it took only minutes to make a tray. She added a second cup of broth for Patsy. Like her mother, she'd survived, but they both needed the restorative liquid to recover.

She tapped on the door then pushed it open with her hip.

"Here we are. I understand someone is hungry?"

Mrs. Finan was sitting with pillows against her back, Patsy curled at her side. It was good for them to be together.

The smell of chamber pots needing to be emptied made her settle the tray across Mrs. Finan's lap and then open the two small windows. Wind stirred the lace curtains, but it also cleared the air. The lingering scent of smoke was less offensive than the chamber pots.

"Thank you, Nurse Piper." Mrs. Finan's voice was stronger since the morning. That and her hunger were both good signs, but her hands shook, and her eyes were swollen and damp.

"See if you can coax Patsy into sipping more broth. I'll send Bart in to empty the chamber pots." The boy had been indispensable during the crisis. He couldn't be more than thirteen, but he'd done the work of a man. He'd even brought Peaches to the boarding house stables and cared for the mule. With Susannah's shoulder only partially healed, she'd relied on him to do the heavy work. And because he'd taken her warnings to wash thoroughly to heart, he'd stayed healthy through it all.

Or maybe he'd simply been destined to survive.

Dr. Peabody had contracted the disease, and he surely knew how to wash and take precautions. Thankfully, Dr. Conkling assured her that the good doctor would also survive.

"Nurse?

Susannah pulled her attention back to Mrs. Finan. "Yes?"

"Thank you. When everyone else abandoned us, you came. I can't help but believe we'd all have died before Mr. Finan returned if not for you." Tears filled the older woman's eyes. And no wonder, with three of her children at the undertaker's awaiting burial.

"You're welcome. Eat now, and see if you can get Patsy to drink. She needs the liquid." She returned to the kitchen. Mrs. Finan would be ready for something more filling soon.

It felt good to do for other people again. Abel had died the past autumn, and she'd been alone for months, seeing almost no one until the neighbors had come to chase her from the soddy. Mr. Hickman had done more for her than she'd done for him. He'd protected her from the boat men, bandaged her shoulder, and guided her to Omaha. She'd done little but cook for him.

She paused by the window and stared at the buildings across the street, some so new the unpainted wood gleamed in the sunshine. Mr. Hickman and Cooter were out there somewhere beyond the buildings.

Her throat tightened, but she swallowed the sense of loss and turned back to the duties at hand. She should be used to saying goodbye to people. She'd done enough of it. And they weren't dead, for pity's sake, they were just... lost to her.

Trooper snorted and shook his head, dislodging a fly that badgered him. Hick rubbed the center of his forehead where an ache had been building since they'd ridden out of Omaha. He glanced at the sun, a scant handspan above the horizon. It was early to find a place to camp, but he was done in.

The sky was clear, no sign of rain, but Hick preferred to camp in the shelter of some trees anyway. They had passed a few isolated soddies—civilization creeping onto the prairie—but it was best to be safe even though nobody had reported Indians in the area. The scrubby trees and brush along the Platte River would hide a fire and scatter the smoke. He aimed Trooper for a likely spot a quarter of a mile in front of them.

Cooter dozed in his saddle, a trick Hick had used more than once during the war, but not while traveling alone. He shot a glance at the young man, chin bouncing off his chest with each step of the mustang. Not quite alone. At least while sleeping, Cooter was quiet.

Hick's headache appreciated that.

He halted Trooper, and Rumpus stopped alongside, waking Cooter.

The little man snorted, looked around, then yawned and stretched his arms. "Looks like a good place to camp." He jumped off the mustang and had his saddle stripped before Hick's feet hit the ground. "I'll mosey down to the river and see if I cain't sweet-talk a fish or two into bein' our dinner."

"Sounds good." Hick barely noticed the lingering soreness in his hip. It didn't compare to the pain in his head. It seemed to take forever to get the tack off Trooper, hobble him, and start a fire. Coffee would have him feeling better in no time.

And yet, it didn't.

Its aroma, which usually smoothed the rough edges of any morning or evening, instead made Hick's stomach twist. He backed away from the smell. But then his insides did something more than twist. He held onto a branch, bent over, and heaved everything he'd eaten that day, and maybe a few things he hadn't even eaten yet. Sweat slicked his face, and his hands shook.

Cholera.

He dug out his canteen and rinsed his mouth, spitting and rinsing twice more before he drank a sip of the tepid water. He didn't want it, but keeping water down was important. He tossed his tarp onto the ground and unrolled his blankets. Cooter would be a while. Long enough for Hick to rest. That should ease his headache, which threatened to beat its way out through his temples.

"Hick?"

Someone shook him, and he groaned.

"Hick? Ya okay?"

Cooter. Why on earth was Cooter shaking him? He'd shove the guy away if he had the energy. All he wanted to do was go back to sleep. A hand came down on his forehead, the pressure adding to the headache, squeezing another groan from him.

"Burnin' up somethin' fierce."

The hand left, and Hick tried to open his eyes. It took effort, and once he did, the world was fuzzy except for Cooter's face, almost nose-to-nose with him. Hick licked his lips.

"Water."

Cooter opened a canteen and lifted Hick's head. He almost called out at the pain, but he needed the water. He drank as half of it ran down the front of his shirt, soaking his neck and chest. It felt good.

Then his stomach rebelled again. He managed to flop over to the edge of the tarp and spew the water on the ground.

"I wish Mrs. Piper was here," Cooter said.

So did he.

CHAPTER 15

S OMEONE WAS BEATING ON the front door. Susannah pushed up from her pillow and fumbled in the dark for her dressing gown. What sort of emergency could it be? Her body ached from lack of sleep, and she winced as she pulled the gown over her shoulder. To be pulled from the first deep sleep she'd managed in days was a cruel trick.

She opened the door to the room she'd taken on the second floor as Mr. Finan emerged from another down the hallway.

"I apologize, Nurse. I'm afraid it took me a bit to wake up." He'd donned pants, but his nightshirt hung over them. "I'll see who it is and what they want."

"I'll go with you. It might be someone needing a nurse."

He paused, glanced back at her with an expression of relief. "That would make sense."

She couldn't blame him for his reaction. He surely didn't want anyone else to be ill, but his house had suffered enough. He didn't need more bad news at his door. She followed him down the stairs.

Mr. Finan opened the door.

"I need Mrs. Piper."

She knew that voice. Even in the fog of sleepiness, it sent a jolt through her. "Cooter?" She stepped around Mr. Finan.

Cooter swiped his hat off. "Ma'am, it's Hick, he's mighty poorly."

"Poorly? How?"

"He's burnin' with the fever, and he chucked up the water he drunk."

A cold shiver rode her backbone.

"Ya gotta come, ma'am. He ain't got much of a chance iffen ya don't."

"Saddle Peaches. She's in the stable behind the house." She turned for the stairs, then stopped and faced Mr. Finan. "Sir, I will need supplies. I can pay you for them."

He raised his hands as if to ward her off. "Nonsense. Take what you need. Is there anything I can do?"

"No. And thank you."

"Will you return?" he asked.

Would she? She paused with one foot on the stairs, one hand on the rail. "I don't know." Would she be able to save Mr. Hickman? Would he agree to take her all the way to Oregon if she did? Or would she contract the disease herself and succumb to it? She looked over her shoulder. "Mrs. Finan and Patsy will both survive. Make sure they take plenty of liquids and only soft foods at first."

"I will."

She fled up the stairs and changed her clothes, packing everything she owned into her sack, saddlebag, and satchel. In minutes, she was lugging them downstairs.

Mr. Finan held a huge burlap sack. "I've put in food and coffee, some clean rags, and three bars of soap. Is there anything else you need?"

"You've been overly generous already."

"Not at all. Here." He took her saddlebags and sack. "Let me carry this for you."

The weight off her shoulder was a relief. They stepped onto the porch as Cooter arrived with Peaches.

"Sorry it took me a bit, but that blamed saddle ain't right. I had to figger how to rig it in the dark."

"I'll check it." She hurried to the mule's side. "Can you tie Mr. Finan's sack to your saddle? It has things we'll need in it."

"Yes, ma'am."

She secured her belongings behind her bedroll and mounted.

Mr. Finan came to her side. "Thank you again, and I hope you can save the man."

"Iffen anyone can, it'll be Mrs. Piper," Cooter said.

"I'll do my best." She gathered the reins and turned Peaches from the hitching rail. Rumpus moved beside her down the dark street.

"Do you have any idea what time it is?" she asked.

"It be past midnight, ma'am. Iffen we ride hard, we can make it to Hick by sunrise."

She glanced at his horse, the buckskin's coat visibly damp even in the darkness. "We can't ride too hard or you risk an injury to Rumpus."

Cooter slapped the animal's neck. "Ol' Rumpus here can run all night and all day. He's tougher than a bag full of bobcats."

"Even so, we won't push the animals beyond what is safe. Mr. Hickman is a horseman. He wouldn't expect us to."

"I reckon that's true, ma'am." But he didn't sound happy about it. It did the young man credit to be so dedicated to Mr. Hickman on such a short acquaintance.

As a nurse, Susannah was duty-bound to answer the call for help, but that didn't account for the way her stomach knotted or the desire to sink her heels into Peaches and race into the darkness to Mr. Hickman's side.

He'd never been so dry. Hick forced his eyes open far enough to spy two canteens within arm's reach. It took all his concentration to pry the lid off one and tip it to his mouth. He took small sips, remembering what had happened when he'd gulped water before. Had it been last night? The purple-gray of pre-dawn surrounded him. Crickets chirped near the river. He could just make out the silhouette of Trooper nearby.

Where was Cooter?

He tried to recap the canteen, but knocked it over, the precious liquid soaking into his blankets. He groaned, then used the damp fabric to wipe his face. Even that small action exhausted him, and sleep reclaimed him.

When next he awoke, a hand held his head and water dribbled against his lips. He sucked it in.

"Slowly now." A woman's voice. Ma? No. Ma wouldn't be there. Ma was back in Ohio on the farm with Pa and his brothers. And she had no use for Hick anymore. Samuel. She'd called him Samuel. Even when his brothers and Pa called him Sam, he'd always been Samuel to Ma. Until the day he and Denny had ridden off to war. That day, she hadn't called him anything at all. Hadn't spoken a word. Had watched him with eyes like flint as he rode away.

Soothing hands and a cool rag touched his face, pulling him away from the painful memories.

"Mr. Hickman? Can you hear me?"

He knew that voice. It was Southern. Deep Southern, like those he'd driven from their homes in Georgia. People who'd been pushed back by other soldiers as he did what he'd been ordered and burned their houses. Flames soared toward the sky. Women cried. And babies. There'd been babies. Innocent little babies he'd turned out of their homes. What would Ma have said about that?

"Mr. Hickman?"

"Didn't want to do it."

Susannah leaned closer to hear what Mr. Hickman mumbled.

"What did you say?"

"I'm sorry, Ma."

He was hallucinating. It wasn't uncommon, especially with severe dehydration. She dribbled a little more water against his lips.

Cooter strode back into the camp, both hands filled with the straps of every canteen they had. If they'd been in town, she would have ordered him to boil that water, but the river was upstream of the disease, and she needed it cool.

"Here you go, ma'am. What else can I do?"

"He'll need broth when he comes around. I don't know what Mr. Finan packed for food, but fresh meat would be best. Can you hunt?"

"Oh, yes, ma'am!" He started toward Rumpus.

"Take the bay."

Cooter stopped and frowned at her.

"Rumpus has been through enough. I'm sure Mr. Hickman won't mind."

Cooter scratched the back of his head. "I reckon yer right, ma'am. I'll have to tether Rumpus, or he'll follow." He shot her a look. "He might kick up a fuss."

"I doubt it. See how tired he is?" The mustang stood with his nose lower than his knees. "And if he fusses, it won't bother Mr. Hickman." But it might keep Susannah awake, which would be beneficial.

Cooter tethered Rumpus and then saddled the bay. The well-rested horse moved out willingly. Trooper, that was what Mr. Hickman had called him.

Rumpus squealed and pulled against his tether until the horse and rider were out of sight, but he settled quietly and dozed within minutes. The poor beast had been ridden to camp, back to town, and returned to camp again without a rest. It took a strong horse to come through it so well.

Susannah bathed her patient's face and opened his shirt to lay on cool damp cloths and bring down the fever. She worked without thinking, treating him as she'd treated so many others, while she fought to keep her eyes open.

Mr. Hickman twitched and groaned, the muscles of his face working. Dreams. And from the looks of it, not pleasant ones. He grimaced and then yelled, "Watch out!"

He was back in the war. She'd witnessed Abel fight the same battle with dreams. Nightmares. The things these men had seen—and done. She shuddered. Her life had been difficult during the war and after, but what the soldiers had been through made her troubles pale in comparison.

It was amazing any of them were able to return to a normal life.

She studied Mr. Hickman's face. The small scar at his temple might have been from the war. If it was, he'd come close to losing an eye. His hair needed a trim and his face a razor. His nose was a little long but straight and centered over a strong chin. He was handsome enough, but not striking, more the steady, reliable type. The type who would have made a good soldier.

One who'd survived.

She lifted his head again and offered more water. He licked the drops from his lips, then his eyes opened wide. Glassy and unfocused, he didn't see her.

"Ma?"

"Shhh. No. It's Mrs. Piper."

"I'm so sorry about Denny. I couldn't save him. I tried."

"Shhh. Drink a little more." She tipped the canteen again, and he took a couple of swallows.

"I didn't know he'd die, Ma." The hazel eyes closed, and he sagged against Susannah.

She lowered his head to the blanket. Who was Denny? Someone important to Mrs. Hickman, so perhaps another son, Mr. Hickman's brother. Susannah closed her eyes and pictured her brothers as they'd ridden off to war, the three of them together. So much family tragedy spread like the roots of a pernicious weed. Where was Mr. Hickman's ma? Did she wonder about the son wandering across the prairie? Or had she died of a broken heart like Mama had?

So many questions.

Susannah rose and stirred the fire. She filled the coffeepot from one of the canteens and set it close to heat the water in case Cooter returned with meat. Then she unrolled her blankets on the far side of Mr. Hickman's tarp. He was too ill for it to be improper.

She was too tired to stay awake.

Hick opened his eyes and blinked against the sun's piercing light where it filtered through the branches. He was flat on his back with the sun directly over him. Why was he there? He searched his memory, pushing against the pain in his head. He'd left Omaha.

Where was Cooter? Hadn't he left with Cooter?

Hick was beyond thirsty. He had to pry his lips away from his teeth. Where was his canteen?

He rolled onto his side. The pain blurred his vision. At least, he thought it was from the pain. Someone lay next to him, but it wasn't Cooter. Long, dark hair flowed in waves down her back. Mrs. Piper? Why was she on Hick's tarp?

What had he done?

The touch between her shoulders was slight, but Susannah never slept soundly with a patient nearby. She turned onto her stomach, raising to her elbows. Hazel eyes met hers, recognition in their depths.

"Mr. Hickman." She scrambled to sit and grabbed a canteen. She eased her hand beneath his head and raised it. "Drink. You need the liquid."

She waited until he'd swallowed three times. From his grimace, it was painful. She pulled the canteen away, and he raised a hand as if to stop her. "No more for a few minutes," she said, "or it may come back up. You're very ill."

He grunted, yet his face relaxed as if he was relieved and not alarmed by her statement of his illness. People sometimes responded to sickness in the oddest ways.

"Cholera?" His voice was little more than a croak.

"I'm afraid so. But you're strong, and you've made it through the night, so there is every chance you'll pull through." There was every chance he wouldn't, but it was best to keep things positive until they knew otherwise.

She offered him three more swallows of water, then lowered his head to the blanket. Heat steamed from his skin.

"Let's roll you onto your back again, Mr. Hickman. I need to freshen the cloths to bring down your fever."

As he did what she asked, his head lolled to the side, lips slightly parted. That was fine. Sleep would do him the most good, that and the water he'd kept down.

She removed the cloths, which had dried against his hot body, and rewetted them from the canteen before covering his chest again. Sunlight penetrated the branches above them, so she used her blankets and rigged a shade for him. She tied the last corner to a low-hanging branch as Cooter arrived. Across the front of his saddle hung a small deer.

"Ain't nothin' but a yearling, but it's meat." He slid off the bay and hauled the carcass down. The horse dropped its head and grabbed a mouthful of grass, unconcerned about the dead animal that landed at its feet. "I'll skin it out directly after I get Trooper settled."

"Thank you, Cooter."

Susannah checked the water in the coffeepot, then stirred the fire again.

"Toss in some green wood, ma'am, and we can smoke the extra meat."

"I'm afraid I don't know how."

The young man grinned. "It's easy, ma'am. I'll learn ya how." He tended the horse, then drew a wicked-looking knife from a sheath on his saddle and set to work on the carcass.

Susannah added chunks of meat to the water and set it to boil with a hefty pinch of salt from the provisions Mr. Finan had packed. Following Cooter's instructions, she built a frame of green willow branches directly over the fire, high enough not to cook, and hung long, thin slices of meat over it. The low heat and smoke would cure it.

Mr. Hickman groaned, so she gave him more to drink and changed the cloths again. Cooter watched while she explained what she was doing and why.

During it all, Susannah marveled at the sense of peace that came over her. They were three people alone on the prairie relying on each other to survive. And yet, it felt so... right.

It felt like family.

CHAPTER 16

"**D**ENNY!"

Susannah jerked awake in the pre-dawn darkness.

"No! Oh, God, no." Mr. Hickman thrashed against his blankets.

"Easy, Mr. Hickman." She scooted closer and pressed a hand to his brow. He was on fire.

Cooter rose and came nearer. "What can I do, ma'am?"

"I need fresh water. Pour what's in those canteens out and refill them. It must be cold if we're to bring the fever down." He'd been much cooler in the evening. It didn't bode well that the fever had spiked again. She did her best to dribble more water into him.

He batted away her hand and opened his eyes. Even in the dim light from the smoking fire, she could see that they were glazed and unfocused. "I couldn't save him." He pawed at his chest. "His blood was everywhere."

She'd rarely heard such gut-wrenching anguish in a voice before.

"Mr. Hickman, you must drink."

"I couldn't save him, Ma. I tried."

He must mean the Denny he'd spoken of before. "Denny would want you to drink. He'd want you to get better, and you must drink to do that."

There was a flicker of something in his expression. As if, for a moment, he understood. She slipped her hand under his head and lifted to his lips the canteen she'd filled with broth the evening before. After the third swallow, she pulled it away, but he'd already sagged back into the blankets.

Cooter arrived with the cold river water.

"Help me undress him."

"Ma'am?" The young man's eyes grew large in the darkness.

"The fever is burning him alive. It's worse than before." She leaned closer to Cooter and whispered, "If we don't bring it down, he will die."

Cooter's voice was solemn when he responded with, "Yes, ma'am."

Between the two of them, they got Mr. Hickman down to his small clothes and covered him with cold, wet cloths. He groaned and shivered. They used all that Mr. Finan had packed, along with one of Susannah's extra blouses. After all, Mr. Hickman had given up a shirt for her wound. It was the least she could do.

Cooter made three more trips to the river for cold water. In between, he fed the fire green branches. The smoke went mostly upright in their little camp, protected as it was by heavy brush, but Cooter said it would cure the meat.

Susannah attempted to get more broth into Mr. Hickman every quarter of an hour or so. Sometimes successfully, and sometimes not. But when dawn finally flirted with the horizon, the fever had lessened.

Mr. Hickman was still alive.

The plop of raindrops and scent of wet foliage woke Hick. A breeze ghosted his exposed arms and chest, raising a chill. He pried his eyes open and stared at the underside of his tarp. It was daylight, but impossible to tell what time. Everything appeared murky beyond the makeshift tent.

Trooper. He must check on his horse. Hick tried to rise to his elbows.

"Mr. Hickman?"

He relaxed into the blankets beneath him, eyes closing. Mrs. Piper would have seen to the old war horse.

She pressed her hand to his forehead and released a loud breath. "The fever has broken."

Fever? Had he been sick? He moved his hands to his chest.

His bare chest.

Where were his clothes?

"Are you chilled?" Her voice came as if from a long distance away.

He nodded, unable to open his eyes again.

She rustled around beside him, making enough noise to keep him awake. Barely. Then her hand slid beneath his head.

He managed to open one eye as she pressed a cup to his lips. The liquid was warm and tasted better than anything he could remember. He swallowed it down, protesting with a grunt when she took it away.

"One cup is enough for now. Sleep again, and I will give you more when you awaken." She covered him with a blanket.

"He awake?" Whose voice was that? The image of a young man swam across his memory, but the name escaped him as darkness closed in.

"The fever has broken, and he drank a full cup of warm broth." Susannah tucked a blanket around her patient. He needed covering with the fever gone.

"Do that mean he'll live?" Cooter's voice was strained, and it matched the creases near his eyes.

"I believe he's out of danger now."

The young man collapsed in the corner of the section kept dry from the tarp overhead. "I don't mind tellin' ya, I was some worried."

Susannah had been too. She desperately didn't want to lose Mr. Hickman. She never wanted to lose a patient, of course, and she refused to dwell on why she felt it so keenly about this one.

She and Cooter had tussled getting the tarp out from under the unconscious man to rig a shelter last evening when rain threatened. Mr. Hickman was a large man but not fat. There didn't appear to be an ounce of extra flesh on him. His height and muscle alone had made it a challenge.

"Animals is all doin' fine. Yer mule had herself tangled in that tether." Cooter pointed at Peaches. "Ya want I should teach her to come to a whistle so ya don't need no tether?"

"I'm not sure Peaches is as trainable as your Rumpus." But it was sweet of Cooter to offer. "She's an independent molly if ever there was one."

He cocked his head at her. "I could try. Looks like we won't be movin' on for a spell."

No, they wouldn't be. It would be days—if not weeks—before Mr. Hickman would be strong enough to travel. He'd come as close to death as one could without crossing over.

"If you wish to try, by all means." She smiled at the young man. "But don't feel badly if she refuses to comply. It's in her nature to be contrary."

The toothy grin she got in reply reminded her so much of John that it brought a stitch to her heart.

"Don't sell me nor that mule short, Mrs. Piper." He winked, then rose and strode toward Peaches in the lingering drizzle.

She might have enjoyed watching, if her eyelids hadn't weighed a ton. When had she last slept uninterrupted? It was her third morning here, and she'd been pulled from her bed to come, so at least three nights. Had she slept the night through her last night at the boarding house? She couldn't remember.

With a sigh, she stretched out on the only blanket not wrapped around Mr. Hickman. His deep, steady breathing lulled her to sleep.

A raging thirst pulled Hick from sleep. He opened his eyes to darkness. He stretched, his hand coming into contact with something beside him. It stirred.

Not something—some*one*.

He rubbed the grit from his eyes, blinked, and turned his head. A thick braid trailed off the back of the head beside him. His touch hadn't awakened her.

Mrs. Piper.

He'd been ill. Cholera. Cooter had insisted on riding back to Omaha for her. Hick'd told the young man not to. Even gotten cross about it. But Cooter had obviously done it anyway.

And Hick was alive.

Chilled, but alive. He rubbed his bare arms.

Bare? Where was his shirt? His legs were also chilled. He reached beneath the blankets. No pants. He was lying almost naked beside a woman he barely knew in the middle of the prairie with no memory of how any of it had happened.

If he hadn't been so thirsty, he might have laughed, but as it was, his throat wouldn't allow it. He raised himself onto one elbow, though it took everything he had to do it. He was as wobbly as a newborn foal.

"Hick? Ya awake?" Cooter's voice came from near Hick's feet, followed by the rustling of movement. "Quiet now. Don't disturb Mrs. Piper," he whispered when he reached Hick's side. "She's worn out with nursin' ya back to life. I promised I'd watch over ya so she could sleep."

"Water." It was the only word Hick could get out past the dryness.

"I got somethin' better." Cooter disappeared, then returned with a cup. "Ya drink all this, and Mrs. Piper says ya can have more iffen ya want. Yer past the danger point now."

The danger point?

Cooter helped Hick sit up, supporting his back and handing him the cup.

Whatever was in it was pure nectar. Warm and savory and not nearly enough. He pushed the cup back at Cooter. "More."

The young man's grin filled his voice. "Comin' up."

It took three cups of the liquid to revive Hick. Or at least somewhat revive him. He finished the third and whispered, "Where are my clothes?"

"I'll fetch 'em."

Cooter returned and, between the two of them, they managed to get Hick dressed and back between the blankets. The drink had revived him, but getting dressed had worn him out. He rolled onto his side and studied the thick braid that hadn't moved.

Mrs. Piper must be exhausted to have slept through all their rustling around and whispering.

How long had he been ill?

It was a question that would have to wait for the light of day, because darkness settled over Hick again.

Susannah poked the fire and set the coffeepot on a few glowing embers. She hadn't brewed any coffee while Mr. Hickman had been so ill. She'd needed the pot to cook his broth. But Cooter had filled her in on the midnight happenings. Mr. Hickman would be ready for coffee when he awoke. She smiled into the rekindled flames.

He'd live.

She'd slept a whole night through, secure in the knowledge that Cooter was nearby if needed. Even so, she rubbed the grit from her eyes. Cooter had gone after fresh meat at dawn. They'd smoked the young deer and had plenty of jerky stored, but fresh was best for Mr. Hickman to rebuild his strength.

He wouldn't be happy with just broth, although she had the last of it heating in the skillet. It would take the edge off his hunger until Cooter returned.

A cough turned her away from the fire. Mr. Hickman coughed again, then pushed into a seated position, but the shaking in his arms was visible.

"Good morning," she said.

He rubbed a hand over his face and blinked at her. "Good morning." His voice was like gravel trickling over rocks.

"I'll get you some broth." She grabbed his cup and a towel to lift the hot skillet.

"I smell coffee."

She grinned. The man loved his coffee. "You do, but it's not ready yet, and you must be thirsty." She handed him the cup. "Drink this first. It'll do you more good than the coffee."

"I doubt that." He sipped, his eyes remaining on her above the cup's brim. "It's mighty fine, ma'am."

"Cooter said you drank three cups last night."

He nodded, then downed the remainder of the liquid. Setting the cup aside, he tried to stand.

"Let me help you." She hurried to his side and supported his weight as best she could while he got his feet under him. They stood there for a moment until he stopped swaying.

"Thank you, ma'am."

"Do you wish to sit by the fire?"

"Eventually, but there's something else I need to take care of first."

"Your horse is fine. Cooter saw to him before he left this morning."

"Yes, ma'am." He glanced away. "But that's not what I meant."

Realization dawned. "Well, I'll be at the fire with my back turned. Don't go too far."

"Nope." His tone was sheepish. "Couldn't if I tried."

She poured the last bit of broth into his cup, then wiped the skillet and returned it to the fire with a spoonful of lard. He needed something easy in his stomach, and he liked her pancakes. Mr. Finan had included several cans of peaches in the sack. It would be like before Omaha. A thought hit her with a finality that stuck.

She wouldn't be returning to Omaha.

Cooter had mentioned a fort to the west, Fort Kearny. It seemed he and Mr. Hickman had planned to stop there to resupply. There would be a doctor there. Susannah would have as much chance of finding suitable employment there as she had in Omaha.

Fort Kearny was also closer to Oregon.

Mr. Hickman joined her by the fire. He sank onto a flat stone Cooter had hauled close.

"If you finish the broth, I'll be able to fill your cup with coffee." She set aside her pancake batter and handed him the cup. "Here you go."

"You're an angel, ma'am." He wrapped his hands around the cup and drained the broth, then handed it back. She refilled it with coffee. He closed his eyes as he drank the first sip. "A true angel."

"For making coffee?"

"That too, ma'am, but mostly for nursing me through the cholera." His eyes met hers with hazel seriousness. "Cooter said you saved my life."

"Only God can do that, Mr. Hickman."

A lazy grin tipped his mouth. "God uses all kinds of angels, ma'am. Not all of them have wings."

Heat crawled up from her collar at his words—or was it from more than his words? She busied her hands finishing the pancake batter and pouring the first of it into the hot skillet. The sizzle and scent filled the space between her and Mr. Hickman.

His stomach rumbled long and loud.

She couldn't stop the laugh that escaped.

He pressed a hand to his middle. "I guess I'm in need of those pancakes."

"I'll fetch a can of peaches to go with them." Cooter had hung her sack of provisions from a tree. The limber branch was easy to bend, but kept their food off the ground and away from coons and possums. He'd rigged a similar one for the provisions he and Mr. Hickman had brought from Omaha. She fished out a can then retrieved her can opener from her saddlebag before flipping the pancake.

Mr. Hickman took the plate after she slid the pancake on it. "I am sorry to pull you out of town though, ma'am. I hope the doctor won't mind you being gone so long as soon as you'd hired on." He ignored the can of peaches and rolled the pancake before stuffing the end in his mouth with a slight groan.

She busied herself making the next one. "There will be time to deal with all that later."

Because she had no intention of turning back.

CHAPTER 17

I T'D BEEN A WEEK since he'd awakened from the illness, and Hick was still sleeping through as much of the day as he was awake. He had no trouble believing he'd been close to death. Closer than he'd ever been before, even during the war.

He fingered the scar on his temple.

Folks tended to assume that soldiers died in battle, and of course many did, but nearly as many died of disease. That'd been true in the early days of the war, at least. Toward the end, the doctors had a better handle on things. Simple things. Like where to dig latrines and the merits of sanitation, a word Hick hadn't even known before the war.

One thing was for sure and certain, cholera had knocked the pins out from under him.

He took one more swipe with a rag over Trooper's coat. The old horse had lost all his winter covering, and his mahogany coat gleamed in the midmorning sun. He'd put on weight since they'd stopped traveling. The break had done Trooper good.

It'd done Hick good too. He flexed his hip—it was stiff but didn't hurt. He was restless to get moving again. The problem was, how did he handle Mrs. Piper? She didn't seem inclined to return to Omaha on her own. He'd suggested that Cooter would be happy to escort her back, but she'd brushed the idea off.

And as much as Hick hated to admit it, he'd be sorry when she left.

She was an excellent cook. What she'd done with that pair of rabbits Cooter had brought in the other night had been nothing short of amazing. He'd eaten his share of stringy rabbit meat roasted over the fire, but...

It didn't matter. Mrs. Piper was needed back in Omaha. There was a doctor waiting for her.

A shrill whistle pierced the air.

That fool boy was still trying to teach the molly to come when he whistled. A horse could learn it—Rumpus proved that—but a mule? A cantankerous one that nipped at Hick every chance it got? Not likely.

"Hey!" Cooter's shout brought Hick's head around.

Trotting toward the young man was Rumpus, followed by the mule. Hick rubbed his eyes with a finger and thumb, then looked again. He couldn't believe it. He was seeing it, but he couldn't believe it. If Cooter could train that ornery mule, he was the partner Hick needed for his horse ranch.

"That's something, isn't it?" Mrs. Piper strode toward him, a wide smile across her face.

"Cooter is some sort of horse trainer."

She stopped next to him and poked him with her elbow. "And Peaches is some sort of mule."

He couldn't argue with her as the evidence trotted toward camp. Instead, he studied her profile for a moment. "What made you name that animal Peaches?"

"Abel bought her when we arrived in Missouri." She glanced up, her dark blue eyes glinting in the sun. "He asked me what I missed most about Georgia. Daddy had planted a pair of peach trees in our garden years before the war." She sighed and watched Cooter fuss with the mule. "I still miss those peaches."

"More than your family?" The words slipped out before he'd thought about them, and he could almost feel her stiffen in response.

"I have no more family in Georgia, Mr. Hickman."

She strode toward Cooter and the mule, her skirts swishing across the prairie grass from hips that swayed in irritation. At him.

He rubbed the back of his neck. He didn't blame her for being vexed. It was none of his business. He couldn't help but feel a tug of sadness for her. She'd lost everything. His family—all but Denny—were safe and happy back in Ohio. Hick rubbed the center of his chest.

A place that would never be home to Hick again because of his younger brother's death.

"Now, Mrs. Piper, don't get me wrong."

Susannah didn't back down as Hick fidgeted with the hat in his hands.

"I'm more grateful than you can know for you coming and nursing me back to health. I truly am. But the prairie is no place for a woman alone."

"You mean for a Southern woman, don't you, Mr. Hickman?" Susannah stuffed the last of her belongings into her saddlebag, releasing her agitation on her hapless spare clothing.

"I mean any woman." He spread his arms as if encompassing the whole of the prairie past their camp. "There are Indians not far from here, and men you can't trust. Bandits. Outlaws. Maybe worse."

She buckled her saddlebag and stood, hefting it to her shoulder, refusing to wince when it landed on her tender but healed scar. "I trust you and Cooter. You're riding to Fort Kearny. If I ride with you, I will be quite safe."

The angles and edges of his face carried the words he didn't say. Susannah had become adept at reading the man. He wasn't happy with her decision. But then, she'd never thought he would be.

Cooter lurked at the edge of camp with his back turned. He had no desire to get in the middle of their muddle. Smart lad.

"Mr. Hickman." He remained mute so she took the reins of the conversation. "You and Cooter are leaving almost this instant, as am I. You can agree to me riding beside you, or I will follow behind. You have no authority to stop me from heading west."

"That's a fact, ma'am." He slapped his hat against his thigh, then stomped off to his horse. He thrust his foot in the stirrup and swung into the saddle without a hitch. The ten days of rest had healed him of more than just cholera. His limp was gone.

He was a strong, healthy, frustrated, irritating man.

Cooter glanced at her and shrugged as he mounted Rumpus, but he waited when Mr. Hickman sent Trooper off at a gallop.

Susannah hooked her saddlebag to her makeshift saddle and mounted. She clicked to Peaches and set her off at a steady trot following the dust behind Mr. Hickman.

Cooter brought his buckskin beside her. "He ain't likely to stay mad very long, ma'am."

"I wouldn't be so sure."

"Oh, Hick's gotta snort and fuss some. He's a man what's used to given orders and bein' obeyed, him bein' in the war and all."

She hadn't thought of it that way, but she couldn't picture Mr. Hickman as a humble soldier. Everything about him pointed to being the man in charge. An officer, even if not a high-ranking one.

"I suppose you're right."

He grinned in response. "I often am, and it generally surprises folk."

Susannah laughed. "You certainly surprised us when you succeeded in teaching Peaches to come to your whistle."

"Oh, that weren't nothin' hard. She's a good mule." He settled back in his saddle despite the bouncing trot, as if he was launching to a long story. "Grandpappy was a mule man back in the hills. He learned me how to work with 'em. When Grandpappy wasn't preachin', he was workin' with his mules."

"Your grandfather was a preacher?"

"Yes, ma'am. He was. And he raised me to do right." Cooter grinned at her, once again bringing John to mind.

"I had a brother much like you."

"Ya never." He learned forward against the pommel of his saddle. "Tell me about him."

For a moment, she stared at the puff of dust far ahead of them. Mr. Hickman was taking his frustration out on that poor horse. No, that wasn't fair. Giving the animal a good run wouldn't hurt it a bit. After days of inactivity, the horse probably needed a good romp. She was simply cross at the way he'd charged off and left her behind.

But Cooter had stayed.

"He died in the fall of 1861 at the battle of Manassas."

"I'm right sorry to hear that." His young face grew serious. "Iffen it pains ya, don't go tellin' me no more."

"It does pain me, but I don't want to forget him. Talking about him will keep his memory alive." It hit her how true that was. "His name was John, and he was the youngest of us four siblings. He had a knack for making everyone laugh."

Talking about him eased the tension from Susannah's shoulders, all the way to her heart. They'd catch up to Mr. Hickman eventually. Until then, she determined to enjoy the beautiful morning and her chatty companion.

What could they be jabbering about back there? Hick turned in the saddle and stared behind him for the umpteenth time since he'd slowed Trooper to a walk. They could have caught up to him an hour or more ago. Why did they dawdle behind? He faced forward again and searched the nearby riverbank for an easy place to water the horses. They'd been on the trail for close to three hours. The animals needed a drink.

He found a sandy area and let Trooper wade into the river. The old horse buried his muzzle in the fresh, cold water and sucked it up. As the others approached, he lifted his muzzle and nickered, his sides heaving between Hick's calf muscles. But Hick wasn't inclined to add to the greeting.

He was still fuming over Mrs. Piper's insistence that she tag along.

Getting used to Cooter was one thing. He was a young man who could take care of himself. It wasn't as if they were at war anymore. Hick pushed the possible threat of Indians aside for the moment.

Mrs. Piper was a liability. She was a woman who needed protection. *His* protection if she continued to ride with him. And he didn't have a clue how to prevent her from doing so. She'd proved more stubborn than her mule when it came to listening to common sense.

"Hey, Hick." Cooter waded Rumpus out beside Trooper. "Hows abouts we stop and do a little fishin'? This appears to be a likely spot."

"Nope."

"Fish dinner would be mighty tasty. Mrs. Piper could—"

"Nope." Hick wheeled Trooper around and headed for the shore.

Mrs. Piper had dismounted and was bathing her face with a piece of cloth while the molly drank beside her. She cast a glance at Hick, then dipped her cloth again and wrung it out.

Hick wrenched his eyes away from the bare throat she exposed to the wet cloth and scanned the area. The land appeared flat, but there were plenty of rolls and folds to the land that could hide danger.

"Thank you for the break, Mr. Hickman." Mrs. Piper gathered her reins and mounted the mule. "It was refreshing."

He grunted, then tapped the gelding's sides and rode on. But he kept the pace to a trot. They hadn't passed a soddy all morning, so they were beyond the edge of civilization. It would be good to remember that and keep his eyes open for danger. Only Cooter had covered that part of the country before. Which reminded him...

"Cooter?"

The young man urged his buckskin away from Mrs. Piper and toward him. "Yeah?"

"You rode this way with the Pony Express, didn't you?"

"Yessir. Many a time."

"How far is it to Fort Kearny?"

The young man rubbed his smooth jawline. "Well, best I can recollect, it were a full day's hard ride and maybe an hour or two more. That were changing horses every ten miles or so."

"That far."

"I guess."

"You guess?" Frustration seeped into Hick's tone.

"I ain't never stopped at the fort, ya see. It weren't on the route." Cooter pointed southwest. "The fort be that way somewheres, but we rode from station to station and they was along the river." He pointed to the telegraph poles that stretched like a high single strand of barb-less fence following the river with enough space for a buffalo or mounted cowboy to walk underneath. "They run them wires along the Pony's route."

"Hm." That didn't help much. They wouldn't be swapping horses or running them. Maybe three days then, or four depending on how far south they had to travel.

Three or four more days of watching over Mrs. Piper.

That wouldn't be too bad. For sure and certain, he was leaving her behind at Fort Kearny, even if he had to sneak off in the middle of the night.

Susannah flipped the fish on the hot cast iron, the sizzle and pop releasing its tantalizing aroma. Mr. Hickman had relented and stopped early enough in the evening for Cooter to do his fishing. Four fat trout in her skillet were further proof that the young man knew what he was about with a hook and line.

That he'd been allowed the time to fish proved, once again, the underlying kindness of Mr. Hickman. She needed to remember that when he tossed scowls her way. That and the way he'd called for Denny in his delirium. Only someone who cared—to his very soul—would be so tormented by such a loss.

She'd considered asking him about Denny, giving him a chance to speak of him. Talking about John with Cooter that morning had eased her grief in an unexpected way. Of course, his resemblance to John had sparked the conversation. It would take something else to spark such a difficult conversation with Mr. Hickman.

It would help if he would speak with her at all.

Never chatty, his stony silence since they'd left camp might as well have been a brick wall. It was the way he averted his eyes from her that hurt, however. It shouldn't, but it did.

She flipped the fish again, then poked at the fresh dandelion greens she'd gathered along the riverbank while Cooter worked his magic with his line and hook. They simmered in Mr. Hickman's coffeepot. She gave the biscuits cooking in his skillet a final turn. They'd have a regular feast for supper. Mr. Hickman needed to regain the weight he'd lost while ill, and Cooter was thinner than a split rail. Their midday break with jerked venison wouldn't fatten either one.

"It's ready. Bring your plates."

Cooter was beside her before she finished her sentence. She cut the extra fish in half, then gave him one and a half.

"No, ma'am. Give that extra to Hick. He's needin' more groceries under his belt."

"So do you. If you turn sideways, you'll disappear."

He grinned wider when she added two biscuits and a spoonful of greens to his plate.

Mr. Hickman handed her his plate in silence—of course. She filled it the same way, but when she handed it back, she didn't let go, forcing him to look at her.

"I hope you enjoy it, Mr. Hickman."

"Can't imagine I wouldn't, ma'am."

"Can't you?" She released the plate.

Confusion clouded his expression. "Ma'am?"

"I've gotten the distinct impression that you don't enjoy my company anymore. I thought it might spread to my cooking as well." That wasn't true, but she was determined to needle some words from him any way she could.

Cooter took his plate and retreated to a spot near the animals.

Out of harm's way.

"It's not that I don't enjoy your company, ma'am." His voice had dropped to a low growl. "It's that you don't belong out here."

She stared at him until he met her eyes and held them. "That's the issue, Mr. Hickman. I don't belong anywhere."

CHAPTER 18

H ICK HALTED TROOPER AND scanned the horizon. There was so much of it. The prairie had flattened out even more, if that were possible, with scarcely a tree except along the river. The river had widened and grown sluggish, its water murky. He didn't relish having to drink from it. It was a good thing they'd filled the canteens before breaking camp.

Then something caught his eye. He squinted and shielded his face from the sun.

Cooter brought Rumpus to a stop next to Hick. "Looks like buzzards to me."

Hick nodded.

"Could be a buffalo shoot. Heard tell men is shootin' 'em dead and leavin' 'em lie after skinnin' 'em."

"Why would they do that?" Mrs. Piper asked from behind them.

"Indians rely on the buffalo." Hick lowered his hand. "If they decimate the herds, they decimate the Indians."

"That's awful," she said.

It was, but war made people do awful things. He'd done awful things. Things that still haunted his dreams.

"Why don't you two ride on along the river, and I'll swing south and make sure it's not someone in trouble."

"Trouble?" Mrs. Piper asked.

He turned to her. She was lovely in the midmorning light. Her dark braid against her shoulder, her face shaded by a straw hat, and her skirt arranged to hide the ridiculous excuse for a saddle while exposing her leather boots. She was too lovely to be there.

Too lovely to be away from his protection.

"On second thought, we should stay together." He glanced at the distant cloud of buzzards. "It could be Indians."

"Heaven help us." Cooter's voice was somewhere between a whisper and a prayer.

Hick added a silent *amen* and clicked to Trooper. The birds were at least a half mile out, maybe farther. It was hard to gauge when the landscape was so flat. Things tended to appear closer than they were simply because he could see so much of the world around him. Growing up in the hilly country of southern Ohio, he wasn't used to the vastness.

He turned in his saddle and motioned to Cooter, who had dropped back to ride with Mrs. Piper. He bridled his irritation that those two enjoyed each other's company so much.

"What d'ya need?" Cooter asked when he drew close.

"I have a bad feeling about this." Hick gave a curt nod toward the birds.

Cooter scratched the back of his neck. "Know what ya mean."

"You ride out and scout the situation." Hick kept his voice low. "I'll keep close to Mrs. Piper, and we'll follow at a fast walk." He pinned the young man with as meaningful a look as he could summon. "If you spot danger, you hightail it back, and we'll get her somewhere safe."

Cooter touched the brim of his hat. "Ya can count on me." Then he planted his heels into the mustang's side. They shot forward as if launched by a cannon.

Hick had to rein in Trooper when the war horse tried to charge in pursuit.

"Where is he going?" Mrs. Piper brought the mule up beside Trooper.

"He'll scout the area."

"Is that safe?"

He glanced at her. Concern creased the skin above her nose. But of course, as a nurse, she'd think along those lines.

"He rode for the Pony Express, ma'am, and that mustang is the fastest horse I've seen in a long time. He'll be fine." He started Trooper forward again. "Best to know what we're riding into."

"I suppose it is." Her voice carried a note of sadness.

"Ma'am?"

Her chin rose as she shifted on her saddle. "Knowing what I'm riding into is a luxury I haven't had for a long, long time."

They had a lot of ground to cover at a slow pace. Hick could keep his eyes open while he listened. Maybe it was time to clear the air between them, to learn more about the stubborn and determined woman riding beside him.

"I know you lost your family in the war, ma'am. I'm sorry about that."

"Thank you, Mr. Hickman."

"And I know you married a Union soldier. But if you don't mind my asking, how did that happen?"

Her lips trembled into a partial smile.

He jerked his attention back to the landscape around them.

"I helped Abel escape from the temporary prisoner of war camp that was erected in our town of Blackshear."

The term of someone dropping their teeth had never meant much to Hick until then. Her father and brothers had fought—and died—for the Confederacy, but she'd helped a Yankee prisoner of war escape?

"I've shocked you, I see."

"It's fair to say you have, ma'am."

She chuckled. "Helping him escape was never my intention. Like so many of the women in our town, I took food to the soldiers when they arrived. As I'm sure you know, our army could scarcely feed itself. But the prisoners..." Her voice trailed off.

After the war, he'd seen a few of the men who'd survived the Southern prison camps. Walking skeletons who'd make Cooter appear fat in comparison. Men who would never be the same after that level of starvation.

She cleared her throat. "I returned to the camp with broth for the prisoners, as much as I could make and carry. Several women helped—it wasn't just me." Her voice dropped to a near whisper. "The poor souls couldn't have taken any solid food in their condition."

He could believe it, and he'd had the benefits of her broth.

"For three days we cooked and served. The camp wasn't a true prison. It had no walls or fence, just armed guards surrounding the tents the men were housed in. Not that they all fit into the few tents they had. Many slept on the ground outside without even a blanket. Their clothes were in tatters."

The picture she painted was too clear, too easy to imagine.

"I took all the clothing in the house that had belonged to Daddy and my brothers." She looked at him then, and the sadness in her eyes moved something deep inside him. Something he tried hard to ignore.

Memories of the war.

"On the night of their third day in Blackshear, a group of men escaped and scattered. Abel, one of many I'd fed and provided clothing for, hid in my gardening shed. I found him there the next morning, almost too weak to stand and wearing Daddy's old suit."

What sort of woman, finding an enemy soldier like that, wouldn't have turned him in at once?

Mrs. Piper's sort.

A woman of deep compassion and practicality. A woman stubborn enough to follow Hick onto the prairie to chase her dreams of Oregon. If anyone could make it there, she could. He mentally shrugged off a grudging—growing—admiration for her.

She'd have to do it without him.

Why hadn't speaking of Abel calmed Susannah as speaking of John had the day before? She shot a glance at the tall man riding in silence beside her. *He* was why. Cooter had been full of questions about John, had encouraged her to tell him more until it'd almost seemed as if they'd both known him.

Mr. Hickman hadn't interrupted once. Hadn't asked a single question. From all appearances, he may not have heard a word she'd said.

Why was it that this one man's opinion mattered so much to her?

She'd been rebuffed by many in the past few years. By fellow Southerners when they learned she was the wife of a Union soldier. By Northerners when she opened her mouth and released her Georgia drawl. By Abel's family when he'd introduced her to them, unable to abide his marrying an enemy—even one who'd saved his life. By shopkeepers and hotel staff along their journey west. By the people in Missouri who'd tolerated her only as long as Abel was alive.

Other rebuffs had hurt, of course, especially Abel's family. He'd been so sure they would accept her. Her hurt from them had mostly been for his sake. She'd offered to leave him, but he'd stood by her. He'd been a good man, one she would forever be thankful she'd saved that fateful night in Blackshear. Given the chance—in spite of everything—she'd do it again.

Samuel Hickman was a good man too, which was why his opinion mattered. As frustrating as he was, she could see past that to the man he was beneath the gruff, inhospitable persona he wore like a coat.

He was hurting from the war, from the loss of Denny, and it'd changed him.

She'd seen enough of wounded soldiers, had doctored those who'd limped home—or were carried—to Blackshear. Men reduced to no more than shadows of their swaggering selves who'd marched out to whip the Yankees in a month.

Men who'd faced hell on earth.

Mr. Hickman stopped Trooper and shielded his eyes from the sun. Peaches stopped a step or two ahead of the horse. A puff of dust on the horizon caught her attention.

"Is it Cooter?" she asked.

"Not enough dust for more than one rider."

They waited, the sun overhead unleashing its full force on the open prairie. Heat waves danced off the landscape even though it was still spring. They played havoc with the dust cloud, making it seem larger and then smaller.

"It's him." Mr. Hickman started Trooper forward.

How could he tell from such a distance? She urged Peaches to catch up, and soon she could make out the yellowish coat of Rumpus, Cooter flattened over his neck and riding hard.

He pulled the horse to a halt, the mustang rearing in protest, but Cooter hung on without seeming to pay any attention. He only had eyes for Mr. Hickman. "Just one wagon, Hick, and no horses or oxen. Them buzzards be wantin' what's inside it."

Mr. Hickman pinched the bridge of his nose. "I suppose there's nothing we can do then."

"Funny thing is, they ain't landin' on the wagon."

"What?"

"I didn't get close enough to see because there ain't no cover nearby, but it seems as if somethin' is keepin' them away."

"You think somebody is still alive in the wagon?" Mr. Hickman's voice was iron-hard.

Cooter didn't flinch. "That's the only way I can see it."

"No Indian sign?"

"None I could see, but someone got the critters what was pullin' that wagon."

Mr. Hickman scanned the horizon, his scowl deepening. "We should avoid it. Mrs. Piper—"

"Did you hear what he said?" She tapped her heels against Peaches. "Someone may still be alive."

"Mrs. Piper." Mr. Hickman lurched forward and grabbed her mule's bridle. "It's too dangerous. If it wasn't Indians, then it was bandits."

"Which doesn't alter the fact that someone needs our help, does it, Mr. Hickman?"

"Ma'am, as long as I'm responsible—"

"You are not." She tugged on the outside rein sharply enough to make Peaches pivot. He had to release the bridle or be pulled from his saddle. "My responsibility lies with assisting those I can. I am a nurse, sir. I cannot leave someone in distress."

"Ma'am, I can't allow you—"

"Mr. Hickman, you cannot stop me." She glared at him, then thumped her heels against Peaches. The mule, already antsy from being part of their tug-of-war, lumbered into a canter before settling into a gallop.

There were words behind Susannah it was probably best she hadn't heard clearly, but the pounding of hooves followed her.

Cooter's horse sprinted past her and took the lead. Mr. Hickman hung back. They kept that pace until Cooter reined in and raised one hand. By then, the canvas of the wagon was visible in the sun. The wind buffeted it, but not enough to keep the black crowd of both buzzards and crows at bay.

It was more than enough wind to bring them the stench of rotting flesh.

Mr. Hickman rode past her and stopped beside Cooter.

She guided Peaches to the mustang's other side. "Why are we stopping?"

"To get the lay of the land, ma'am." Mr. Hickman didn't look at her, his eyes seeming to rake in every aspect of their surroundings.

"Look there." Cooter pointed at something poking from the back of the wagon when a buzzard attempted to land. "That sure enough looks like a gun barrel to me."

Someone was alive in there—surrounded by the stench of death.

Hick had no idea how they were going to approach the wagon without being sitting ducks for whoever was inside with a rifle. The land around it had all the contours of a kitchen table.

"How do ya reckon we should go about this?" Cooter asked.

Hick turned to Mrs. Piper. "You stay here ma'am, we'll find out what's happening." He touched his heels to Trooper's sides.

"We just ridin' up on that?" Cooter asked.

"Yup."

"Ain't ya worried about what's scarin' them crows?"

"Yup."

"Then why is we just ridin' up like we's goin' to a Sunday picnic?"

Hick rubbed his jaw, never taking his eyes off the wagon. "Whoever's in there is surrounded by that smell."

"And?"

"Would you be in there if you could be anywhere else?"

Cooter snorted. "Ain't likely."

"Me neither. And I figure it's the same for whoever's in there."

"Reckon they's hurt?"

"Likely."

The odor magnified as they drew near. How on earth could anyone be in that wagon with whoever was dead?

At a walk, offering no movement toward his rifle and keeping his hands away from his sides—Cooter doing the same—they gave whoever might be watching plenty of warning. As soon as they were within shouting distance, Hick hollered, "Hello, the wagon."

A rifle barrel poked from the canvas covering.

"We're friendly. Just wondering if you could use a hand."

The rifle barrel wobbled, and Hick shot Cooter a glance. The other man's face was creased in a combination of baffled and appalled that matched how Hick felt.

"Is it all right if we ride in?" Hick shouted.

A long minute passed, and then another. The rifle barrel wobbled again.

"Reckon whoever it is ain't strong enough to hold that thing steady?"

"Could be." That would explain a lot.

"What're we gonna do?"

What indeed? Trooper stomped at the flies that buzzed around them. Going forward, they'd have more to contend with. Still, there was nothing for it. He wasn't going to leave anyone there... in that. He tapped the horse's sides, but the animal balked, not that Hick could blame him. Memories of bloated bodies—both human and horses—littering battlefields and cooking in the heat assailed him.

"We're going to ride around to the other side of your wagon. That all right with you?" he hollered.

The rifle barrel wobbled again, but didn't disappear and didn't fire. That was something. He glanced back at Mrs. Piper to be sure she'd stayed put, then reined Trooper in a wide circle around the wagon. The gagging stench was slightly better once they were upwind, but not much. The rifle barrel, or maybe a second one, protruded from above the wagon's high seat. Then it wobbled. The same one then, held by the same unsteady hands.

Hick dropped the reins and held his hands up. "We're riding in now. Just coming to offer help. Nothing to be afraid of."

"'Ceptin' maybe a bullet," Cooter muttered as he lifted his hands.

"Whoever it is has had more than enough time to shoot us."

"That ain't exactly a comfortin' thought."

It wasn't. But Hick had a hunch. A hunch that made him want to lean over and lose the fine breakfast Mrs. Piper had cooked them.

Guiding Trooper with pressure from his legs, a maneuver made more difficult by the old horse's perfectly sound judgment to get as far away from that stench as possible, they approached one slow step at a time.

The rifle barrel continued to wobble, at one point disappearing and then reappearing before he could draw an easy breath.

"My insides is squirmin' somethin' fierce," Cooter said.

That was a good description. Too good. One Hick didn't need to hear.

"Can you call out? Tell us your name?" he asked.

Silence except for the reluctant thump of the horses' hooves. They approached to within a dozen feet and stopped, both horses shifting and snorting. Even a trained war horse wasn't immune to the smell of a days-old decaying body. Or bodies.

"We'll dismount now." He did and handed Trooper's reins to Cooter. No horse was going to stay ground-tied under the circumstances.

"Grandpappy'd say that this here's where the fat hits the pan. Go easy."

"I'm walking in, nothing in my hands." Hick kept them raised to chest level. He was within six feet of the front of the wagon when a head poked above the high seat. A small, bonnet-covered head. His hunch had been correct, but seeing it hit him hard anyway.

A child.

"Stop right there, mister." The high-pitched voice wavered through the air between them, the child's attempt to be brave more like a cry for help.

CHAPTER 19

"**I** WANT TO HELP you, missy. Seems to me you got more trouble than you can handle on your own." Hick made his voice as soothing as he could, like he would have for a spooked horse.

The rifle barrel wobbled again, probably too heavy for her little arms.

"Me and Cooter here, we figure you need a hand burying some folk in there with you."

The girl sniffled, then wiped her nose with the back of her wrist, nearly dropping the rifle in the process.

"I gotta keep the birds away."

"That's why we need to bury them, missy. To keep the birds away permanently."

The rifle barrel tilted down.

"I got a shovel, but I can't leave the wagon because of the birds."

That was a problem.

"How many are dead in there with you?"

"Five."

Lord, have mercy. "Anyone else alive?"

"No." He barely made out that one word, laden as it was with a world of grief and despair.

"I'll tell you what. Why don't you let me and Cooter borrow the shovel out of your wagon. We'll dig while you keep the birds away, all right?"

Silence hung between them for a long moment. He smacked a fly that landed on the back of his neck. If she didn't decide to trust him, what could he do? Six months ago, he'd probably have left Cooter hanging in that willow tree. A year ago, he might have ridden away from the reeking wagon in front of him.

But not anymore.

"All right, mister."

Relief washed over him.

"Can you toss out the shovel? Do you have a pick?"

The wagon creaked and rocked, then a shovel appeared over the top of the seat and tumbled to the ground. "I'll push the pick out the back. It's too heavy for me to lift over the seat."

"That's a good girl. We'll dig five holes for you."

"You can just dig three. My brothers can be buried together. I think they'd like that." The last word ended with a shaky half sob.

The pick landed on the ground moments later. Hick walked to the back of the wagon, scattering buzzards and crows as he went, and looked into the grayest eyes he'd ever seen. Curly hair, matted and unkempt, hung around a freckled face. Why, she couldn't be more than ten years old.

"Your brothers, are they older or younger?"

"Younger."

Lord, have mercy. "You just keep those old birds away, and we'll do the rest." He turned with the pick in his hand.

"Mister?"

He looked back over his shoulder.

"Much obliged."

His throat tightened into a knot, and he nodded before walking to Cooter.

"She's mighty young, ain't she?"

"Yup. Whistle Mrs. Piper in. We're going to need her help with that little girl."

Cooter stuck two fingers in his mouth and let loose one of his piercing whistles. It hadn't stopped before the mule was galloping toward them.

Cooter looked around. "I'd like to dig away from that stink, but I don't suppose we want to try movin' those bodies very far."

"Don't think so."

"I'll picket the horses over there." He pointed to some scrub-by-looking bushes growing around a clump of rocks.

Mrs. Piper rode in and handed her reins to Cooter. "What's the situation?"

"A little girl, ma'am." Hick cleared his throat. "The rest are dead. Five of them. Her whole family, I suppose."

"Do you know why?"

"Nope, ma'am. But it wasn't Indians or the girl wouldn't be alive."

His eyes met hers and her brows raised. "Cholera?"

"That'd be my guess." It was the type of thing that would leave a little girl an orphan on the prairie.

Mrs. Piper's insistence on coming west with them had a silver lining, after all.

The stench was overwhelming, even from a distance, but Susannah gathered her skirt and rushed toward the wagon. She kicked at a couple of the bolder crows as she ran, swatting away the flies. How could that poor child stand it inside the wagon?

A pitiful little girl with curly red hair peeked out of the back.

Susannah reached the edge and lifted her arms, and the poor mite fell into them, her body trembling.

"Oh, my dear." Susannah smoothed down the mass of tangled hair that reeked to high heaven. "Let me get you out of this wagon."

"No!" The girl pulled back, shaking her head. "I have to keep the birds away."

Susannah looked over her shoulder. Mr. Hickman and Cooter had gathered a shovel and pick. Both wore neckerchiefs over the bottom half of their faces. It probably didn't help much, but it couldn't hurt. The first *shurf* of the shovel into the dirt sent a cloud of black wings into the sky. She turned back to the girl.

"What's your name, dear?"

"Bonnie."

"Listen, Bonnie. These men will see everyone buried properly, and as long as they are beside the wagon swinging those tools, no nasty old bird is going to disturb your family. I promise."

Large gray eyes studied her face, then the girl looked back into the wagon.

What Susannah saw tore her heart to shreds. Evidence that it was cholera flooded the wagon's bed and teemed with flies. She had to get the little girl away from it. "We can walk to the river and get you cleaned up. That way, when it's time to say a few words over the graves, you'll be more presentable."

Bonnie turned back to her, a single tear clinging to her lashes.

"I think your mother would approve."

The little chin dipped and raised, but the gray eyes never left Susannah's face.

"Do you have a change of clothing in there?" And please, let it not be covered in anything nasty. Or crawling.

Another nod, and Bonnie opened a trunk, pulling out a green dress, a handful of underthings, and a pink-and-brown wool shawl.

"You won't need the shawl. It's very warm."

"It's my momma's."

"Then bring it." Susannah offered her arms again, and this time she swung Bonnie to the ground where the girl's legs buckled. Susannah supported her. The poor dear weighed less than half a sack of flour. "When was the last time you had anything to eat or drink?"

The girl squinted and then shook her head. "Maybe the day before yesterday."

She was dehydrated. The lone tear made sense. Susannah scooped her up and carried her on one hip. "She needs water and washing. We'll be back after you've buried her family."

Mr. Hickman nodded.

"Ya go on, little missy." Cooter pulled his neckerchief down. "Me and Hick, we're goin' to take care of everythin' here."

Bonnie nodded.

Susannah strode to Peaches and unstrapped a canteen, opened it, and handed it to Bonnie. "Not too much or too fast, or it'll come back up." She kept her hand on the canteen to be sure the girl obeyed. Then she set her down. "Hold on to my skirt if you need to. I'll just get a few things from my saddlebag." She rummaged for a rag, a piece of toweling, her comb, and a precious bar of soap she'd been hoarding for months. It wasn't the harsh lard soap she normally used but a special bar Abel had bought for her. It smelled of roses, and Bonnie needed it now more than Susannah ever had.

With the supplies, she carried the girl to the river, had her drink from the canteen again, sat her on the bank, and stripped off her shoes and socks, knocking off several crawling maggots in the process. She'd have to be sure and shake out her own clothing afterward. Susannah pulled the back of her skirt between her legs and tucked it into her front waistband, exposing her legs. "Come on, Bonnie. We'll need to wash your clothing anyway, so you might as well get it wet too."

The little girl took her hand and walked into the river.

Susannah let Bonnie sit in the shallows while she washed the clothing, including the dress from the wagon after she'd discovered maggots on it and the shawl. She spread the garments on nearby bushes to dry, then unwrapped the special soap.

"Come here and smell this." She held out the bar.

The little girl's eyes widened when she got her nose over the bar. "My grandma had soap like that," Bonnie said. "We could sniff it, but we weren't allowed to use it."

"Well, today, you get to use as much of it as you want." It was little enough that Susannah could do for the poor orphan.

Since the men would be occupied for a while, Susannah removed her dress and shook it fiercely to dislodge any crawlies that might have transferred from Bonnie. She washed the dress and then bathed herself with the fragrant soap.

Once both of them were thoroughly washed and dressed in their still-damp clothing, it was time to return to the wagon and the burial. Bonnie appeared on the verge of collapse, so Susannah scooped her into her arms. They approached the animals first so Susannah could pack her belongings into her saddlebag and listen for the sound of shovel or pick. There was none, so she offered Bonnie one more drink, hugged her for a moment, then said, "It's time to say your goodbyes."

After stomping down the loose dirt on the last grave, Hick picked up a stone and slung it at a pair of buzzards. The ugly, bald-headed birds squawked and flew away. There were still a number of crows hopping around and pecking at the leavings in the wagon. He and Cooter had cut off the canvas to wrap the bodies.

Cooter straightened and stripped his hat off as Mrs. Piper approached with the little girl in her arms. Both had wet hair hanging loose down their backs and damp dresses that clung to them. In the case of Mrs. Piper, the dress clung in all the right places.

Hick pulled his attention away and stomped on the dirt a few more times.

"Stop!"

He froze and met the little girl's eyes, swimming with unshed tears.

"Don't step on them."

"He has to, little missy." Cooter stepped forward. "We have to pack the dirt back real tight. Iffen we don't, might be some coyote would dig 'em back up."

"He's right, Bonnie." Mrs. Piper hugged the girl. "These men know what they're doing."

Bonnie. So that was her name.

"If you tell us your family's names, Bonnie, we can say a few words over them now." Mrs. Piper's voice was soothing and calm. Being a nurse, she'd likely been in similar situations before, having to comfort the family of the dead.

"Ma and Pa are Nancy and Herbert. My brothers are Clem, Rupert, and Robby. Clem's the oldest, he was named after Grandpa Sorrel. Rupert and Robby are twins. Robby's real name is Robert."

The magnitude of her loss hit Hick like a kick to the belly. Burying the bodies had been a chore that needed doing. Hearing their names, learning something about them, made them... real.

As real as Denny.

He rubbed the center of his chest.

"Cooter, maybe you could say a few words over the graves for us?" Mrs. Piper asked.

Relief flowed through Hick like sweet molasses. He wasn't sure he could have pushed the words past his tight throat. And Cooter's grandfather had been a preacher, so it was fitting.

"Yes, ma'am." Cooter brushed the dirt from the front of his clothes. "Little missy, do ya want to say anything first?"

Bonnie shook her head and buried her face in Mrs. Piper's shoulder.

Cooter coughed, stuck his thumbs in his suspenders, and spoke at length about a family he'd never met and the God who loved them above all else.

Hick's throat closed even tighter, as if the words were also spoken for Denny. Because his brother hadn't had such a eulogy. Until that moment, it hadn't even occurred to Hick. In the middle of a war, there wasn't time for the niceties one normally expected. But when Cooter slapped an *amen* on the end, Hick whispered the word for Denny.

And for the first time he could remember, the pain didn't spark in his chest at the thought of his brother.

"This little girl needs to eat, and I suppose you men have worked up a hunger." Mrs. Piper eyed them both. "But I suggest we move a mile or so along the river."

Away from the smell and the flies and the lingering crows.

Hick met her direct look. "That would be welcome."

"Bonnie?" She leaned over the little girl still in her arms. "Do you wish to say goodbye while the men ready the horses and Peaches?"

Hick and Cooter strode away, but a glance back seared a picture in his mind that he knew he wouldn't soon forget. A lovely woman and a little girl kneeling beside fresh graves.

"Kinda chokes ya up, don't it?"

"Yup." He clouted Cooter on the shoulder. "Nice words you spoke over them."

That brought the young man's grin back. "Done a hundred of 'em with my grandpappy. He trained me real good."

"I hope he trained you to wash clothes too."

Confusion replaced the grin. "Why?"

Hick brushed several crawlies off the young man's sleeve. "Because you're covered in more than just dirt."

That sent Cooter off in a hop-slap-dance that would have been funny in any other circumstance. But Hick did his best to slap his own clothing to remove any vermin. He'd bathe in the river as soon as they set up camp. They'd traveled far enough today.

And they needed to figure out what they were going to do with a little orphan girl.

CHAPTER 20

C OOTER HAD BROUGHT FISH back after he and Mr. Hickman had bathed and changed clothing. The young man's face had fallen when Susannah told him she would stew them. But little Bonnie needed something easier on her stomach than fried or roasted fish, and there were so many fresh edible greens breaking through the spring ground to stew with it. Judging from the way Cooter leaned over the pot and closed his eyes, her meal was going to pass muster. She gave the concoction one last stir and moved it away from the direct heat of the fire, then flipped the biscuits.

"Mrs. Piper?" Hick squatted on the other side of the fire.

"Yes?"

"I think you and me and Cooter should talk before the girl wakes up."

Cooter sat to the side of the fire. "What is there to talk about?" He picked up a stick and poked at the flames.

Mr. Hickman nodded to the girl sleeping on Susannah's bedroll, where she'd been since they'd set up camp. "What are we going to do with her?"

"What can we do with her?" Susannah's heart squeezed for the poor girl. "She'll have to come with us, of course."

"To the fort?" Mr. Hickman shook his head. "A fort is no place for a little girl, ma'am."

"It's a far cry better than leavin' her here." Cooter shot Mr. Hickman a disbelieving look.

"I didn't mean we should leave her here." Irritation colored his tone. "But maybe we should try and find her a family."

"Say." Cooter sat up straighter. "Why don't we try and find *her* family?"

Mr. Hickman tossed a piece of bark into the fire. "We just buried them."

"No. I mean, she must have other family somewheres." Cooter warmed to his idea, his face flushing. "She's old enough to know where, and we could deliver her."

"What if her family is back east, say, in Kentucky?" Because Susannah had no wish to go back there.

"We ain't gonna know till we ask her." Cooter glanced at the sleeping girl. "That's where we gotta to start."

He was correct, of course, but from the thundercloud on Mr. Hickman's face, he wasn't happy with the obvious.

"The stew is done. I'll wake her." She spared them each a glare. "The child needs food. Let her eat her fill before you pepper her with questions."

They glanced at each other in that way men had of talking without words. But she was reassured they'd comply, so she went to Bonnie.

"Wake up, sweetheart." She smoothed the mass of dry curls away from the girl's forehead. She really was a darling little thing. Her freckles and reddish hair collided with her pale skin in an impish way. "Wake up, you need to eat now."

Bonnie yawned and stretched but didn't open her eyes.

"Come on, sleepyhead." Susannah lifted her and carried her to the fire. The men had searched the wagon for anything usable, including a plate and cup, some silverware, the pot the stew was cooking in, and another skillet. They'd have brought more, but they could only carry so much on the already loaded animals.

Bonnie stretched again as Susannah lowered her to the ground, and by the time she passed the plate loaded with fish stew, the girl's eyes were open and eager. They ate in a companionable silence, listening to the birds and the sighing of the wind through the bushes along the river.

The little girl cleaned her plate and ate one biscuit but declined any more. Her stomach couldn't hold too much food at once.

Mr. Hickman and Cooter, on the other hand, finished the rest between them.

It seemed Susannah was destined to collect people in need of feeding out.

Mr. Hickman cleared his throat. "Bonnie, where were your folks heading out here on the prairie all by themselves?"

She wiped her mouth with the back of her hand. "Wyoming. My Aunt Sadie Mae and Uncle Will live there."

"Why were they by themselves and not with a group of wagons?" he asked.

"Because of the cholera in Omaha." She glanced at Susannah. "Ma said it'd be best to get us children away from there." Her chin dropped to her chest. "But it didn't matter. They all got sick anyway."

And yet, surrounded by the illness, Bonnie hadn't sickened. It made no sense. But disease was like that sometimes, taking the strong and leaving the weak.

"How old are you, Bonnie?" Susannah asked.

"Eight. We had my birthday dinner before we reached Omaha. Ma fried prairie chickens."

"Bonnie." Mr. Hickman leaned his elbows on his knees. "What happened to your horses or oxen that pulled the wagon? Did you set them loose?"

She shook her head, her eyes growing large. "Indians took them."

That had both men sitting up straight and scanning their surroundings. The child's words sent a cold chill over Susannah's shoulders.

"They didn't bother ya none?" Cooter asked.

"I laid real still next to Ma. She'd just passed that morning. The wagon shook some, so they must have looked in, but I kept my eyes shut. They spoke words I didn't know and left."

Smart Indians didn't want anything to do with the white man's sickness. They'd learned. Plenty of them had died in the learning.

"How long ago?" Mr. Hickman asked.

Bonnie's face creased in thought. "Maybe three days ago? Pa had unhitched the horses when we stopped and picketed them near the river. After he and the boys died, Ma told me to untie them. She was sick then too. But the horses didn't go far." Her shoulders slumped. "After the Indians left I checked on them, and they were gone."

"You're a very brave little girl, Miss Bonnie," Mr. Hickman said.

Cooter nodded. "The bravest I ever met."

Susannah pulled the girl against her. "You survived an awful time, but you did survive. And now you have us to help you." She sent a very pointed look at each gentleman across the fire. "You rest now. We'll be watching over you."

The girl went limp against her, clutching the damp pink-and-brown shawl and melting Susannah's heart.

They'd been riding all morning, Hick taking the lead while Cooter rode behind Mrs. Piper and chatted with the girl. They'd learned a little more about her aunt and uncle, but not much. The couple had settled in Wyoming in the foothills of the mountains. Hick hadn't been there yet himself, but he knew there were a lot of mountains and plenty of foothills. Finding an aunt and uncle—Miss Bonnie wasn't sure of their last name—would be a near-impossible task.

Or maybe not. There weren't many white couples there if what he'd heard was true. If they could find any white couple in those mountains, likely they'd either be her aunt and uncle or would know of them. Maybe. But he and Cooter couldn't manage it alone.

Which meant Mrs. Piper needed to stay with them—*if* they decided to try and find the couple.

He ground his teeth as he scanned the never-changing flatlands. A flash of white was the rump of an antelope in the distance. The river continued on its sluggish journey to their right, wide and brown as a butternut. The brush that grew near it, twisted by the constant wind, couldn't be called trees. And the sky above was a cloudless pale blue, the sun beating on them with all the warmth of full summer. At least, if they'd been back in Ohio. He had a feeling it would get much hotter in this vast openness by midsummer.

A peal of giggles from behind brought him back to the problem at hand—Miss Bonnie and Mrs. Piper.

His plan had been so simple. Work a few jobs, save enough to buy some stock, head west and raise horses. Finding jobs had been easy enough. There were always horses that needed to be broke. Earning enough to buy horses had been something different. Wages were thin following the war. He'd been on four different farms and ranches since the war, including the Bar Arrow for a few months, and he had a small stake hidden in his saddlebag and a few coins in his pocket. It should have been enough to buy a quality stallion to put with the wild mares he planned to catch.

Until he was saddled with a partner of sorts, a widow woman, and an orphan girl. What was a man to do?

A puff of dust on the horizon caught his eye. He pulled Trooper to a halt, wishing he could gauge distance better. He half-turned in the saddle and held a hand out, palm toward those following.

Cooter saw it and moved Rumpus sideways in front of the mule. The young man had good instincts.

Hick scanned the area again. To the south was a thicket of brush that might mean a fold in the land. He'd seen several places where what looked like brush had turned out to be the tops of trees growing in a ravine.

The puff of dust grew larger.

He motioned for Cooter to follow but kept Trooper at a walk. No sense raising enough dust to be spotted by whoever was coming their way. Cooter followed suit, and the mule with Mrs. Piper and Miss Bonnie followed him. The land rolled in that deceptive way it had, hiding the dust cloud, but also hiding them. Hick released a breath of relief when a ravine, a shallow one, opened in front of him.

Trooper picked his way down the steep side, sliding on his haunches at one point. Rumpus, as a true mustang, handled the descent with no problem. Hick reached the bottom and turned as Mrs. Piper's molly came down the embankment as sure-footed as could be.

"What'd ya see?" Cooter asked.

"Dust cloud, moving fast."

"Injuns?"

Hick shrugged as Mrs. Piper joined them, her eyes wide and uncertain.

"Just a dust cloud, Mrs. Piper," Hick said. "Figured we'd let whoever it is pass on by."

"Could be some soldier boys from the fort," Cooter said. "We must be gettin' purdy close by now, and they throw a wide loop out here."

No doubt their patrols covered a lot of territory, and they could be soldiers, but something in Hick's gut said otherwise. He dismounted and dropped the reins to ground-tie Trooper. "I'm going to climb to the top and keep watch." He shot Cooter a *stay with the women* look.

Cooter touched his hat brim in response.

Hick scrambled up the embankment, glad that his hip was fully healed. Twice rocks slid out from under him, but he regained his balance and made it to the top. The dust cloud was almost directly north of them. Maybe a dozen and a half horses ridden by—

Indians.

Hick pointed toward the trees. Cooter grabbed Trooper's reins and shepherded the animals and women into the trees growing on the west side of the ravine.

The Indians didn't slow. They were riding fast. Men on a mission. Running toward something? Or running away from something? The hairs on the back of Hick's neck prickled. The burden of responsibility pressed against him.

Again.

If he hadn't left Trooper below, he'd be tempted to ride away and leave the others behind.

Except he wouldn't.

Between his Pa's upbringing and the cavalry's training, he wouldn't be able to walk away from his responsibility—however much he didn't want it.

He watched until the dust cloud was a small puff to the east, then retreated into the ravine.

Cooter trotted Rumpus to meet him, Trooper following. He stopped beside Hick and gave him time to mount. "I left the womenfolk in the trees. What was it?"

"Indians. Maybe eighteen of them riding hard and fast."

Cooter rubbed the back of his neck. "Up to mischief, ya reckon?"

"Don't know." Hick glanced at Mrs. Piper and Miss Bonnie, visible in the thin stand of trees. "At least they are heading away from us. We'll stay here for our noon break." He glanced at the sun. "It's a little early, but we don't need to raise any dust for a while."

Afterward, they'd ride hard for the fort. What they'd do once they arrived... that was a problem for another day. Maybe he'd luck out and someone at the fort would know of Miss Bonnie's kinfolk. Maybe Mrs. Piper would stay on and work for the fort's doctor. Maybe she'd meet some nice officer and...

And maybe Hick could get on with his life.

It'd been two days since they'd hidden in the ravine from Indians. Two days for Susannah to do some deep soul-searching. She hadn't been ignorant of the risks between Missouri and Oregon. There had been plenty of reports of Indians battling with the army as well as reports of civilians attacked, both homesteads and wagon trains.

Hearing about it and narrowly escaping it were two different things.

Susannah shifted on the hard saddle, settling Bonnie's limp form more securely against her. The girl's head rested between her breasts. She slept a lot, which was to be expected after the trauma and her lack of nutrition for who knew how many days.

In her heart, Susannah knew that her soul-searching had everything to do with Bonnie. By herself, she was more than willing to take the risks involved in reaching Oregon. It wasn't right, however, to subject the girl to the same risks.

Mr. Hickman must feel the same way. He'd pushed the horses and Peaches hard. Their lunch breaks were short and their evenings and mornings without a fire. The lack of coffee had that man even more taciturn than normal.

Or maybe he was struggling with the same soul-searching.

What would they do with Bonnie if no one at the fort had any word of her aunt and uncle? There would be no orphanage on the prairie. According to Bonnie, her grandparents were deceased and the only aunt and uncle she knew were those in Wyoming. One couldn't expect an eight-year-old to know everyone in her family if they hadn't lived close.

Susannah's parents had moved to Blackshear from North Carolina before Susannah's birth. She'd met Daddy's sister once and knew that Mama had two brothers, but she couldn't say she actually knew any of them. She had no idea where any of them were anymore, or even if they were still alive.

Peaches stepped in a hole, lurching to the right. Bonnie awoke with a soft cry. Susannah tightened her grip on the girl and steadied them both while Peaches got her feet firmly underneath her again.

Cooter trotted up beside her. "Ya all right, Mrs. Piper?"

"We are." She freed one hand to pat Peaches on the neck. "She stepped in a hole, but she's agile and didn't dump us."

"She's a right fine mule."

"I'm not sure everyone thinks so." She lifted her chin toward the back of the man riding a ways in front of them, scouting for the fort.

"Hick's a horseman. Ain't too many horsemen who'll give the time of day to a mule."

Was that all it was? A simple prejudice? The habit Peaches had of nipping at him probably didn't help. She stifled a smile. The molly didn't nip at anyone else. Perhaps she knew prejudice when she saw it.

"Mrs. Piper?" Bonnie rubbed her eyes and yawned. "I need to find a bush."

"I'll be just ahead, ma'am." Cooter touched his hat brim and urged Rumpus forward.

Susannah stopped her mule and dismounted, and her feet prickled when they touched the ground. She'd been in the saddle for a long time. She swung Bonnie down and they walked to a scrubby patch of brush. Susannah scanned the area for snakes, then turned her back and spread her skirt wide to give the girl some privacy.

Cooter had reached Mr. Hickman. They'd stopped their horses, backs to her and Bonnie. Susannah had felt safe with Mr. Hickman from the start, but seeing those two now, keeping watch, she was thankful beyond words for their presence.

If she were brutally honest with herself, part of her soul-searching was dreading being separated from them at the fort. Her heart prickled much like her feet had moments ago.

She couldn't afford to grow attached, not to a man who had made it very plain that her presence was unwelcome.

CHAPTER 21

H ICK AND THE OTHERS rode into the fort before noon on the third day after the Indian sighting. They'd swung too far south and might have missed it altogether if Cooter hadn't spotted it while scouting. The young man had sharp eyes, no doubt.

The fort sat on a modest rise less than a mile from the Platte River. Buildings of lumber, many of sod, and a whole field of canvas tents stood in the open without any type of palisade, not even a rail fence to separate it from the surrounding prairie. If not for the parade ground and powder magazine, it might have been the beginnings of a town in the middle of nowhere. The place was a beehive of activity. Dust thickened the air from horses' hooves, men's boots, and wagon wheels.

Hick's insides rolled and jerked at the sight.

He hadn't expected to have such a reaction. The war came flooding back, as if the past two years hadn't happened. He could almost hear the cries of the wounded and smell the rotting carcasses of horse and human, the lingering acrid scent of gunpowder.

"Where ya reckon we oughta start?"

Cooter's voice shook the specter of the war away. Hick'd stopped Trooper at some point but couldn't remember doing it. Mrs. Piper stared at him, concern knitting her brows. He coughed, more to gather his wits than to remove the dust from his lungs.

"Headquarters, I suppose." He pointed to the largest wooden structure. "There."

"Mr. Hickman." Mrs. Piper angled her mule next to Trooper. "Are you all right?"

"Just gathering my thoughts, ma'am." Which was more or less true.

He clicked to Trooper. The old war horse stepped lively, ears pitched forward like he was coming home. The atmosphere didn't spook him, at least.

Hick's skin was trying to crawl out from under his clothing.

A corral filled with horses, rough-looking stock, gave him hope for employment. His hip was up to it, and he needed the money. They rode straight to the large building.

At the door, a soldier stood straighter than the flag pole.

"We'd like to see the man in charge," Hick said.

"Colonel John Gibbon is the commanding officer."

"Would you tell him we're two bronc busters looking for work?"

"Wait here." The man pivoted as only a well-trained soldier could do and entered the building.

"Guess we'll just wait out here," Cooter said to the soldier's retreating back.

If Cooter'd thought they'd be invited in for tea, he was sorely mistaken. But then, Cooter'd never been in the army.

Lucky for him.

The soldier returned. "Colonel Gibbon will see you. This way."

Hick glanced back at Mrs. Piper and Miss Bonnie, waiting behind them on the mule, then followed the soldier into a large room and down a short hall, where he rapped on a door.

"Enter," commanded a voice from inside.

The soldier opened the door and stepped away.

Walking into that room resurrected a whole lot more memories Hick would rather stay buried, but he clicked his heels and stood straight. "We're bronc busters looking for work, sir."

The colonel eyed him up and down from behind his scarred desk. "Bronc buster with a military background, I take it."

"Union Cavalry, sir." Hick didn't offer any particulars.

Colonel Gibbon raised an eyebrow as if expecting more, but then flicked a glance at Cooter.

"I were busy with the Pony Express, and then ridin' shotgun for the stage."

The colonel grunted. "So you both know horses."

Hick nodded.

"As luck would have it, we took possession of a herd of mustangs last week. Either of you familiar with mustangs?"

"They's my favorite," said Cooter. "Ya get 'em broke right and they's no stoppin' a mustang. They's tough."

"Yes, tough and wily. Several of my men are limping proof of that." The colonel stood. "Report to Sergeant O'Reilly in C Company. He'll get you settled. We don't normally work on Sundays, but we're behind, so you can start first thing in the morning."

"What day is this?" Cooter asked.

The colonel's brows pulled into a forbidding line. "Saturday, of course."

"Thank you, sir." Hick left before the colonel could ask why they didn't even know what day it was. He stepped out of the building and stopped short.

A gaggle of women in wide skirts surrounded Mrs. Piper. Above their heads, Miss Bonnie sat by herself on the back of the mule. He and Cooter were blocked off by a sea of calico.

When he came to a stop, bonneted heads turned as if pulled by a string, and assessing eyes took him in from hat to heels. Not one of them looked impressed. Not even a little bit.

He pasted on his best Sunday-go-to-meeting smile, touched the brim of his hat, grabbed Trooper's reins and strode toward the corrals with Cooter on his heels.

"Hick?" Cooter turned his name into a question.

A question that would surely be more annoyance than not. "What?"

"Don't ya think maybe we should see Mrs. Piper settled before we meet the sergeant?"

"Nope."

"But her and Miss Bonnie, they's goin' to need—"

"Whatever they need, that horde of women can supply better than you or I can."

Cooter's face pulled into a grimace. "But Hick, ya know what they'll think once they learn the truth."

Hick growled under his breath. "What truth?" Not that he needed to ask.

"That she ain't yer wife."

No. She wasn't. He wasn't responsible for her. And what he'd told Cooter was the truth. Those women could supply what she and Miss Bonnie needed far better than he could.

"Hick?"

He pulled a long breath through his nose and let it out before stopping and looking at the other man. "Now what?"

"Ya ever think about maybe marryin' Mrs. Piper?" The lines on Cooter's face were a mixture of curiosity and concern with maybe a little puzzlement on the edges.

"Nope." Hick started walking again, fully aware that he hadn't told the truth. He had thought about it, for about as long as it took a tumbleweed to blow across their path. He wasn't going to marry anyone. Mrs. Piper might be in a tough place for a bit, but she'd move on and make it to Oregon somehow. That was her goal.

Not his.

Mrs. Hardy had introduced herself to Susannah as the highest-ranking officer's wife, explaining that Colonel Gibbon was unmarried. That the woman had a high opinion of herself was obvious. Still, she could be very helpful to Susannah and Bonnie.

"Your husband is a man on a mission." Disapproval filled the woman's tone.

Susannah had a feeling she was about to sink whatever good opinion of her the woman may have had. "He isn't my husband."

A dozen pairs of eyes speared Susannah on the spot, several hands covered mouths, and one woman even took a step back. Mrs. Hardy stiffened, disapproval coming off her in waves.

"I see. Well. That changes things." The woman shot a glance at Bonnie atop Peaches. "And the girl? You don't appear old enough to be her mother."

"Bonnie Sorrel, the only survivor of a cholera outbreak that took her family. We happened across their wagon a few days back."

That earned a flicker of pity from the women, but only for a moment.

"We have no empty houses at present that would suit you." Mrs. Hardy broke her eye contact. "There is an empty shack along the supply row. That should do, don't you think, ladies?"

There was a vigorous murmur of assent with a bobbing of heads. If the forceful woman had told them to fetch a rope and hang Susannah, they'd likely have had the same reaction. Daddy had always said a body had just one shot at making a good first impression.

Susannah's shot had failed... miserably.

"Ladies, let's show her to the shack." Mrs. Hardy plowed a path through the women, and they fell in step behind her.

"Come on." Susannah lifted her hands to help Bonnie off the mule. "Let's see what kind of shack they have for us, shall we?" At least they would be inside and off the ground.

"What about Mr. Hick and Mr. Cooter?" The girl's gray eyes pooled. The poor thing. She'd lost everyone she loved, and now those two lummoxes had walked away as if she didn't exist. Susannah could smack the both of them for the girl's sake.

And maybe a little for her own.

"We'll see them again." The fort wasn't very large. They'd strode off in the direction of the horse corrals, so they'd gotten jobs as they'd hoped. "We'll see them often, I'm sure."

Bonnie slid into her arms as a young soldier took Peaches by the reins. "I'll see to your mule, ma'am."

"Thank you." He didn't look old enough to shave. Not as old as Cooter.

"Come along, Mrs. Piper," Mrs. Hardy called over her shoulder.

Susannah grinned at Bonnie, getting a weak smile in response, and hurried after the other ladies. They stopped in front of a shack—that was the only word for it. At least it was constructed of lumber and not a soddy. Its door hung askew from the top hinge, the bottom one having gone missing. There was a window opening, but no glass or oiled hide to cover it. Oddly enough for a shack, it had a covered porch that protected the door and window. That was a plus. Several of the women entered, filling the small room inside. Susannah stopped in the doorway and lowered Bonnie to the porch.

Mrs. Hardy stood in the doorway, hands on her broad hips, and gave a firm nod. "This will do. I'll have someone bring you a scrub bucket and rags to clean with." She pointed to the window. "And a piece of cloth to cover that." She looked at Bonnie. "The girl deserves her privacy."

The underlying meaning was as clear as the sun overhead—Mrs. Hardy didn't care at all about Susannah's privacy. If she'd harbored any illusions about finding a place for herself in the fort, the stout woman had slapped the lid on them.

Susannah had been judged and convicted of being a loose woman—without a trial. If she hadn't spoken with a Southern accent, would any one of the women ringed around the shack have at least asked her story as they'd asked for Bonnie's? Probably. Fort Kearny in Nebraska wasn't far enough away from the war.

What would she do if Oregon wasn't either?

Hick's irritation at Cooter's line of questioning had subsided by the time they reached the corrals. It was easy to spot the man in charge—he was shouting orders in a thick Irish brogue. Hick approached him.

"Sergeant O'Reilly?"

"That's right. Who be wantin' ta know?"

"I'm Hick and this is Cooter." Hick tipped his chin toward the crowded corral. "Colonel Gibbon hired us to break out these mustangs."

"Glory be, and did he now?" The barrel-chested man thrust his thumbs behind his suspenders. "Ye be horsemen, then?"

Cooter clipped his heels together and bowed from the waist. Rumpus knelt down on one foreleg and pressed his forehead to the ground.

Hick about swallowed his teeth.

Sergeant O'Reilly laughed and slapped his thighs. "By golly, ye are."

A bugle sounded from across camp, playing a tune Hick knew well.

"Ah, well, after a bite o' lunch, we'll see what ye boys can do." He raised one eyebrow. "I caution ye ta eat lightly. These beasties will shake it out o' ye after." He laughed and headed in the direction of the bugler.

Hick tied Trooper to the fence, waited for Cooter to secure Rumpus, and then followed.

"He seems a jolly sort," Cooter said.

"For now." Hick had fought beside that type before. They could be some of the fiercest warriors when it came time. "When did you teach Rumpus to bow like that?"

"Back when I broke him out. It was just somethin' I taught him to pass the time. I seen a trick rider do it once in a circus show I snuck into."

"He know any other tricks?"

"A few." The young man grinned. "He's a smart one, Rumpus is."

"Let's hope a few of those other mustangs are as smart."

"The thing is, the smart ones be the hardest to train." Cooter tapped one finger against his temple. "Ya gots to outsmart 'em, and it takes time."

"And time is something we don't have." Not according to the colonel. "Best we start after lunch like the sergeant said."

"But the colonel—"

"Here's your first lesson in the army." He shot Cooter a pointed look. "Always keep the officer closest to you happy. Life is better that way."

The young man's Adam's apple bobbed a couple of times. Good. No sense of him thinking this would be a lark. They weren't in the army, but they were working for it.

The thought rode Hick's shoulders like an ill-fitting saddle.

Lunch was the typical army issue of beans and beef and biscuits. Nothing like what Mrs. Piper could do with the same staples, but it was filling. Hopefully the women would see that she and Miss Bonnie were fed. Or at least had a place to prepare something for themselves.

Not that it was any of his concern. Not anymore.

They returned to the corrals and looked over the milling stock in the largest one. The mustangs were rough, remnants of their winter coats still clinging to them, hooves chipped from living wild. More than one rolled the whites of its eyes in Hick's direction. Frightened. And why wouldn't they be? Their world had been turned upside down.

"These be the wild ones." O'Reilly pointed to the horses, one foot on the bottom fence rail. "Over there"—he jerked his thumb at a smaller corral—"be those my men are already working with. And this one"—he pointed to the smallest corral, which was empty—"be the training corral. Now." He rubbed his hands together. "Which beastie catches yer eye?"

"The blue roan." Hick pointed to the tallest animal in the bunch, its head high and nostrils wide.

O'Reilly clouted him on the shoulder. "By all that's holy, you are a horseman. He be the pick o' the lot. Three men have tried, and three men have put him back in that pen. Two o' them are limpin' still."

If Cooter was right, that meant the blue roan was one of the smart ones. A stallion and well put together. Hick would be happy to have a horse like that on his ranch someday.

But first, he had to break this bunch out for the cavalry. That meant working alongside the soldiers. Living among them. He refused to rub the skin that crawled behind his neck.

Riding across the prairie with Mrs. Piper suddenly didn't seem like the worst thing he could be doing.

CHAPTER 22

"**M** A'AM?" THE YOUNG SOLDIER who had taken Peaches approached with her saddlebag, satchel, and sack. Susannah's heart lurched. She'd left them in the hands of someone she didn't know, when her entire life's savings were inside. When had she grown so complacent?

Since she'd been with Mr. Hickman.

Since she'd felt safe.

"Thank you." She took the items from him, along with a bucket filled with the things Mrs. Hardy had promised. "Where is my mule?"

"In the mule stable, ma'am. She drank her fill, and I settled her with enough hay to keep her happy." He took a step back.

"Soldier, what is the doctor's name here at the fort?"

"Captain Newmyer is the regimental surgeon, ma'am."

"And where is his office, or quarters, or wherever he works from?"

He pointed back toward the building Mr. Hickman and Cooter had entered. "It's around the backside of that building." He cast her a quizzical glance. "Are you or the little girl ailing, ma'am?"

"No. I'm a trained nurse. I will inquire about employment with him."

The young man gave her a sheepish look. "Captain Newmyer is a good enough sawbones, ma'am, but he's rougher than a dry cob. He ain't likely to take on a... woman nurse."

What he didn't say came through loud and clear. Word had already spread across the camp about what kind of woman Susannah was, according to Mrs. Hardy.

She thanked the soldier and entered the shack, Bonnie clinging to her side.

The shelter had walls, a floor, and a roof that looked solid enough, but without a proper door or a set of shutters that locked...

How was she to keep them both safe from men who'd come to see if the rumors were true?

The dark bay Cooter was on hopped and twisted across the training corral, but the young man never shifted in his saddle. His body rocked and bent, his free arm swinging for balance. Hick lifted his foot to the bottom pole and cheered with the soldiers who'd stopped by to watch the fun. Cooter rode the horse like a burr rode a collie dog.

"He wasn't havin' me on. That youngun can sit a horse." Sergeant O'Reilly plopped his forearms on the top rail near Hick. "I could do the same meself at his age."

Hick gave the man a sideways glance. A bit paunchy at the waist and hair the color of yesterday's ashes, but the breadth of his chest and the thickness of his arms and neck said the sergeant wasn't a man to tangle with.

"He's good," Hick said.

The sergeant turned, one elbow on the fence, and looked at Hick. "The boys say ye roped the blue roan first thing, even after I warned ye."

"He's the best of the bunch."

"Aye, that he is, but he'll take too long ta break out. Leave him be and work on some we can get under a pair of blue britches as soon as possible. We have dire need for horseflesh I can put soldiers on. Now."

"You're the boss."

The other man grinned. "We're goin' ta get along just fine." He half-turned but moved back. "If ye want ta be workin' that roan on yer own time, o' course, that'd be somethin' else entirely, if ye get my meanin'."

"Yes, sir. I believe I do."

With a clout to Hick's shoulder, the sergeant strode off, already yelling at some hapless soldier caught sauntering when he should have been stepping lively. It sent a chill over Hick despite the sun burning down, bringing back too many memories.

If he hadn't needed the money for a good stallion—like the blue roan he'd roped and done some groundwork with—he'd never have stopped at the fort.

That wasn't true, though. He'd had to stop for Mrs. Piper and Miss Bonnie.

Where had they gone?

Renewed shouts pulled his attention back to the corral. Cooter was still on the dark bay, and it was cantering around the enclosure. Time for Hick to rope another horse and take his turn in the training corral. He untied Trooper and swung into the saddle, then shook out his rope. Another soldier opened the gate to the large pen as he neared. Trooper waded into the crowd of horses like he owned it. The blue roan squealed and reared, beating the air with his front hooves.

Just you wait, mister. Your time is coming.

Hick twirled his rope and dropped the loop over a black mare with one white stocking. Trooper anchored his feet, and Hick dallied the rope. The old war horse had taken to ranch work like a pro. Hick slapped Trooper's dusty neck once the black stopped fighting.

"Come on then, let's teach her a thing or two."

He might not know much about women like Mrs. Piper, or little girls like Miss Bonnie, but with a mare like the black, Hick was right in his element. He could even forget the uniformed men around the corral... for a little while.

They'd not been invited to dinner by any of the ladies—of course—and they surely wouldn't be welcome in the men's mess hall, a lengthy structure that was more than half tent. Susannah dug into her sack. They still had a good quantity of jerky from the two deer Cooter had brought back to camp while Mr. Hickman recovered. Thankfully she'd stowed it in her sack. The shack had no fireplace, not that she had anything to burn. From the odors around the mess hall, the cooks there burned coal.

A luxury she couldn't afford even if they'd sell her any.

"It's peaches and jerky for dinner." She gave Bonnie her most cheery smile. "And then we'll walk about and see the rest of the fort. How does that sound?"

"Will we see Mr. Hick and Mr. Cooter?" Hope brightened the girl's eyes.

"I guess we'll find out."

That seemed to satisfy the girl, so after their meager meal, they walked into the cool of the evening. The prairie was like that, burning hot at midday and downright chilly once the sun hung low in the sky. Nothing like the sultry Georgia evenings she'd grown up with.

They drifted toward the horse corrals, Bonnie pointing out all sorts of things that caught her eye. She was an intelligent and inquisitive child. Susannah had answers for only some of her endless questions. After all, she'd never been in an army fort before either.

The sidelong glances from the few soldiers they passed brought on another kind of chill.

As they neared the corrals, a familiar slight figure leaned against a rail of the smallest one. His attention was on the horse in the corral, a dashing blue roan with its head in the air, front hoof pawing the ground in front of Mr. Hickman.

"There's Mr. Cooter." Bonnie pointed.

"Shh. We must be quiet while they work with the wild horses." Susannah whispered. "And don't run. We don't want to spook them."

Bonnie nodded, her face too solemn for one so young.

They walked to the corral hand in hand. Cooter nodded a greeting.

"Miss Bonnie, Mrs. Piper." He twisted his hat in his hands. "I'm right glad to see ya. Did ya get a place to stay?"

"Of a sort."

He cocked his head, but a squeal from the corral distracted them. The blue roan had reared, front feet lashing out toward Mr. Hickman, but the man was far enough back to be out of danger. He had his hat off, waving it in a non-threatening way, his voice a gentle murmur.

"Ain't he somethin'?" Cooter asked.

Did he mean the horse or Mr. Hickman? Not that it mattered, because either one fit the description. The horse for its beauty and spirit, the man for his quiet confidence. And his own version of beauty and spirit.

"Ain't he scared, Mr. Cooter?" Bonnie's eyes were round as river pebbles.

"Nah. Hick knows what he's doin'. Why, he'll have that stallion eatin' outta his hand afore next Sunday, mark my words."

Bonnie scrunched her nose. "When is next Sunday?"

Cooter leaned his shoulder against the corral rail and crossed his arms. "Tomorrow is Sunday, so the next Sunday be just seven days after."

Sunday. A day of rest.

Susannah kept her eyes on the man in the corral while her mind whirled. She couldn't approach Captain Newmyer on Sunday about a possible nursing position. The young soldier hadn't given her much—any—hope, but Susannah wasn't going to give up without trying. She and Bonnie needed to eat, for one thing, and they had nobody else to support them.

She knew all too well what the other options were for a single woman without employment. Marriage, or turning into the type of woman Mrs. Hardy already deemed her to be. Unless, of course, Mr. Hickman decided to try and find Bonnie's aunt and uncle. Because if he did, he'd need Susannah to accompany them. Two men weren't fit to take a little girl to the mountains by themselves.

If only she could find a way to convince the stubborn man to make the effort.

Once they were in Wyoming, it wouldn't be that much farther to Oregon. At least, she didn't think it was. There were mountains to cross, to be sure, but she'd already crossed the longest stretch of land between Georgia and Oregon. Abel had marked Missouri as the halfway point on his map. She'd survived it all, including losing her husband, so the mountains didn't frighten her. Abel and she had traversed mountains during their flight north and into Kentucky to meet his family. The mountains of Wyoming couldn't prove any more disastrous than that trip had.

She'd been a dutiful wife and written Abel's parents of his death. Not that they'd deserved it after the way they'd treated him for marrying "Southern trash" like her, but out of respect for Abel, she'd done it. Although she'd felt the need to wash her hands afterward.

Nothing to the west frightened her, but the man approaching the snorting horse in the corral? He did. Because he had too much power over her future. If he saddled up and rode away, she could probably afford train tickets back to Omaha for her and Bonnie. Maybe. It would likely take every penny she'd hoarded away and sewn into her spare petticoat.

But if she could convince him to go in search of Bonnie's kin, then she had a chance of convincing him to take her all the way to Oregon. The mountains might not frighten her in and of themselves. But traveling them alone?

Susannah Mary Jessup Piper might be a lot of things... but stupid wasn't one of them.

The horse blew out a mighty snort, wheeled, and raced around the enclosure.

Mr. Hickman turned, and when he spotted them, his eyes clashed with Susannah's.

The way her stomach tightened was another reason to fear this man. Against her better judgment, she found herself thinking of him far too often. And while she tried to tell herself it was due to his infuriating stubbornness and frustrating silences...

Her response to him was far too much the response of a woman to a man.

CHAPTER 23

T HE BLUE ROAN TORE past him, flinging dirt around the corral. It snapped Hick back to the business at hand, which was training horses and not considering Mrs. Piper. Most definitely not considering Mrs. Piper. He slapped his hat on his head when Sergeant O'Reilly joined the others at the rail. Maybe he'd better find out what brought the boss there after hours.

"We have been assigned a shack down that way." Mrs. Piper pointed to the east. "I'll have to figure out a way to cook our meals, but other than that, Bonnie and I will be comfortable enough."

"Do ye have enough food then?" the sergeant asked.

"For now, yes, thank you." Then Mrs. Piper turned her smile to Hick. "He's a beautiful animal."

"Oh, Mr. Hick." Bonnie bounced on her toes. "I was scared for you."

Answering the child gave him a reason to look away from Mrs. Piper. Her smile, when it was that genuine and natural, had a way of tying his tongue in knots.

"That horse isn't a mean one, Miss Bonnie."

"He's not?" She peeked around him. The horse had stopped its wild flight and pawed the ground behind Hick, its rhythmic thumps displaying the animal's disapproval.

"Nope. He's just trying to figure things out." Hick dropped to one knee and looked her in the eye. "He's used to being the boss, you see, telling the mares and young horses what to do. He won't accept me giving him orders until he figures out that he can trust me."

"That's what makes Mr. Hick such a good horseman," Cooter said. "He knows how to read 'em."

Hick stood. "And you know how to stick with them."

"I'd say the two of ye make a first-class team." O'Reilly gave a nod. "Just don't be takin' too long ta get the job done. I need those horses last week." Then he winked. "'Tis glad I am ta see ye workin' that one. I wouldn't mind him for me own mount. But mind ye work the easier horses first."

"Oh, we done worked three apiece betwixt lunch and supper," Cooter said. "Ya got some nice ones in that bunch, for sure and certain."

"That we do, boy-oh." The sergeant turned to Mrs. Piper. "Has anyone shown ye around the fort, ma'am?"

"Only as far as the shack." Mrs. Piper stroked Bonnie's hair. "We are out to explore it now."

The sergeant offered his arm. "Then, please, allow me ta escort ye. Our soldiers may not all be angels, ma'am. 'Tis better if ye don't wander into some areas by yerself."

Her eyes met Hick's for an extended moment, and then she slipped her hand into the sergeant's elbow, the other hand holding one of Bonnie's. "Thank you, Sergeant..."

"O'Reilly, ma'am." He stepped away from the corral, Mrs. Piper with him. "Those buildin's over there, now ye want ta stay away from 'em durin' the day..." His words drifted off with the distance.

Miss Bonnie peeked over her shoulder, then wiggled her fingers at Hick. He raised a hand in return. Mrs. Piper didn't look back.

And Hick shouldn't want her to. Just like he shouldn't be irritated at her walking off with O'Reilly.

But he was.

"Am I mistakin', or did the sergeant just make off with our girls?" Cooter asked.

"Our girls?" His gut reaction aside, those two didn't belong to him and Cooter. They should be back in Omaha, safe in a town where Mrs. Piper had a job waiting.

"We got first claim on 'em, don't we?" Cooter looked a bit confused. "After all, ya rescued Mrs. Piper from them men at the river—the ones what shot her—and we rescued Bonnie and buried her kin."

"They'd be better off without us."

"How ya figger that?" Cooter's tone was nothing short of incredulous.

"They'd be in Omaha in a real house—not here in a shack surrounded by men even O'Reilly doesn't trust."

Cooter studied the trio in the distance. "Ya thinkin' they still need our protection here in the fort?"

"She's a handsome woman, and this place is crawling with men." He shot Cooter and side glance. "What do you think?"

The younger man settled his hat more securely on his head. "I'm thinkin' we best find that shack and maybe pitch our camp nearby."

So much for delivering Mrs. Piper and Miss Bonnie to the fort and walking away. That was what he wanted, wasn't it?

If so, then why did his spirit lift at the thought of camping near them again?

It didn't take Susannah long to figure out that Sergeant O'Reilly considered himself something of a lady's man. His descriptions of his exploits and importance at the fort were typical of a man in his position, midway between the grunt soldiers and the real power. She'd seen the same when she'd fed and tended the prisoners back in Blackshear.

His less-than-subtle hints of availability for moonlight walks were easy enough to deflect, and he was an engaging companion who included Bonnie in his comments and took pains to point out things that might interest a girl of her age. Despite his preening and suggesting, he seemed harmless enough while providing a diversion from Susannah's worries.

The fort wasn't what she'd thought it would be. For one thing, it was small. They strolled around the entire perimeter in about thirty minutes. Which was fine, the sun slipping beneath the horizon and the landscape lit only by its reflection in the clouds.

"Thank you for the tour, sergeant." Susannah put an arm around Bonnie and drew her close. "It's time we retired for the night."

He glanced at Bonnie, then back at her, understanding clear in his eyes despite the gathering darkness. "Aye, ma'am. I'll walk ye ta yer door."

"Ain't no need of that, sergeant." Cooter's voice came from behind Susannah, and she turned. "Me and Hick will see 'em there safe enough." The young man's grin conveyed nothing unusual, but something in his voice caught Susannah's attention. As if, in the most amiable way possible, he was letting the sergeant know that she and Bonnie were under his protection.

Mr. Hickman trailed behind the younger man, his face shadowed by his hat, but even in the darkness, it was plain there was no smile there. Did he feel the same way? Would he once again offer her his protection?

Because if she'd read him correctly, he'd like nothing better than to head for the mountains and leave her behind. He'd certainly been adamant that she should have returned to Omaha. And got madder than a wet hornet when she'd refused.

The thought that he'd ride on and leave her in Fort Kearny had plagued her for the past few days. After arriving and seeing the fort, she'd probably have nightmares about being left there. It held nothing of promise for her or Bonnie.

Bonnie's aunt and uncle were between the fort and Oregon. Both of them needed to head west, and the man approaching them was the one who could make it happen.

The one she wanted to make it happen.

"Well, then I'll leave ye with a 'good evenin'." The sergeant took her hand and bent over it in a partial bow. "'Tis been me pleasure, ma'am." Then he did the same with Bonnie. "Good night, Miss Bonnie."

The little girl took a step behind Susannah, cheeks pink, almost hiding in the folds of Susannah's skirt.

"Thank you, sergeant," Susannah said. "It was a lovely walk."

He left them, and Cooter knelt in front of Bonnie. "Ain't no cause to go a-hidin', Miss Bonnie. The sergeant was just makin' nice."

Hick grunted. It was one of those grunts that could mean anything—or nothing.

"Which shack is yours?" Cooter asked.

"Follow us." Susannah took Bonnie's hand, and they led the way.

"They put you in there?" Disapproval oozed from Mr. Hickman's voice when they reached it.

Susannah didn't blame him. In the darkness, the shack looked a little less cozy. A little less safe with its door hanging askew.

"Well, it be a good thing me and Hick decided to pitch our camp nearby." Cooter swung his saddlebag from his shoulder. "Ain't it, Hick?"

The tall man eyed the structure, then sized up the clouds that were fast losing their colorful display. "If you don't mind, ma'am, it'd be nice to have a roof over our heads. Wouldn't be surprised if it rained tonight, and that porch is plenty wide."

Susannah hadn't been aware of the tension in her shoulders until it melted away. "That would be more than fine, Mr. Hickman. Please, make yourselves at home." Nobody could enter the shack without stepping over the men. She touched the sleeve of his shirt, drawing his attention. "And thank you."

His hazel eyes appeared darker in the shadows, but for just a moment, the corners crinkled. His lips never moved, but it was a smile of sorts. And it warmed her inside in a way she hadn't felt in a long time.

A way she hadn't thought she'd ever feel again.

Susannah had washed their clothing the day before and dried it on a rope Cooter had strung for her. It had rained Saturday night, so her Sunday afternoon wash dried without any added dust. Even so, she gave her skirt a vigorous shaking before pulling it on. She wanted to look her best before she approached Captain Newmyer. Not her prettiest, but her cleanest and most efficient. Those were the qualities a doctor should look for in a nurse.

Bonnie buried her nose in her freshly laundered skirt. "It smells so nice."

"It was good to wash out the sweat and dust of the trail."

She'd laundered Mr. Hickman's and Cooter's spare clothing as well. They'd need that regularly if the dust rising above the corrals was any indication. But it was little enough in exchange for the protection they offered, and the food. They'd sneaked biscuits from the mess hall for her and Bonnie yesterday and included a bit of bacon this morning.

The morsels were welcome additions to the jerky and canned food, both of which would run out in a few days if not supplemented.

She straightened her blouse and tucked it inside in her skirt, wishing she had something shiny to check her reflection when she patted her hair. Nothing felt out of place.

"You look real fine, Mrs. Piper." Bonnie had dressed and waited by the door. "Can we go now?"

"Yes. You'll stay at the corral until I return?"

"I will."

She was such a solemn child, but how could she be otherwise?

"No matter who may ask you to walk with them, or offer you something, what will you say?"

"No, thank you, I must stay with Mr. Cooter and Mr. Hick."

"And if they tell you it'll be all right?"

Bonnie straightened, her little chin lifting in a way much too old for her, but effective. "Thank you, but I prefer to stay."

They'd practiced the lines the day before. Susannah was still worried about leaving the child with the men, not that they wouldn't protect her, but they had their hands full and couldn't give her their undivided attention.

But Susannah couldn't appear asking for employment with Bonnie at her side.

"Let's be off then." She pushed the door open and closed it behind them. Mr. Hickman had produced the tools and hardware necessary to repair it.

They approached the corrals from upwind, keeping out of the worst of the dust. The rain had helped, but with so many hooves and boots and wheels, the soil was soon loosened and billowing in the wind. Cooter was in the saddle on a dark bay, putting the animal through its paces. Mr. Hickman sat astride Trooper, keeping watch.

"Thank you for watching Bonnie." Susannah stopped beside the horse.

"No problem, ma'am." He slid out of the seat and sat behind his saddle before leaning down. "Hand her up."

Susannah lifted her to Mr. Hickman's strong hands. He settled her in the saddle, and she beamed down at Susannah. The girl liked horses almost as much as the men, it seemed. Susannah was relieved that he'd keep her close.

"I'll return when I can."

He touched the brim of his hat. "Good luck, ma'am."

She marched toward the building Sergeant O'Reilly had pointed out on their walk the other evening. It was both infirmary and the captain's office. A young soldier stood guard at the door and straightened at her approach.

"I'd like to speak with Captain Newmyer."

The young man blinked, then he shifted his feet. "Captain don't like to be disturbed, ma'am."

"I understand." The open window behind the man probably led to the doctor's office. She raised her voice a notch. "I promise I won't take up too much of his valuable time."

"He's a very busy man."

"I'm sure he is, being the only doctor in the fort. My daddy was a doctor, and I'm a trained nurse, so I fully understand."

"He's—"

"Send her in, Johnson." The bellow came through the open window.

Susannah resisted the urge to smile, even when the young man rolled his eyes.

"This way, ma'am."

She stepped through the doorway and into the familiar scents of alcohol, camphor, and strong lye soap. They greeted her like old friends. She needed that before facing the man whose roar had granted her entrance.

The young soldier opened a second door and stepped aside.

Susannah entered a room that resembled a bear's den she'd once seen in the forest near a lake they'd visited when she was a child. The floor along the walls was packed with stuff, leaving only the middle as an inhabitable space. Some of it she could identify, but much she couldn't, other than the books. Books were stacked everywhere, as many as a dozen high in places. In the middle of it all, a square desk rose from the jumble.

Hunched behind it was a bear of a man who matched the surroundings. His hair was iron gray, and a full beard of the same color hid most of his face. Penetrating blue eyes met hers from behind gold-rimmed spectacles. "What do you want?"

"Captain Newmyer?"

"You knew that before you got here." He scanned her from head to toes, giving no hint to his conclusions. "What do you want?"

"Sir, I am a nurse—"

"I heard that already. What do you *want?*"

He wasn't going to make it easy, but Susannah refused to let him bully her. "Employment, sir."

He barked a laugh that contained no humor. "Not interested."

"Captain Newmyer, I am fully trained and qualified to—"

"This is an army infirmary, ma'am, not a hospital. I don't need a nurse. I have all the orderlies I can keep track of."

"Orderlies aren't trained—"

His fist connected with the desk, making several items on it jump. "Mine are. I train them myself."

The soldier who'd first mentioned Captain Newmyer to her had been correct. He wasn't going to budge.

"I thank you for your time, sir." Her voice was frosty, but she didn't care. Without employment, she and Bonnie would have to return to Omaha—spending every penny she'd hoarded for a new start in Oregon.

Back stiff, Susannah left the room and strode past the young soldier, ignoring the expression of sympathy he shot her.

She and Bonnie had enough food for a few more days, maybe a week with the men smuggling them more from the mess hall, but after that...

Mr. Hickman and Cooter had weeks of work ahead of them with the wild horses. They wouldn't leave the fort until they'd been paid for that job.

For the first time in a long time, Susannah had no idea what to do.

CHAPTER 24

THE YOUNG CHESTNUT BENEATH Hick would make a fine mount. He'd
started the colt a week before, the same day Mrs. Piper had been
turned down by that idiot doctor, and the colt was ready to be stabled
with the regular mounts. He'd need a rider with good hands for a while
yet, but he was the best of the bunch Hick had broke so far.

He stopped the horse and dismounted, taking a moment to rub
the animal's damp neck. The chestnut nuzzled his other hand. A fine
animal.

"Ya done in there, Hick?" Cooter called from the back of Rumpus
as he towed a reluctant black colt with a crooked blaze behind.

"We'll get out of your way." Hick led the chestnut out of the training
corral and held the gate for Cooter.

As they passed, the black took a kick at Hick. It missed, mostly
because Hick was watching for it. The black had already proved he
was trouble.

"That one will never be the horse you are," he told the chestnut.
"Nor measure up to the blue roan either." The stallion was coming
along—slowly. But unlike the black Cooter was snubbing to a post, the
roan wasn't mean. He was smart. Almost too smart. He kept Hick on
his mettle.

Hick closed the gate and stripped the training saddle from the
chestnut, giving the animal a good brushing. He mounted Trooper and
led the other horse to Sergeant O'Reilly across the yard at the stables.
The man saw him coming and walked to meet him. Hick stifled the
surge of resentment that shouldn't be there. If the sergeant walked out
with Mrs. Piper most evenings, what was that to him?

"Got another for me, do ye?"

"Yes, sir." Hick handed over the lead rope. "This one is something special. If you're still looking for a new mount for yourself, I'd recommend him. But whoever he winds up with, make sure they've got soft hands. He responds best that way."

"Most of 'em do." The sergeant peered past Hick. "Like a good woman."

Hick twisted in the saddle. Mrs. Piper approached the corral with Bonnie. He glanced down at the sergeant, who seemed to have forgotten the horse on the end of his rope.

Hick cleared his throat. "I should have two more to bring you before supper, and Cooter might have another."

O'Reilly blinked, then nodded toward the corral. "Not that one, I'll wager."

"Nope. That black will be one of the last." Hick reined Trooper round and headed back to the corral. He touched his hat to Mrs. Piper. "Ma'am. Miss Bonnie."

"Mr. Hickman, I know you are busy, but I really must speak with you." The urgency in her tone said he wasn't going to be able to put her off. He'd sensed her wanting to talk to him for the past few evenings, and he'd done his best to avoid it. He didn't have any answers for her. At least, none she wanted to hear.

He dismounted and motioned to Miss Bonnie. She hurried to him, and he swung her atop Trooper. "You take care of old Trooper while I speak with Mrs. Piper."

"I will." She flashed her dimples at him. She'd started to come out of her shell of grief, and that made him glad. For her. A child shouldn't have to survive what she'd been through. For the first time in months—maybe years—when he got to feeling overwhelmed by the war, he could pull himself out of it by thinking of Miss Bonnie and how bravely she was handling her sorrows.

Maybe he could start to see his blessings again.

But first he had to hear out Mrs. Piper.

Cooter leaped into his training saddle and hung on as the black sunfished around the corral, kicking up a thick cloud of dust. Hick wouldn't admit it out loud, but he was glad he hadn't roped that particular animal. He could stick a saddle with the best of them, but Cooter was in a class by himself.

"Mr. Hickman?" Mrs. Piper's voice pulled him back to the issue at hand. He had a pretty good idea what it was, so he followed the woman a few paces away from Miss Bonnie. The girl didn't need to overhear.

"Since I have no employment, and our food is all but gone, I need a plan for Bonnie and me." She got right to the point.

"I can see that, ma'am." What she expected him to do, he had no idea. Except that wasn't the gospel truth. Somehow, without outright saying so, she'd made it plain that she'd like to see Bonnie delivered to her aunt and uncle in the foothills. The aunt and uncle who could be anywhere within tens of thousands of acres of unmapped wilderness.

"I worry for Bonnie," she said.

He cut a glance her way and couldn't find anything but honest concern in the dark blue of her eyes. If she were trying to manipulate him, it didn't show. And he couldn't deny the loving care she'd given the orphan girl. Miss Bonnie was plenty easy to care for, but Mrs. Piper went above and beyond. She'd make a fine mother.

That thought put a crimp in his middle.

"I know, ma'am. Life dealt her a losing hand, for sure."

"I don't think it has to end that way." She shielded her eyes from the sun, gazing at Cooter in the corral. "Cooter agrees that we should try and find her family."

"We buried her family."

She sighed, and the look she shot him said he was better than that.

He shifted his feet, trying not to act like a schoolboy caught in a lie.

"Her aunt and uncle must be frantic wondering what happened to her family."

Oh, good. More people for Hick to feel accountable to. He stripped off his hat and raked his fingers through his sweaty hair. "Ma'am, I don't know what you expect of me, but—"

Miss Bonnie's ear-splitting scream cut him short. The girl pointed toward the corral and screamed again.

Hick raced toward the black horse, plunging and kicking its way across the corral, the limp form of Cooter dragging behind by one stirrup. He plucked Bonnie from Trooper and vaulted into the saddle as more soldiers arrived. One swung the gate open, and he spurred Trooper through. The black reared in front of them, but old Trooper reared in response, his neck out and teeth bared. When both animals hit the ground again, Hick pitched forward and grabbed the black's bridle.

Three soldiers swarmed over Cooter and got his foot loose. Hick pulled the black away while Mrs. Piper raced to the young man's side. He had his hands full with the horses that still wanted to fight, but her crisp directions to the soldiers helped slow the pounding of his heart.

She wouldn't be issuing those orders if Cooter was dead.

After assuring herself that Cooter was alive and that his back wasn't broken, Susannah ordered several soldiers to carry the unconscious young man to her shack. She snatched Bonnie and carried the girl with her behind the men.

"Carefully now." She huffed to keep up as Bonnie clung to her. "Don't let his head fall back."

Once in the shack she had him placed on the only bed, the one she and Bonnie shared from a platform Cooter had fashioned for them. They'd be sharing the floor for the foreseeable future.

"Someone fetch me a fresh bucket of water." She lowered Bonnie to one of the chairs and rolled up her sleeves as she spoke.

"What else can we do?" one of the soldiers asked.

"Pray." She shooed them out of her way and unbuttoned Cooter's shirt. The mark on the front of one shoulder was the size and shape of a horse's hoof. She traced the area with her fingers to a knot of bone in the wrong place. The shoulder was dislocated.

She pressed gently along his ribs. He grunted, but nothing shifted beneath her fingers. That was a blessing.

She was unfastening his trousers when Mr. Hickman arrived in the doorway.

"Ma'am?" He turned the one word into a question, but she didn't have time to soothe his qualms at the moment.

"His shoulder is dislocated. I'll need your assistance in a moment to correct that." She shot him a glance. "You've done that before, I assume?" Many men had become adept at the more basic procedures during the war, the doctors being too busy with amputations and other more serious cases.

"I know what to do."

"Good."

"But Miss Bonnie, ma'am."

Susannah closed her eyes and pulled a steadying breath through her nose. She hadn't forgotten the girl, but it dawned on her that Bonnie might not be able to handle one more calamity in her young life. How best to address that and tend to Cooter?

Like Daddy would have.

"Come here, Bonnie."

Mr. Hickman made a sound somewhere between a grunt and gasp, but Susannah ignored him.

"I could use your help." She held out her hand to the girl.

Bonnie slid from the chair and came to her side.

"I must remove Cooter's trousers to examine his legs for broken bones, but first, his boots need to come off." She took the girl's hands and slid them under Cooter's leg above the boot. "You lift that leg just about this far"—she showed Bonnie a four-inch spread with her forefinger and thumb—"when I say, and keep it there while I work off the boot, okay?"

Her gray eyes were awash with unshed tears, but Bonnie nodded.

"All right... now." Susannah slid the boot as gently as she could while Cooter stirred. "Keep the leg up, that's a girl. You're doing a fine job." They repeated the process for the second boot, and Susannah handed both of them to Bonnie.

"Cooter is going to want these boots cleaned up when he awakens. Can you see to that?"

"Yes, ma'am."

Susannah cupped a freckled cheek in her hand. "Thank you. That's a real help. Stay on the porch while you do it, okay?"

Mr. Hickman moved out of the girl's way, then reached through the doorway and grabbed a bucket from whoever delivered it.

"Set that by the bed." Susannah grabbed a clean rag from the table and tossed it in the water. "Now let's see his legs."

"Maybe I should do that part, ma'am."

She turned and almost bumped her forehead against Mr. Hickman's chin. He'd bent that close. Probably so Bonnie wouldn't overhear. She shifted back a few inches, met the clear hazel of his eyes and turned back to her patient. "I'm quite capable, I assure you."

"I know ma'am, but..."

"I'm a nurse, Mr. Hickman. And a widow." She worked Cooter's trousers and long johns off as she spoke. "I'm not unfamiliar with the male anatomy."

"I didn't think you were. But Cooter here might not appreciate—"

Susannah sucked in a loud breath, which brought Mr. Hickman's chin back to her side, level with her eyes.

"At least it hasn't punctured the skin." She exhaled the breath, still staring at the misshapen and discolored area below Cooter's right knee.

"I'll go for the doctor," Mr. Hickman said.

Susannah grabbed his sleeve and hung on. "No."

"Ma'am, that's work for a doctor."

"You haven't met him. I have." How to make him understand? She didn't want that boorish, arrogant bear of a man to touch Cooter. "I can set his leg." She turned her head, their faces a scant handspan apart. "If you'll help."

Why wouldn't she allow him to go for the doctor?

Hick wanted to protest, but there was something in her eyes that stopped him. That and the rumors he'd picked up about Captain Newmyer. He wasn't well respected by the men under his care. Mrs. Piper had done nothing *but* earn Hick's respect—many times over. He needed to trust her.

"Tell me what to do."

In under ten minutes, Cooter's leg was set and his shoulder popped back into place. The young man had moaned both times, which Mrs. Piper said was a good sign, but he hadn't awakened. She bathed his face, removing the layers of corral dust and exposing skin too pale for Hick's liking. Then she moved down his body, cleaning away the grime except for the area covered with a piece of toweling to preserve Cooter's dignity.

"Oh."

He leaned closer to see what had brought her response. She cradled the arm she was washing, studying a nasty bruise that marred the skin around Cooter's wrist. She rotated the hand, pressing here and there as she did so. Cooter moaned again.

She lifted her eyes to Hick's. "Badly sprained, but I can't feel anything broken."

Hick studied his mostly naked friend. It would be a long time before Cooter forked a bronc again.

Miss Bonnie appeared in the doorway with Cooter's cleaned boots.

Mrs. Piper flipped a blanket over the injured man, then turned to the girl. "You've done a fine job. Cooter will be so pleased."

The little girl took a tentative step into the single room of the shack. "Is he...?" She swallowed and tried again. "Is he going to die?"

Mrs. Piper opened her arms. Miss Bonnie dropped the boots and ran into them, burying her face against the woman's neck.

"Shh, now. It will be all right." She squatted on the floor and rocked the girl side to side. "His leg is broken and will need time to heal, so we'll have to take good care of him." She pushed the girl away, wiped the red curls from her damp face, and lifted her chin. "But with our best care and prayers, he should be fine."

Hick released a deep breath.

"Why doesn't he wake up?" Bonnie asked.

"There's a frightful bump on the back of his head." Mrs. Piper touched the back of Miss Bonnie's head. "Probably where he hit the ground. That often makes it hard for someone to wake up for a while."

"But he'll be okay?" The little girl's words wobbled.

Mrs. Piper nodded. "I believe he will." Then she stood and faced Hick. "But he won't be helping to break any more of those mustangs, I'm afraid."

"Nope, ma'am. He won't." Hick smashed his hat back on his head. "Which means I best get back to work."

She touched his sleeve. "And we can talk after?"

There was a vulnerability in her face that hadn't been there before Cooter's accident. A vulnerability that tugged at something deep inside Hick. He gave her a curt nod and left.

Two soldiers were still hanging around outside the shack. They fell into step beside Hick.

"He going to pull through?" the taller one asked.

"Mrs. Piper thinks so."

"Is she any good, as a sawbones, I mean?"

"She is." He paused and faced the men. "What happened in that corral?"

"Cooter slipped sideways on that nasty bronc," the tall one said.

The shorter one added, "And before he could right himself, that devil drove him right into the rails. He got his head up but took a hard hit to the shoulder. That knocked him out of the saddle."

"His foot wouldn't have caught in the stirrup, but the leather twisted and trapped his spur," the tall one said.

Hick resumed walking. An accident. A bad one, but an accident. Nothing would have changed if he'd been standing at the rail and watching. He couldn't have prevented it.

But if he hadn't been distracted, if he hadn't stepped away with Mrs. Piper, he might have reached Cooter faster. His friend might have fewer injuries. Once again, Hick had allowed someone close and then let them down.

Cooter was alive—no thanks to him.

The urge to toss a saddle on Trooper and ride away was strong. More than strong. It practically hummed through his veins.

CHAPTER 25

S ERGEANT O'REILLY HAD ARRANGED for Susannah to be given coal and
food in exchange for caring for Cooter. That he'd made the rations
generous—enough to feed her and Bonnie too—hadn't passed her un-
noticed. And the man was a frequent visitor to the shack, supposedly
to check on Cooter, but often lingering on the porch in the evenings,
even though Susannah didn't encourage him.

It'd been a week since the terrible accident. Cooter was healing as
well as could be expected. He was still in bed, but she planned to
fashion a crutch for him to start using soon. Once he could hobble to
the porch, he'd be happier. Thankfully, his major injuries were all on
one side of his body, so the other side could work the crutch.

"You'll stay on that bed and behave yourself while we check
on Peaches?" Susannah speared Cooter with her best no-nonsense
nurse's look.

"Iffen ya'd help me to a chair, ma'am,"—Cooter managed to get his
elbows under him and lifted into a half-seated position—"I'm sure I'd
feel some better."

"Tomorrow. If"—she held one finger up—"you behave yourself today."

"What difference would one day make?"

"The difference between that broken bone in your leg shifting or
not. And if it shifts, the difference between you walking with a limp
the rest of your life or not."

Cooter practically melted back onto the mattress, defeat in his
expression.

"Don't worry." Bonnie smoothed the hair from Cooter's forehead.
"Tomorrow will be here before you know it."

As it was barely past breakfast, Bonnie's assertion was a stretch, but Cooter smiled at her like he was stuck on a ledge and she'd handed him a rope. He truly did dote on the little girl.

"Okay, Miss Bonnie. I'll keep myself right here on this bed until ya tell me different."

The little girl nodded, then made eye contact with Susannah and winked.

The little minx.

"Let's check on Peaches." Susannah led the way to the mule's stable. They didn't visit often. The mule stable was on the far side of the fort's grounds. But Susannah missed her mule's steady presence. Missed her last link to Abel.

They hadn't reached the end of the row of storage shacks before Sergeant O'Reilly joined them.

"Top o' the morning, ma'am. Miss Bonnie."

"Good morning, sergeant," they answered together.

"How's the patient?"

"Mr. Cooter wants to get out of bed," Bonnie said.

The sergeant nodded. "No man wants to be lyin' abed when there be work ta be done. Where be ye ladies off ta?"

"To visit Peaches." Bonnie bounded on her toes.

Susannah had to glance away from the sergeant's baffled expression lest she laugh outright. "Peaches is my mule."

"Oh."

What was it about men and the name Peaches? "We haven't been to see her lately."

"I'm sure she be gettin' the best care, ma'am."

"Yes, but she's my mule, and I want to see her."

"I want to see Peaches too," Bonnie said.

"Then shall we all visit the beast together?" The sergeant's smile was aimed at Bonnie, but his eyes locked onto Susannah.

She needed to make it clear that she wasn't interested in his attentions, but it wouldn't be very ladylike to say so bluntly. Or in front of Bonnie. He wasn't disagreeable, in personality or appearance, but she just didn't...

Didn't what?

It would solve so many of her problems if she were to remarry. It could even solve Bonnie's if the man were willing to take the child too. And Susannah would never accept a man who wouldn't. She was entirely too attached to Bonnie for that. If she couldn't deliver her to her real family, then Bonnie would stay and become part of hers.

That was not negotiable.

Could she marry another man she didn't love? She and Abel had married out of obligation on his part and necessity on hers, but they'd grown to care for each other. Their marriage had been too short but left her with some wonderful memories. Not the fiasco with his family, of course, nor the intolerance of those who judged her harshly due to her Southern accent—and judged him harshly for marrying her. But Abel had been kind and generous, loving and steadfast to the end.

Could she find anyone like him again?

She pushed the image of Mr. Hickman from her thoughts. That door wasn't open, and she had no reason to believe it ever would be. Quite the opposite, in fact.

Sergeant O'Reilly was listening to Bonnie explain how she'd been helping Cooter. The girl was doing her best to imitate Susannah, which was very endearing. Everything about Bonnie was endearing. If Susannah married again, she could justify keeping the girl. That was tempting.

She gave the sergeant a second look.

He had made his attraction to Susannah clear without being obnoxious. He was providing them with food that allowed them to stay in the fort. He sought Susannah out every evening and was pleasant and kind.

But it wasn't just about Susannah.

Bonnie deserved to be reunited with her real family. And the only man who could do that was Mr. Hickman. The same man who dragged in after dark and left again before sunup, working twice as many horses as a man should. Wearing himself thin. Was he doing it just to break the horses for the army?

Or was he also avoiding Susannah?

The sergeant had assigned two of the younger soldiers, Wilson and Top, to assist Hick since Cooter's injury. Even with them to catch and saddle, strip and groom, and finish riding out the almost-ready stock, Hick was exhausted. He dropped to the ground beside the blue roan, having finally ridden the stallion that day. He'd had to slow down the special horse's training to fit in all the others, but this evening, he'd put his weight in the saddle for the first time, and the stallion had accepted it.

The victory should have been sweeter, but Hick was too tired to enjoy it.

He handed the animal to Top, then stripped Trooper and rubbed the old horse down. He'd let the soldiers care for their animals, but not his own. He turned the horse into a corral with Rumpus and several other mounts. Trooper dropped to his knees with a groan and rolled to scrub his back in the dirt. Hick waited until he'd lumbered back to his feet and shook off the excess dirt before heading to the shack.

Cooter sat on a chair with his leg on a crate in front of him. He grinned at Hick. "Ya look like ya been ate by wild dogs and barfed over a cliff."

An apt description of how he felt. "I'd love to spend a day in a chair on that porch."

"No, ya wouldn't." The grin slipped from Cooter. "And I'm right sorry—"

Hick raised his hand to ward off yet another apology. Cooter had done nothing wrong. Breaking horses was dangerous work. Accidents happened.

Which was why Hick shouldn't have left the corral while Cooter had been on that rank horse.

He sank to the porch boards and leaned against the side of the building, every muscle protesting even that much movement.

Mrs. Piper appeared in the doorway with a plate of biscuits and fried pork.

His stomach growled like it hadn't seen food in a week, not just since noon. But then, noon had been close to nine hours past.

"You skipped supper again, I imagine, so I made you a plate." She handed it down to him with a fork.

"Thank you, ma'am." The food wasn't hot, but that didn't matter. He wolfed it down and drank the cup of water she'd set next to him. Miss

Bonnie appeared with a dipper and filled the cup again. It wasn't coffee but killed his thirst.

"Thank you, too, Miss Bonnie." The girl dimpled and glanced at Mrs. Piper.

They could be mother and daughter.

A bite of biscuit caught in his throat, and he gulped the water down to clear it. What was he thinking? They weren't a family. Couldn't be a family.

"How many horses ya gots left to break?" Cooter asked.

Hick bit off a chunk of pork, chewed and swallowed before he answered. "There are eight more that I haven't been on yet. Wilson and Top are riding those that just need more time spent on them."

"What about the blue roan?"

"Do you mean Cobalt, Mr. Cooter?" Bonnie asked.

The young man looked startled. "Cobalt?"

Bonnie nodded, her red curls bouncing on her back. "Mrs. Piper says the prettiest blue she could think of was cobalt. She says it's a blue stone."

Cooter rubbed his chin. "Well, I reckon Cobalt would be a right fine name for that animal then."

Hick chewed on the name along with his last biscuit. It wasn't a bad name. The horse had muscles like stone. It was a far cry better than Peaches.

"I rode Cobalt"—he nodded at Bonnie's wide grin—"this evening."

Cooter bolted upright on his chair. "Ya done it? How'd it go?"

"Didn't buck once."

"Aww... I knowed ya could do it." Cooter slapped his good leg with the flat of his hand. "I should of been there to watch."

Mrs. Piper gathered Hick's plate and fork and stopped in the doorway of the shack. She glanced down at Cooter. "Tomorrow."

"Honest?" The hope and longing in the young man's voice was unmistakable.

She pressed her hand on his shoulder. "Honest. And next week, you can ride again. A month is long enough for bones your age to have knit."

Hick would have those last horses ready in that same week, and then he and Cooter could head for the foothills. He glanced at Mrs. Piper still standing in the doorway. The question was there in her eyes, but he looked away.

He didn't have the answer she wanted.

Mr. Hickman and Cooter strode away from the shack, the younger man leaning on a cane Sergeant O'Reilly had brought him. Susannah sighed.

"You sound sad." Bonnie blinked up at her. "I am too. I'm going to miss Mr. Cooter being here on the porch all day. Are you?"

If it were only that.

The mustangs were green broke enough for the soldiers to ride. Cooter was healed enough to ride Rumpus. The men were on their way to see Colonel Gibbon about getting paid.

And Susannah had no idea what would happen after that.

Would they return to bid them farewell at least? Or would they saddle and ride away without a backward glance? Cooter would come back, she was fairly certain. Mr. Hickman, however...

She should have confronted Mr. Hickman directly. Should have pressed him about finding Bonnie's aunt and uncle. She should have—

Bonnie tugged at her skirt. "Are you?"

Susannah blinked. "Am I what?"

"Are you going to miss Mr. Cooter now that he's healed?"

"Yes." She squeezed the girl's shoulder. "Very much." Not to mention the food that would stop coming to the shack. Her dress was looser around her middle. Mr. Hickman had often needed a meal when he returned sometime near dark. She'd scrimped to stretch every bit that she could.

She'd gladly continue to scrimp as long as he'd keep returning.

Susannah strode to the fire they'd been using for cooking and heating water. She poked the lingering coals and poured water into the pot to heat. She would wash the breakfast dishes and then... wait.

Waiting wasn't something she did very well.

"Sergeant O'Reilly is coming our way." Bonnie's voice carried a pleased lilt to it. There was no doubt she enjoyed the man's visits. Over the past two weeks, Susannah had watched the two together. She was convinced that the sergeant enjoyed the little girl's company as well.

What did it say about Susannah that she'd wondered if he only pretended interest in Bonnie to try to win her affections? The thought made her cringe inside. She stood and shielded her eyes from the sun's early glare.

"Good morning, Sergeant O'Reilly," Bonnie said.

"Good mornin', darlin'." He reached Bonnie and swung her in the air, but his eyes sought Susannah's, and he lowered the giggling girl to her feet. "The fellows are done with the mustangs, and a fine job they did of it too."

"Good morning, sergeant." Susannah wiped her hands on her apron. "What can I do for you?"

His eyes took on a gleam that made her want to look away, but she didn't. He was a good man, of that she had no doubt, but...

"I was wonderin', darlin'," he spoke to Bonnie. "Would ye be mindin' it too much if Mrs. Piper and me took a stroll by ourselves this mornin'?"

Bonnie's eyes rounded, and she glanced at Susannah.

"It's all right, Bonnie," Susannah said. "We won't go far, I promise. You'll be able to see us from here."

The little girl nodded and sat on the edge of the porch, swinging her feet.

"Mrs. Piper?" The sergeant offered his arm.

Susannah slipped her fingers around his elbow, and they strolled down the row of shacks. Since they were the only ones who lived in them—the others were used for storage—they met no one else.

"Mrs. Piper, I have a feelin' ye know what I'm wantin' ta discuss with ye."

A heaviness settled on her shoulders and pushed against her chest. "I suppose I do."

"'Tis only that a handsome widow woman like yerself, well, ye need a man ta be lookin' after ye proper-like." He raised his free hand. "Not that I think there be anythin' improper between ye and the gentlemen who brought ye here. They've both threatened the lives of any man who dared suggest otherwise."

"They are very protective of Bonnie and me."

"And yet." He paused and gave her a searching look. "Neither seems ta be offerin' ye more than that, if ye don't mind me pointin' it out plain-like."

She did mind, actually, but it was the simple truth. The ache it caused around her heart was the reason she'd have to rebuff the sergeant. She'd married Abel in haste and from necessity, but she'd also been free to do so.

Her heart was no longer free.

Willing or not, it had attached itself to Mr. Hickman. That infuriating, kind, stubborn, and loyal man... who didn't want her.

Something must have shown on her face, because the sergeant shook his head. "There's no point in me goin' on with my speech, is there." It wasn't a question.

But it still deserved an answer. "I'm afraid not."

"Mrs. Piper, if ye ever need me, ye know where ta find me." He moved a step away, letting her hand fall from his arm. "I mean it. Those are not empty words."

"I know. And I appreciate it. If things were different..." She gripped his forearm for a moment, then let go. "But they aren't, and it wouldn't be fair to you."

"I expect it's right ye are, darlin'. But ye can't blame a man for tryin'." He walked away with his head held high but without the normal swagger in his step.

Susannah had thought there'd be a sense of relief when they reached an understanding, but there wasn't. She'd hurt a good man—and she'd been hurt by another good man.

There was nothing left to do but saddle Peaches and make for the nearest railroad station to purchase her tickets back to Omaha.

CHAPTER 26

"**S**ERGEANT O'REILLY IS FULL of praise for your efforts with the mustangs." Captain Gibbon drummed his fingers on his desk. "That man's praise is not easily earned, I assure you."

"There were some fine horses in that bunch." Hick glanced at Cooter, who nodded. "They made us look good."

The captain pointed at Cooter's cane. "Not all of them."

"No, sir, yer sure right about that." But Cooter grinned. He'd never held it against the black beast who had nearly killed him.

"And now, since my attempts to persuade you to join our ranks have been in vain, there is nothing left to do but settle up." Captain Gibbon pulled a thin leather wallet from his desk.

Hick leaned forward, one hand on the desk until the captain looked at him. "I'd take the blue roan as my portion of the payment."

Cooter's breath half hissed and half whistled past his teeth.

"I hear that's a mighty handsome horse." The captain placed the wallet on the desk and leaned back in his chair. "But your proposal is interesting."

As thin as the wallet was, Hick had a good chance to ride off with the stallion who would start his herd.

"Why the blue roan?" the captain asked.

"I want to start my own herd of horses when I get to the mountains. I'll need a quality stallion for the mustang mares Cooter and I plan to round up."

That had the captain leaning forward. "And what are your plans for the blue roan's offspring?"

Hick didn't miss the gleam in the officer's eyes. He crossed his arms and tipped his chin in the direction of the stables. "Why, to sell them to the U.S. Army, of course."

"Trained?"

"Fully broke and ready for patrol."

The captain eyed Cooter up and down. "Are you in this with him?"

"I guess I am." Cooter's thin chest puffed a bit. "We's a team, me and Hick."

The captain drummed his fingers on the desktop again. "If I let the stallion go for half your wages—paying out the other half—will you agree to give me first options on your horses in three or four years?"

"Yes, sir. That I will."

The man stood and they shook hands. Moments later, Hick and Cooter were outside the office building with their money and the blue roan's bill of sale in their pockets, heading for the stable. Hick had hoped he'd be able to get the roan—Cobalt, as Miss Bonnie had named him—but hadn't dreamed he'd draw half pay as well.

"That were some dealin' ya done, Hick." Respect flowed with Cooter's words. "I had no idea ya were gonna say that. About knocked my knees out from under me."

"I had to try. Cobalt has everything I want in a herd stallion."

"He is a beauty." Cooter slowed down. "Uh-oh."

Heading straight for them was O'Reilly, and he didn't look pleased. There was no way, coming from that direction, he could know about the stallion yet. But he was pounding the ground like it had insulted his mother.

"Hickman."

"O'Reilly." Since they were no longer employed by the army, and since the man looked like he'd rather throw a punch than speak, Hick didn't feel the need to address him more formally.

Cooter took a step to the side—out of harm's way.

"What are yer intentions regardin' Mrs. Piper and Bonnie?"

The bark of the sergeant was drawing a crowd, men hanging back but listening close. More than one of them would have gladly gone sniffing around Mrs. Piper if O'Reilly hadn't made his interest clear from the beginning. Hick should be grateful to the man for that, but this public display was a little too much.

Hick clenched his fists but kept them tight to his sides. "What business is that of yours?"

O'Reilly took a step closer, the man's breath reaching Hick when he spoke. "She turned me down, and what reason would she have other than ye?" He kept his voice too low for the onlookers to hear.

"Mrs. Piper is an independent woman." That was an understatement. "She makes up her own mind."

"Have ye made her a promise?"

"I still don't see that it's any of your business." Hick got the words out between his teeth, stifling the urge to plant a fist on the man's chin. "She's turned you down."

"Listen here—"

"Nope, you listen." Hick closed the slight distance left between them, his words barely more than a whisper. "We're riding out of here tomorrow, me, Cooter, Mrs. Piper, Miss Bonnie, and the blue roan stallion the captain just gave me in payment. And you're not going to get in our way."

"Ye'd do that ta her? In front o' the whole fort? Ye'd shame her that way?"

"She wants to find Miss Bonnie's family. I'll help her do that."

"Without making an honest woman o' her?"

"If you don't realize she's the most honest woman in this fort, then she was right to turn you down."

The sergeant's nostrils flared, and Hick tensed for the first punch, but it didn't come. The man seemed to take notice of the onlookers for the first time, then he speared Hick with a scathing look. "Get out o' my fort."

His fort? Captain Gibbon might have something to say about that, but Hick let it go, and the man stormed off.

"I was awaitin' for the battle, I gotta say." Cooter stepped to his side. "When did ya decide to go after Miss Bonnie's kinfolk?"

When had he? Maybe when the sergeant's breath had fanned his face.

Cooter cleared his throat. "Ya know, what he said was some true."

Hick swallowed a growl that tried to push past his throat.

"It'd be better all the way around iffen ya got hitched to Mrs. Piper afore we ride out." Cooter rocked from his heels to toes and back again. "Mrs. Piper is a fine woman, make any man a good wife." He nodded toward the fort's administration building. "The chaplain's a fair man. He'd get it done right."

"I'm not marrying Mrs. Piper." He rounded on Cooter and practically spit the words. "Not today, not tomorrow, not ever." Then he strode for the stable. He needed to calm down. He needed to think. He needed Trooper's steadying presence.

He needed to figure out why his last words to Cooter had revived the pain in his chest.

She'd been a fool, a proud and stupid fool. Susannah folded her extra clothing and stuffed it in her saddlebag. She'd already packed the rest of her belongings and Bonnie's in her sack and satchel. They had precious little food, but it would have to do until they reached the train station.

It would be a hungry ride back to Omaha.

What if Dr. Conkling or Dr. Peabody had no job for her when they returned? It had been weeks since she'd ridden out with Cooter in a mad dash to save Mr. Hickman's life. The cholera outbreak would be over, perhaps the need for a nurse gone. But she wouldn't know if she still had a place until they arrived.

The bottom line was—Susannah had run out of options.

She'd refused Sergeant O'Reilly for a very uncertain future. With Bonnie to look after, there was no way she could travel to Oregon. That door was closed. Every door might be closed.

Susannah dropped onto the thin mattress and buried her face in her hands. She didn't weep. She didn't even want to weep. She just wanted to give up.

"Mrs. Piper?" Bonnie's tentative voice came from the doorway.

Susannah rubbed her forehead and then looked up. "Yes, Bonnie?"

"Are you ill?"

She didn't believe in lying to people, not even children, but Susannah wasn't physically ill. She was spiritually and emotionally ill. A child of eight couldn't understand. Or at least, she shouldn't be able to. It wouldn't be right to burden the little girl with Susannah's worries.

"Just tired, love." She held out her arm, and Bonnie scooted under it, snuggling close despite the summer heat. "It's been a long day already, and it's still morning."

That brought a giggle, which eased Susannah's despair. They may not have much, but she and Bonnie had each other.

Maybe that was enough.

Maybe that was more important than reaching Oregon.

Cooter had wandered off, leaving Hick in the stable to groom Trooper and calm down in the cool of the building. He should groom Cobalt too, but he was too tense. The mustang stallion would sense it and react. Old Trooper knew all of Hick's moods including those he should ignore. Hick gave the bay coat one last wipe with a rag, and the old horse yawned.

"Some help you are." He patted the animal's rump and was putting the grooming tools away when the unmistakable voice of Mrs. Hardy came from the stable's doorway.

"Mr. Hickman." The woman actually put her hands on her hips as if dressing down a child. "I hear you plan to ride off to God knows where with Mrs. Piper and that girl."

"Ma'am, I fail to see where that is any of your business."

"As the ranking officer's wife, I am of course concerned about the women in this fort."

"Oh, are you?" Hick took a step forward. There were several other women arrayed behind Mrs. Hardy, and they took a collective step in retreat, but the old battle ax kept her hands on her hips and her chin in the air. "So concerned that you and your flock invited her to join you for meals? Or took her food? Or inquired after how she and Bonnie were faring here?"

The gaggle behind her twittered at that, but he wasn't interested in them.

"I assisted her in finding lodging—"

"A broken-down shack hardly fit for the mice that called it home. And you never crossed the threshold again."

"Well, I understood that she was under *your* protection. That you were sleeping at the shack."

"She was and is under my protection." If she'd accepted O'Reilly, Hick would be out from under that obligation. Instead, he found himself still burdened with her. Even though that *burden* didn't seem so... burdensome anymore.

"Then I could hardly condone the other good women"—she waved a hand at the sea of calico behind her—"of this fort to fraternize with a kept woman."

"Kept?" Hick's voice rose. He drew in a long breath and lowered his voice. "I was sleeping *outside* the shack. Mrs. Piper isn't a kept woman. She earned her keep by nursing Cooter when he was—"

"The fort employs a perfectly good doctor—"

"The man's a quack and you and everyone else here knows it."

She puffed herself up like an overstuffed turkey. "Mr. Hickman, I believe—"

"Mrs. Hardy, I don't care what you believe." His arm brushed her shoulder as he passed her in the doorway.

She'd completely undone the calming he'd worked so hard to achieve. First O'Reilly, then Cooter, and now Mrs. Hardy. Why did everyone think he needed to marry Mrs. Piper?

His anger drained and his steps slowed as the truth hammered its way through his defenses. As much as he hadn't wanted anyone—anyone at all—to be dependent on him, and as much as he'd fought against getting close to people, he'd been raised better than he'd been acting.

If Ma could see him now, what would she think? The memory of her disapproval hurt. It hurt in the same deep soul-wrenching way he'd felt while Denny died in his arms. It hurt the same as when he'd decided not to return home after the war, so he wouldn't have to face Ma again.

A man couldn't spend his life running from his past. Running from his pain.

His steps slowed until he was barely moving, each footstep heavier than the last. He'd written his folks a short note letting them know he'd survived the war and that he was heading west. Nothing more. He'd convinced himself it was all they'd want to know after what he'd done. But in truth, he'd couldn't have written much more without apologizing—as he had when he'd written them of his brother's death—for taking Denny into the war with him.

For causing his brother's death.

He lifted his head, the shack in sight, Mrs. Piper on the porch watching his approach.

If he took her to the mountains, he would cause another form of death for her. No respectable man would have her as a wife. She'd be known as his kept woman. She'd not land another job as a nurse with that sullied reputation. The western territories were vast and thinly populated, so the only gossip there would blaze a path like a twister.

Bonnie came through the shack's doorway. Mrs. Piper's arm encircling the little girl as if by instinct. A woman and a child looking to him. Depending on him. The war-wounded part of him wanted to execute a military-style about-face, saddle Trooper, and ride long and hard.

But he was a better man than that. At least, he had been. Something inside stirred, something that was... what? Cautiously eager? Hopefully uncertain? Willing to be that man again? And perhaps, with Mrs. Piper's help, he could.

If she'd have him.

Could it be that Mr. Hickman was reluctant to say goodbye? Susannah rubbed Bonnie's shoulder, the little girl tight against her side as if aware that something was about to change.

Well, there was no keeping the truth a secret. They were about to part ways with the tall man ambling toward them.

She'd had many hard thoughts about Mr. Hickman—and many soft ones that she'd have to forget—but she couldn't read his face as he drew closer. Something had changed. The air between them, prairie dry and dusty, held a charge she couldn't name. Sorrow, perhaps? Was he truly sorry to see them leave? That idea plucked at the soft thoughts she needed to pack away in the back of her mind.

He stopped short of the porch, removed his hat and tapped it against his thigh, dust puffing from the battered, sweat-soaked felt. He looked toward the corrals, then turned back to her. He needed a shave and a haircut and a bath. His clothing was as much dirt as threads, and the boots he'd bought in Missouri were as worn as the rest of him.

But her heart gave a painful thump anyway.

"Mrs. Piper?"

"Yes, Mr. Hickman?" Always they were formal with each other, but it didn't seem right, somehow, at this moment of parting. "Samuel?"

His head jerked up, and surprise relaxed the hard plains of his face. He shuffled his hat from one hand to the other, cleared his throat. "Could we take a walk, ma'am?" He glanced at Bonnie and then back to her.

"Bonnie will be fine as long as we stay in sight of the shack, won't you, love?"

Bonnie nodded, eyes far too large in her freckled face. She didn't know what was happening, but she'd find out soon enough that it would be just the two of them.

Susannah squeezed her shoulder, then stepped off the porch.

She walked beside Mr. Hickman until they were well out of earshot of the shack.

Then he stopped and faced her. "Ma'am, I know we've had our differences..."

"We have, but we've pushed through them." And in hindsight, he'd been right more times than she wanted to admit.

He glanced at his hat, then raised his eyes to hers. "I guess what I need to say is, if you want to go west with me and Cooter to find Bonnie's kin..."

Shock doused her like cold water from a stream. "You'd take us?" She held her breath in case she'd misunderstood.

"Yes, ma'am. Under one condition." His Adam's apple bobbed behind the neckerchief tied at his throat, but he didn't continue.

She sighed, then closed her eyes for a moment, steeling herself for whatever may come before looking at him again. "What is your condition?"

"We get married by the fort's chaplain first."

CHAPTER 27

S USANNAH'S EARS WERE BUZZING, and she swayed. Mr. Hickman's hands cupped her elbows, steadying her. His voice came as if from a distance.

"I know this is sudden, ma'am."

Sudden? A tornado was sudden, a runaway horse, but this... this was impossible. He'd all but painted a board sign with "don't get close to me" and hung it around his neck. And now a proposal of marriage? It made no sense.

"Why do you wish to marry me?"

He studied his boots, hands still on her elbows, not more than a foot between them. "Because it's the right thing to do." He raised eyes to her that were clear and serious, their hazel depths threatening to draw her in.

"Mr. Hickman—"

"I liked when you called me Samuel." His voice was rough, tight. "Ma called me by that name. To everyone else, I was just Sam. Then in the army, Hick."

In his fever dreams by the river, he'd called out to his ma. She mattered deeply to this man. "Samuel, I don't know what to say."

"Say yes, and I'll find the chaplain. Say no, and I'll see you and Bonnie to the railroad." He looked around. "You can't stay here."

"So it's all up to me?" That didn't seem right.

"My part was the asking, and that was hard enough." A shallow smile twitched his lips. "But the yes or no is up to you."

"You didn't ask." That shouldn't hurt, but it did. "You made it a condition." Like a business arrangement.

She glanced at Bonnie. The little girl leaned on the porch rail, watching them. What they decided would affect her the most. Well, not the most. Heat flushed through Susannah. She kept her face averted for a moment while it passed, then lifted her face to the tall man still holding her by the elbows.

"I will marry you, Samuel."

He cocked his head. "Why? You asked me, so I guess I can ask you."

What could she say to that? There were so many reasons hitting her from every direction. Because it was best for Bonnie. Because it was best for Susannah herself. Because she felt safe with him. Because he was heading west where she most wished to go. And because her heart fluttered in an unexpected way whenever she spied him in the distance. What it did when he was this close... well...

But she left all those thoughts inside. "As you said, it's the right thing to do."

He dropped her elbows and slapped his hat on his head. "I'll find the chaplain." And with that, he strode away, a man on a mission. A man with a purpose.

A man soon to be her husband.

She'd done it again. She'd agreed to marry a man she barely knew. No, that wasn't fair, she knew Mr. Hickman—Samuel—better than she'd known Abel when he'd proposed. At least he *had* proposed. Not on bended knee as every little girl dreamed, but with an open honesty missing in the present offer of marriage.

Susannah hadn't been fully honest with Samuel, and she was fairly certain he hadn't been fully honest with her.

That wasn't a very good start to a marriage.

She glanced at Bonnie again, whose head had turned to watch Samuel walk away. But unlike the other times he'd walked away, this time Susannah knew he'd be back.

And the next time he walked away—he'd take them with him.

Cooter appeared at Hick's elbow, marching beside him.

"Did ya ask her?" Cooter asked.

He searched the young man's face without slowing. "How'd you know?"

Cooter shrugged. "There's somethin' different about ya, I guess. She say yes?"

"Yup."

Cooter clapped Hick on the shoulder, and then coughed at the dust that billowed. "When ya gettin' hitched?"

"On my way to the chaplain's now."

With that, Cooter stopped cold and grabbed Hick's sleeve, stopping him as well. "I don't know much about women nor weddin's nor such like, but even I know somethin'." He eyed Hick up and down, mouth twisting into a frown.

"What?"

"Ain't no polite way to go about sayin' it, Hick, but ya need a bath. And a shave. And maybe even a new set of clothes." Cooter nodded. "Man oughta make an effort for his bride."

"It's not like that between Mrs. Piper and me."

"Ain't it?" Cooter's eyebrows lifted in a challenge.

Hick growled under his breath. He'd run the gauntlet of emotions already that day. He wasn't sure he could do one more thing. But he ran his hands over his clothes and had to admit Cooter had a point. None of his other clothing was fit to stand before the chaplain in either. He'd best visit the sutler's place first. Then he could pump water and bathe at the stables. All that fuss for...

Susannah.

There was no doubt she was worth it.

"Come on," he said. "You need clothing too if you're going to stand up with me."

Cooter grinned like a possum on a holiday.

It took them longer than Hick imagined to buy new outfits. He'd bought extra socks and long johns and shirts too. No telling how far they'd be from a trading post or sutler's once they reached the foothills. Since he'd drawn half pay and had his stallion, he could afford it. He was looking at a fine leather halter when Cooter joined him.

"That would look right smart on Cobalt," Cooter said.

Hick grunted and added it to his pile on the long counter. He'd already set an extra length of rope there with his pile of new clothing, as well as an adz and several other tools they'd need to build a cabin.

Cooter's purchases were wrapped in brown paper and tied with string.

"We still leavin' in the mornin'?" he asked.

"Yup."

"We'll need provisions."

"I figured Mrs. Piper would see to that. She'll know what best to purchase."

Cooter grinned at him.

"What?"

"She'll be Mrs. Hick afore the sun sets. I like the sound of that."

Hick's insides did an unsettling flip as he turned his back on the other man and paid for his purchases. "Let's go." He'd never thought about a Mrs. Hickman other than Ma. That would take some getting used to.

The stable was fairly quiet, the soldiers off on some detail or another. Hick pumped water into two buckets and hauled them into an empty stall. He fished a bar of soap from his package and stripped down. The water was cold, but it felt good to get clean. He'd even thought to buy a length of toweling, so he dried off and dressed in his new suit.

Cooter washed while Hick shaved and the young man emerged looking even younger. "I reckon we's off to the chaplain's next?"

Hick stowed his dirty clothing and the rest of his purchases in the manger of Trooper's stall. The old horse wouldn't bother them.

The chaplain had a desk in the corner of the administration building. They were halfway there when it occurred to Hick that the man might be out on patrol. It wouldn't be unusual. He was the chaplain but also a soldier.

"What if he isn't there?" he asked Cooter.

"Aw, he likely is."

"But what if he isn't?" Irritation crept into Hick's voice, but he couldn't stop it. He didn't even know why he was irritated. It wasn't like he was looking forward to the marriage.

Was he?

"We'll find out in a few more steps." Cooter's grin was back.

Hick fought the urge to knock it off his friend's face.

His friend. Not just a wife, but a friend, not to mention a little girl, were all looking to him. Hick fought the panic that threatened to rise in his throat as they walked up the steps to the administration building.

The soldier at the door allowed them in. The chaplain was hunched over his desk but glanced up at their approach.

"I'd like you to marry me and Mrs. Piper." Hick blurted the words as if they'd been burning his tongue, then he flushed like a schoolboy, fists tightening at his sides.

The chaplain leaned back in his chair, fingertips steepled and pressed to his lips. He eyed Hick and then Cooter and then Hick again. "Is the lady willing?"

"Of course she is."

"When would you like the nuptials to take place?"

"This afternoon."

The man's palms hit the desk. "Why the rush?"

"We're leaving in the morning, and we'd like to be married before we ride on." Maybe not *like* exactly, but they were agreed on it at least.

"There are those within the fort who will be glad to hear it."

The old battle ax and her crowd, no doubt. "I'd appreciate it, Chaplain, if you didn't mention it until after we've gone."

"There must be witnesses."

"Cooter here will be a witness, and Miss Bonnie Sorrell."

"She's but a child, not old enough—"

"The girl is old enough to sign her name on a piece of paper." Hick leaned over the desk. "She's old enough to have buried her whole family and survived."

"It's highly unusual." The chaplain stood. "But you make a convincing argument." He pulled a watch from his pocket. "Shall we say seven o'clock?"

Hick nodded. "Do you know where Mrs. Piper's shack is?"

"I do."

"We'll see you there."

What was Hick going to do with himself for the hours in between? He was too dressed up to work with Cobalt and too keyed up to sit and wait.

He'd never planned to marry after the war. It was more than just not wanting to be responsible for someone else. It was... knowing how unworthy he was. He hadn't kept his own brother safe. He'd done things he was ashamed of, things he could never forget. Things that would live with him always.

He'd be bringing all that into the marriage with Mrs. Piper. Would Mrs. Piper—Susannah—be able to bear it?

Bonnie remained still on the chair while Susannah finished brushing the child's hair dry. The reddish curls had a mind of their own, wanting to tangle in the brush, Susannah's fingers, and each other.

"Ma always said my hair was a trial." Longing filled the little girl's voice. She hadn't spoken of her family often.

"I'm sure she didn't mean that in a bad way."

"My brothers all had straight hair like her. Pa had curls."

Susannah knelt beside the chair. "There, you see? She married your pa with his curly hair, so she must have admired it."

Bonnie's lips trembled but tipped up in a slight smile. "I never thought of it that way."

"She probably meant your hair kept her busy when she had so many other things to do. But I'll bet she enjoyed the time spent brushing it, even if other work was left undone."

"I never thought of that, either." Something like hope glimmered in the gray depths of her eyes.

"That's because you were a little girl, and little girls aren't supposed to think of things like that. But now"—Susannah rose—"you are going to stand up with me and Mr. Hickman."

Bonnie smoothed her hands down her clean dress. "Ma made this for me."

"She'd think you look beautiful in it, and so do I."

"Mrs. Piper?"

"Yes?"

"Once you're married, will you be called Mrs. Hick?"

"Mrs. Hickman." The name felt strange on Susannah's tongue, but she'd need to get used to it. "His last name is Hickman."

"But Mr. Cooter calls him Hick."

"He said the men in the army shortened his name that way. But his real name is Samuel Hickman."

"Will you still call him Mr. Hickman?"

"No. I will call him Samuel when he's my husband."

Bonnie swiveled on the chair and looked up at Susannah. "Are you happy to be marrying him?"

Out of the mouths of babes.

Susannah searched for an appropriate answer. "I am glad we're getting married. It's not seemly for a man and woman to travel together if they aren't."

"But we all traveled here without you being married."

"That's true, but there was no one to marry us until we reached the fort."

Bonnie nodded as if that satisfied her, and Susannah let out a soft sigh. If only the answer satisfied her as well. It should, but it didn't.

Still, she'd taken measures to be ready. She'd donned her best dress. She had no flatiron to press out the wrinkles, but she'd shaken it and dampened the worst of the creases to ease them. She'd bathed and dressed her hair in a simple braid she'd pinned up. Without a mirror, it was the best she could do. Bonnie was also bathed and dressed, and once Susannah had finished with her hair, there was nothing else to do but wait.

What was taking Mr. Hickman—Samuel—so long?

Had he changed his mind and ridden away?

Of course not. He was a man of his word. She knew that, but her nerves were getting the best of her. She gave Bonnie's hair a few more strokes, then gathered the curling mass and secured it at her nape with a ribbon.

"There. You look beautiful."

"So do you." The little pixie smiled at her. "I'm sure Mr. Hick will think so too."

Since she'd taken the time to tidy herself as best she could, she certainly couldn't deny that it mattered. But supper mattered, too, and if she didn't start something, they'd all go hungry. She was tying her apron on when a knock sounded on the door.

"Yes?" she called.

"It's Cooter, ma'am."

Susannah opened the door, which she'd only closed in the summer's heat for their bathing and dressing.

The young man was dressed in new clothing, so new the store-bought wrinkles remained. But he held up a stringer of fish. "I did me a little fishin' at the river. Figgered we'd need a good meal under our belts for tomorrow's travelin'."

"Oh, good!" Bonnie crowded into the doorway. "Fish is my favorite."

"Well, ya look pretty as a wildflower, Miss Bonnie," Cooter said.

Bonnie clasped her hands in front of her skirt and swayed side to side. "Mrs. Piper helped me. I'm going to stand with her for the marrying."

Cooter beamed. "Me too. I'm standin' with Hick."

"And where is...?" But before Susannah could finish the question, Samuel came into view. She sucked in a quick breath. He also wore new clothing.

Susannah glanced down at her best dress. It was clean but worn and faded. She lifted her face to catch Samuel looking at her. What did he see?

A poor widow.

She should have dug into her hoard of coins and gone to the sutler's. She'd almost done that but decided it wouldn't matter.

She'd been wrong.

It had mattered to Samuel.

He stopped at the edge of the porch. The silence stretched thick between them.

Cooter coughed. "Miss Bonnie, how about we get these here fish cleaned?"

"I don't know how."

"I'll show ya. Ain't nothin' to it." He held her hand and led the little girl to the back of the shack, where they'd rigged a makeshift table for such work. But he just about stared a hole through Samuel on the way past.

What was that all about?

"Mrs. Piper." Samuel removed his hat.

"Susannah."

He met her eyes then, and she tried to read his thoughts but failed.

"Susannah, Cooter and I were at the sutler's, but we didn't buy any provisions for the trip. I reckon you'll know best what we need.

The chaplain won't be here until seven, so we have time." He pointed toward the sutler's store.

"Give me a moment." She whirled and dug through her satchel, extracting a handful of Yankee coins from her petticoat. With those in her pocket, she took a deep breath and plunged through the doorway.

"Cooter, start the fire, will you?" she called around the corner of the shack. "We'll return directly."

Samuel held out his arm, and she slipped her fingers around his elbow as if...

As if they were a couple.

CHAPTER 28

I T HAD TAKEN EVERYTHING Hick had in him to approach the shack. He'd wasted several hours pacing in the stables while Cooter went fishing. Pacing and telling himself all the reasons why he shouldn't go through with marrying Mrs. Piper.

Susannah. He needed to think of her that way. Because he *was* going through with it. He might not be the honorable man his parents had raised him to be, but he wasn't going back on his word.

The war had taken a lot from him, but he still had some decency left.

And then he'd seen them, Susannah and Bonnie, looking so much like a mother and her child. Both of them looking to him for his protection, his provision. Both in dresses that'd seen better days, Bonnie's dress barely reaching below her knees.

They needed clothing. Why hadn't he thought of that before going to the sutler's? At least he had the excuse of their provisions for the return trip.

But when they arrived, Susannah insisted on paying for the new dresses she bought for herself and Bonnie. Where had she gotten the money? Store-bought dresses were costly so far away from civilization. The sutler didn't carry many, but Susannah had found two that satisfied her.

While she'd been busy, Hick had asked the sutler to add several dress lengths of material to his order. When the man had asked which bolts, Hick had pointed to a lavender print and a yellow. He knew nothing about women's clothing, but he remembered his sisters liking those colors.

Hick had also bought a pack saddle. He'd ride Cobalt, since the horse needed hours spent under saddle to finish his training, and that would free up Trooper to haul their added provisions. He was a little sad to use the old war horse that way, but Trooper wouldn't balk. He was as steady and trustworthy as any animal Hick had ever known.

Then, just before he settled his bill, Hick spied a mule saddle hanging on the back wall. Susannah's so-called saddle couldn't be comfortable, and he doubted its reliability in rugged terrain. He pointed to the saddle and haggled the sutler down on the price. After all, with so many horses around, who else was going to purchase the thing?

The scent of fish frying broke him out of his thoughts. Mrs.—Susannah, still wearing the old dress covered with an apron, flipped fish in the pan.

Hick glanced at the sun. The chaplain would be there within the hour, yet Susannah seemed as cool and composed as always.

While his insides were tussling like a pair of mule deer with antlers locked.

Bonnie came out of the shack and sat beside him on the edge of the porch. "Mr. Hick?"

"Miss Bonnie."

"Cooter says you're going to try and find Aunt Sadie Mae and Uncle Willie for me."

"We'll do our best."

"What will happen if you can't?" She blinked at him. "Find them, I mean."

Susannah must have heard, a wrinkle forming between her brows as she turned to him.

All those other children he'd ridden away from—children silhouetted by the flames engulfing their homes—flashed across his mind's eye. He'd done nothing to help them. He'd followed orders. He'd ridden away.

"Mr. Hick? What will happen to me?"

She needed an answer, and he didn't have one. He couldn't push away the faces of all the other children he'd ridden away from. Children outlined by the fires burning their homes.

"Why, Miss Bonnie." Cooter hunkered down in front of the girl, pulling her attention away from Hick. "Ya stay with us. We ain't about to leave ya on yer own. Right, Hick?"

"That's right." He closed his eyes to remove the images that haunted him. Opening them, he forced out the words. "You'll stay with us."

Those gray eyes blinked at him again. "Like a family?"

Cold washed over him despite the sun's rays still baking the prairie around them. He swallowed against the dryness of his throat and refused to look at Susannah. Even so, he could almost feel her urging him to say the right thing. "Of course, Miss Bonnie. Just like a family."

She gave him a solemn nod, but Cooter grinned from ear to ear. And when he faced Susannah, what shone in her eyes knocked any remaining breath from him. When was the last time anyone had look at him with admiration in their eyes?

"And here comes the chaplain to make it all proper-like." Cooter stood.

He was early.

Panic—there was no other word for it—fired through Hick's limbs.

"We'll need a moment." Susannah grabbed Bonnie's hand. "Cooter, move the fish away from the fire." And then she disappeared into the shack with Bonnie, closing the door behind them.

The chaplain shook Hick's hand and attempted small talk, which barely registered. Cooter took up the slack, his gift for gab finally expressing itself in a useful way until the door opened and Susannah invited them in. They'd already decided to hold the ceremony inside, away from prying eyes, despite the heat.

She'd changed into the new dress, its deep blue a match for her eyes. Bonnie looked several years older in her new dress. Almost a young lady. And they were watching him. He stepped into the shack and tossed his new hat onto the bed. The table held a cup with a tangle of wildflowers, a strip of toweling covering its rough surface.

The chaplain arranged where they stood and started to speak. Hick knew the words. He'd heard them when his sisters had married and again when his friends had. He'd even stood up with a few of them. But this time, they were aimed at him like a sniper's rifle.

It was hard to breathe in the close confides of the shack. Hard to concentrate on the chaplain. Hard to ignore the flowery scent of the soap Susannah had used on her hair as she stood beside him.

He'd never noticed how dainty she was before. Her strength of personality somehow conveyed a larger person, but she barely reached his shoulder. Not that he'd want to tangle with her despite her size. She'd proved herself a force to be reckoned with.

"Do you have a ring?" The chaplain's words smacked his wayward thoughts back to the issue at hand.

"I didn't think—"

"I don't need a ring." Susannah's voice was unruffled, such a contrast to the battle going on inside of Hick.

But then... she'd been married before.

He'd said all the right things at all the right times, but Susannah knew Samuel's heart wasn't in it. He was an honorable man, doing the honorable thing, but he might as well be approaching a

gallows instead of a plate of fried fish.

Once the chaplain left, Susannah had changed into her old dress and finished cooking their meal. It was a bit surreal, knowing that she was married again, handing the plate to the man who was now her husband.

Her first night with Abel had been no different from the nights of their harrowing escape from Georgia. He'd been barely strong enough to stand for the pastor they'd approached once they arrived in a small town in Tennessee. Yet he'd been determined to marry her. To protect her as much as he could for what she'd done by giving her his name and respectability in the eyes of the world. They hadn't truly been man and wife until more than a month later.

"Thank you, ma'am." Samuel took the plate. "I mean, Susannah."

His sun-darkened skin flushed, and her cheeks heated in answer.

What did he expect of her next? There were Bonnie and Cooter to think of. They hadn't discussed anything like... sleeping arrangements.

Did he even find her attractive?

She busied herself serving the others, then added a crispy brown fish and a biscuit to her own plate. The last thing she wanted to do was eat. Her stomach was still in knots over the events of the day, but they were leaving in the morning, and she'd need the strength.

They ate their supper in silence, even Bonnie and Cooter. But once the plates were down to just bones, Cooter stood and took Susannah's plate.

"You and Hick go take a walk. Me and Miss Bonnie will get the washin' up done."

"Yes." Bonnie took Samuel's plate. "And then Mr. Cooter is taking me to visit Peaches."

Samuel stood, brushed off the front of his shirt, and offered Susannah his arm without a word. She glanced at Cooter, but at the jerk of his head toward Samuel, she grasped his elbow and walked into the evening with... her husband. In the opposite direction from the mule stable.

Had they planned this?

"I know everything happened in a rush today," Samuel said once they neared the edge of the fort's grounds. "And maybe I didn't handle things as well as I should have. If that's so, then please accept my apology."

"You've no need to apologize to me." But it touched her that he had, all the same.

"If I'd been the man I should have been, we would have been married when we arrived." He turned his head toward her, but didn't stop walking. "It would have saved you a lot of grief from the fort's busybodies."

She had to ask. "What changed between then and now?"

He stopped, the sun behind them casting long shadows. "I don't know." He removed his hat and wiped his brow before resettling it. "Maybe I needed my eyes opened."

"What opened them?" She needed to know.

He looked away for a moment, but then back to her, his face calm and serious with just a hint of tightness around his eyes. "O'Reilly. He confronted me with the truth."

The truth? Susannah paused a moment. Did she really want to know? Or was ignorance bliss for now? "What truth is that?"

His pause was twice as long as hers had been.

She liked that he thought about his response, but she had to use all her self-control not to fidget.

"At first, the truth that my behavior was not honorable. That if we rode out of the fort with you and I unmarried, it would forever mark your reputation."

The wind kicked up a dust devil a few yards ahead of them, its swirling funnel a good approximation of her emotions. "But then?" She was in this far, she needed to know the rest.

"But then..." He cleared his throat. "I knew I didn't want you to stay and marry him. And I didn't want to put you on the train heading east. I wanted you to go west with us, to help us find Miss Bonnie's family."

Dare she ask? How could she not? "Why?"

"I've never met a woman like you, Susannah. And after the war, I never wanted to." His voice was low and rough. "But the thought of sending you away..." His voice trailed off.

She squeezed his elbow and leaned against him for a moment. "I'm glad. I'm glad you didn't marry me just because it was the right thing to do."

"Are you?"

The intensity of his question startled her, and she took a small step away but didn't release his arm. "Yes, I am. I think we can have a good future together, Samuel. If I didn't, I wouldn't have married you."

There. The truth was out—of both of them. She relaxed and fancied she could feel the same from him. They may have agreed to marry without their true feelings spoken, but they'd gotten there before the end of the day.

She glanced over her shoulder. The shack was no longer in view. "We have a ready-made family."

One side of his mouth ticked up. "So it seems. Are you sure you want to be married to a man who collects stray people instead of stray puppies?"

Susannah laughed then. A real laugh, from somewhere inside that had been closed off for a long, long time. "I'll forever be grateful that I was one of those you collected."

Turning to face her while she laughed, he searched her face. He brought his hand to her neck, and her laugh faded. He cupped her cheek, his long fingers tangling in the hair behind her ear.

She didn't move, didn't make a sound, as he closed the distance between them. When his lips brushed hers, the jolt of her response shocked her. In a pleasant way. She let her hands rest on the front of his shirt, and when he raised his head, she tugged on the fabric to draw him back.

The kiss that followed was... magical.

It proved beyond a doubt that Susannah was ready to be married again. At least, married to the man in front of her. The man who held her close as she buried her face against his shirt, still scratchy in its newness.

"I'm sorry we don't have anywhere private to go." His shrug moved the fabric against her cheek. "I never thought... that is... I didn't think you'd..." His breath rustled her hair. "It seemed too bold of me to assume you'd want more than my name, under the circumstances."

She lifted her face, his so close she only needed to raise on her toes to kiss him again. "There will be a right time for everything, Samuel." Then she gave in and stretched toward him. She never made it to her toes, because he met her more than halfway.

A much better start for their marriage.

CHAPTER 29

A FTER A NEARLY SLEEPLESS night, Hick whistled as he cinched the loaded pack saddle onto Trooper. Cobalt and the mule were already saddled and ready. Trooper turned his face as if to say, *What's this thing all about?* But he accepted the new saddle without a hitch.

Susannah's mule had been something else altogether. She'd not taken to the fancy new saddle he'd bought her. Ungrateful beast. Cooter had jumped on and held tight while the ornery molly had pitched and bawled and let the whole fort know of her displeasure. Thankfully, Susannah and Bonnie had remained at the shack packing the last of their supplies and had missed the show. He didn't need either of them being afraid to ride the mule. Not that the molly ever misbehaved for Susannah. Once she'd thrown her fit, she'd settled down. She seemed to be in good order for the journey.

"Guess we's as ready as we'll ever be." Cooter was sitting sideways on Rumpus, rubbing his mostly healed leg. The bucking ride on the mule probably hadn't helped it any. "Good to see ya in a chipper mood."

"We're leaving the fort behind." Which was true. Getting away from any reminders of the war picked his spirits up considerably. "Finishing the journey to a new beginning."

"A beginning that includes Mrs. Pi—Hickman."

Hick had spent a mostly sleepless night thinking about that and remembering her kisses... wondering when they'd find that right time to indulge in more. He thumped the pack saddle to be sure it was secure, then took Trooper's lead rope and mounted Cobalt. He'd already ridden the kinks from the blue roan after saddling, but the stallion still danced a few steps before settling into a walk.

Cooter tossed one leg over the saddle and followed, leading the mule. "How long you reckon it'll take us to reach them mountains?"

"You'd know better than me. You've been this way before with the Pony Express."

"Well, that there's the truth, but it were some time ago, and I were a-ridin' like the devil himself were on my tail." He scratched above his ear. "Still and all, I guess maybe two full weeks, dependin' on the weather and all."

And traveling with a woman and a child. He and Cooter could cover fifty miles of flat ground in a day if they pushed it. But there was no way he'd subject Susannah and Bonnie to that kind of hard riding. He'd studied the map posted outside the fort's headquarters. Cooter was maybe a little optimistic with two weeks, but by three they should be there.

Finding Miss Bonnie's relatives, however, would have to wait until they got a cabin built. Hick squinted into the sky. It was already mid-summer, and winter came early in the mountains. The cabin had to come first.

"It's Peaches!" Bonnie's voice cut through Hick's musings.

The little girl barreled toward the mule. Hick raised a hand to warn her off, but the silly molly perked her ears and trotted toward the child, practically towing Rumpus behind. When she reached Bonnie, she dropped her head, long ears swaying, and closed her eyes as the girl stroked her face.

Didn't that just beat all? Where was the wild molly of half an hour past?

Susannah exited the shack and pulled the door shut behind her. She was... breathtaking. Wearing the old dress, hair covered with a straw hat pulled low to protect from the sun, but it didn't matter. She was still the best-looking woman in the fort. Maybe even the whole state of Nebraska.

And she was his.

Susannah had determined not to let things be awkward between her and Samuel. They'd made it through breakfast with the normal conversation, ninety percent supplied by Bonnie and Cooter. But as she'd packed their belongings for the last time, apprehension had settled in like it owned her.

Samuel tied his horses and came to help her with her saddlebag and sack. She kept hold of her satchel. She'd have to tell him of the money before long. After all, according to the law, it was his now. Strangely enough, that didn't create even a prick of resentment.

"I can add your sack to Trooper's pack saddle, but your mule will have to carry both your saddlebag and Miss Bonnie." He glanced at the now docile molly. "Doesn't look like she'll mind much."

"She's a good mule. She's never balked at what I've asked her to do." Why did that send his eyebrows to his hat line?

"If you say so, ma'—um. If you say so." He colored slightly behind the day-old stubble on his face, and she strode to Peaches's side before he could see her smile. She started to hoist the saddlebag, but stopped. "What is this?" She patted the saddle.

"You couldn't ride all the way to the mountains on that thing you called a saddle." He gestured to what looked like a brand-new saddle on Peaches. "The sutler had that one hanging on a wall. Seemed better for you, Miss Bonnie, and your mule."

He'd bought Peaches a new saddle? She blinked back moisture. How had she forgotten the kindness in this tall man beside her? "Thank you. We'll all be better off for it."

He lifted the saddlebag from her hands and secured it behind the saddle and over the crupper. Then he assisted her in mounting, settling Bonnie behind her on top of the saddlebag, which would act like an extra seat for her.

Susannah secured her satchel to the saddle's horn before hooking her knee over it. It wasn't a sidesaddle, but still an improvement over her rickety converted pack saddle. "I guess we're ready."

Samuel looked up at her for a long moment, then untied his horses and mounted. With a click to his horse, he led the way out of the fort. She nudged Peaches to follow, and Cooter brought up the rear.

It was finally happening. She was moving west. Maybe not to Oregon, but to the mountains. To a place where North and South had never collided.

Would it be far enough to leave the past behind?

They were five days on the trail when Hick spotted hoofprints in the mud. They'd been riding within sight of the river since they'd left Fort Kearny, but it was the first time they'd seen anything or anyone other than the train chugging on the other side.

He stopped Cobalt, the blue roan having settled into trail life with little fuss. But then, the stallion likely knew the territory. His band of mustangs had probably ranged here before they were captured.

The prints were of unshod horses. Not a cavalry patrol, that was certain. An itchy feeling crawled across the back of Hick's neck. He'd learned to heed such feelings during the war.

Cooter rode beside him, leaning half out of his saddle, scanning the ground. "Don't like the look of those."

"I don't either."

Cooter straightened. "I left the women behind to find a bush."

Hick nodded. That would buy them a few minutes. "Those prints are fresh."

"Uh-huh."

"Ride Rumpus forward, then back him off."

Cooter raised a brow at him, but urged his mustang into the mud, then backed him next to Hick again.

The prints Rumpus left were not as deep as the others. The younger man rubbed his jaw. "Ya thinkin' what I'm a-thinkin'?"

"There's no mustang out there heavier than you and Rumpus combined." Even though Cooter didn't weigh much more than a sack of cornmeal, his saddle and gear weighed nearly as much, doubling the load on Rumpus.

"What we goin' to tell the womenfolk?"

"Nothing." He scanned the land to the south, the direction the hoofprints followed. "Nothing until we have to."

"I figger they were through here hours ago, maybe dawn," Cooter said.

Hick nodded. Four or five hours maybe, not enough to fully dry the mud pushed up by the hooves. Not nearly enough for him to relax.

He'd known from the start he was likely to encounter Indians on his way west, but in the beginning, he hadn't figured on a woman and a child. Cool sweat broke across his brow. That old feeling of wanting to run goaded him. Cobalt danced beneath him, picking up on his restlessness. He needed to keep tighter control of himself.

Then Susannah brought her mule beside him, and his world evened out. That's the only way he could describe the sensation. The restlessness melted away in the reflection of her dark blue eyes.

"Thank you for the stop. We needed it." Her smile was relaxed, trusting, and entirely too captivating.

He needed to keep his mind on their surroundings. He needed to protect her. That was the mission he could not fail. Not this time.

"This is a natural ford." He pointed to the wide expanse of the river. The Indians would know the best places to cross. "Cooter and I are thinking about crossing to the north bank. We need to cross somewhere." But was the main Indian camp in that direction? Would they be riding into something worse?

"There's a better ford down the way." Cooter pointed west. "I remember it." The look he shot Hick said there was more to his comment, but he wouldn't voice it in front of Susannah and Bonnie. Hick would have to trust him.

For that matter, Hick would have to trust himself.

They usually stripped the tack off the horses and Peaches when they stopped for a rest and meal at noon. Susannah was untying the straps of her saddlebag when Samuel put his hand over hers, stopping her.

"Leave them on today."

Behind him, Trooper and Cobalt still carried their saddles, even though both were hobbled and grazing.

"What happened?" She kept her voice low, although Bonnie had already headed for the riverbank.

"Nothing. But it's best we stay prepared to ride."

Samuel dropped his hand, but she took hold of his sleeve before he could turn away. "Tell me." She removed her hat so she could see his face without the brim in her way.

The sigh he released confirmed her suspicion. Something had changed. "It might be nothing."

"Or it might not." She tugged on his sleeve. "I'm not a child, Samuel. I prefer to know what's happening."

He rubbed the back of his neck, then faced her fully. "Those hoof-prints by the crossing a ways back, they were probably Indians."

Oh. She'd seen them, of course, but had assumed they'd been from a wild herd. Wild animals used the natural fords of the river just like... Indians.

"We'll ford the river after our break and continue on the other side. With any luck, we'll reach the end of the railroad tracks in two or three more days."

"Another Hell on Wheels town." She'd seen enough of the first such town they'd passed to know she didn't wish to stay in there. And that one had been half deserted since most of the town had been disassembled and moved farther down the newly laid tracks.

"We won't stay there, but maybe we can pick up a few more supplies."

"At outrageous costs." It was time to tell him. She searched for the right words. "Samuel."

His hands cupped her elbows, concern settling on his brow. "What is it?"

"I should have told you before, but there never seemed to be the right time."

That brought a twitch to his lips. "We aren't very well acquainted with right times, are we?"

"No. We haven't been." She answered his smile. "But this is important. You see, I sold everything but Peaches before I left Missouri."

"If you need anything, I'll try to find it in the rail town. There isn't likely to be more than a trading post for supplies once we cross over into Wyoming Territory."

"It's not that, it's that I have money."

He jerked his head back a fraction, eyes intent on her face.

"Legally, it's yours now. I should have told you sooner." She nodded toward her saddlebag behind Peaches's new saddle. "It's in my satchel, sewn into an old petticoat."

Understanding relaxed the lines around his eyes. "That's why you were so worried about your belongings the night we met."

"The night you rescued me, you mean. Yes. There is a considerable sum. Enough to set me up in Oregon."

The tenseness returned twofold, even his fingers at her elbows seemed to radiate it. Or maybe it was wariness?

"Is that what you still wish? To continue on to Oregon?"

She shook her head. "That dream was mine with Abel. I would have done my best to continue on without him, to fulfill that dream, but now..." She straightened the hem of the vest he'd worn since they started on the trail, avoiding his intense hazel eyes. "Now there is you and me."

A *whoosh* of breath reached her before his lips pressed against her forehead. She leaned into the pressure.

They hadn't kissed since their walk the evening of their wedding. Susannah had thought about it—more than once—but there was no privacy with Cooter and Bonnie along. Nothing to seclude them in the miles of flat prairie. And Samuel's attention had been needed elsewhere.

There was always the possibility of Indians.

Goosebumps rose on her arms, but she stepped into Samuel's embrace, shielded from the others by the bulk of Peaches. With the smooth leather of his vest beneath her cheek, the scents of horses and dust and sunshine clinging to him, life seemed loaded with possibilities.

It was hard to imagine anything could harm her with him nearby.

CHAPTER 30

H ELL ON WHEELS WAS an apt name for the town they rode into. Susannah shivered as a flash of lightning zigzagged across the sky behind the tents, some with false wooden fronts, that lined the single long street. Noise billowed above the roll of distant thunder from several establishments that were doing a brisk business in the evening.

Saloons, no doubt.

Samuel leaned toward her while keeping Cobalt under control. The stallion fretted about the coming storm—or perhaps about the town. "I'll try to find us a room for the night. Someplace that'll stay at least mostly dry."

"Samuel, look." Susannah pointed to the far end of the street. A crude cross rose in the gathering darkness. A church?

"It's worth a try." He tilted his hat against the rain and urged his horse forward.

Fat raindrops soaked them as they approached the wood-and-canvas structure attached to the cross.

"That do look like a sanctuary to me." Cooter hopped off Rumpus and banged on the wooden door. Nobody answered. He tried the doorknob, and it turned. With a glance back at Susannah and Samuel, he pushed it open.

The rain was pelting them now. Susannah gave Bonnie her arm and swung the girl to the ground. "Go with Cooter." The girl ran as Susannah dismounted.

"You too. I'll strip the horses and find a place to tie them." Samuel had to raise his voice above the thunder rumbling overhead.

Cooter and Bonnie disappeared into the building as a stranger appeared in the doorway.

"I'm sorry if we're intruding," Susannah said. "We're looking for a place to stay dry for the night."

"This is the best place." He stood aside and let her pass. "I'll help your man."

Her man. The words warmed something inside her, but she didn't have time to dwell on it.

"Bonnie?"

"Over here." The little girl popped up from behind a piano. How on earth had they managed to get a piano clear out here? "Listen." She disappeared behind the instrument.

Susannah started to rebuke her for touching it when music filled the church. Beautiful music.

Samuel, Cooter, and the man from the church dumped their belongings in a pile inside the door, faces wet and eyes alight with wonder.

Susannah hadn't known either, but it was obvious that Bonnie was incredibly gifted.

Samuel and Cooter disappeared again, then returned moments later, wetter than ever. The man from the church was sitting in a chair by the doorway, head back and eyes closed. Praying? Maybe enjoying the wealth of sound Bonnie coaxed from the ancient instrument in need of a good waxing and tuning.

Susannah hadn't moved, and Samuel came to her side, one arm slipping across her back as if it were the most natural movement in the world. She leaned against him—an equally natural reaction—until the sound died away.

Bonnie's freckled face appeared from behind the piano, curly hair wayward from the rain and wind, her bonnet trailing by its strings down her back. "They have a piano."

"Indeed, we do." The man slapped his thighs and stood. "But no one who can play it so beautifully as you just did, young lady."

Bonnie came around the instrument and, much to Susannah's surprise, she curtsied.

"Thank you, sir."

"Folks call me Pastor Mark, and this"—he opened his arms taking in their surroundings—"is my humble church."

The canvas above them billowed and snapped with the wind, the torrent of rain making it hard to hear the man's words. But it was dry and safe.

"The horses and Peaches?" she half-shouted to Samuel.

"In a shed behind the church, thanks to Pastor Mark." He tipped his head toward the other man.

Pastor Mark waved off the thanks. "You are in need, and the church can supply. Is that not what the church is for? Meeting the needs of the flock?"

That was what it should be for, but Susannah knew it wasn't always the case. The church that she'd grown up attending had backed the Confederacy and its insistence on slavery. Daddy had struggled with that, and their attendance had declined until, after Mama died, they'd stopped going altogether. She wasn't sure she was part of any flock anymore.

"We are indebted, nonetheless." Samuel removed his hat and shook the rain from it. "Is there a hotel among the businesses where we might find a room for the night?"

Pastor Mark glanced at Bonnie, then back to Samuel, shaking his head. "Not a place you'd want to be in."

Susannah rubbed her hands up and down her arms, chilled in spite of the humidity under the canvas. She didn't need to be told what sort of establishments populated the town. Saloons and brothels were the booming businesses of any Hell on Wheels. But this one also had a church, and for that, she was grateful. Maybe that gratitude means she still belonged to the flock after all.

"You are welcome to sleep in here. Services won't start until ten o'clock tomorrow. And even then, you can leave your things in a corner. It's not like the place fills up." He beamed at them. "You'll join us, of course?"

Samuel cleared his throat.

"We'd like that just fine." Cooter stuck his hand out to Pastor Mark. "I'm Cooter, and this here is Mr. and Mrs. Hickman. That little girl what played such purdy music is Miss Bonnie."

"Perhaps, Miss Bonnie, you'd be willing to play for us tomorrow during the service?" the pastor asked.

She clasped her hands in front of her and faced Susannah. "May I wear my new dress?"

"Of course you may." Anything to help keep that look of delight on the young girl's face.

Samuel shifted beside Susannah. He hadn't said anything, but she sensed that he wasn't pleased by the turn of events.

"We can afford a day of rest, can't we, Samuel?" she asked.

The eyes that met hers lacked any of the delight of Bonnie's or the glowing approval of Cooter's.

Samuel's eyes were... haunted.

Hick dumped the bedrolls on the wooden platform that held the piano and pulpit. It was large enough for the four of them, and dry. He'd moved their saddles and provisions to the wooden benches, water having seeped in around the canvas sides into the dirt floor.

Pastor Mark, it turned out, had a small tent room off the back of the church. He'd bid them good night and retired there shortly after the worst of the storm blew over.

"Pastor Mark is awfully nice." Miss Bonnie smoothed out her bedroll.

"He's a man of God, Miss Bonnie." Cooter sat cross-legged in the middle of his bedding. "Like my grandpappy. Men of God has a callin' to help them what's in need."

The little girl wrinkled her nose for a moment. "Are we needy?"

Susannah chuckled—a sound Hick was growing very fond of. "We needed a dry place to sleep. I suppose that makes us needy for the night."

Miss Bonnie's yawn was followed by a grin. "And I get to play the piano again tomorrow."

"That were some purdy music," Cooter said. "Who learned ya to do that?"

The grin slipped from Bonnie's face. "Ma played. I watched her and learned from as early as I can remember." Her chin wobbled. "We couldn't bring our piano with us in the wagon. Ma cried over that."

Susannah held out her arms, and the little girl sank into them.

The sight brought a knot to Hick's throat. He could picture a day in the future when Susannah offered another child comfort. Their child.

But first, they needed to get to Wyoming and get a cabin built. Not waste a day attending church services.

He scratched the days-old growth on his cheek. It wasn't the wasted day that was bothering him, and he knew it. It was the church part. Hick had been raised going to church every Sunday, sitting in the pew between his youngest sister and... Denny. He hadn't been in a church since his brother had died in his arms. He didn't deserve to be.

God may forgive the sins of some, but Hick knew the Bible well enough to know what had happened to Cain after he'd killed his brother, Abel.

As sure as if he'd pulled the trigger, Hick had killed Denny.

He'd been the one to talk Denny into joining the war. He'd been the one to volunteer for the scouting duty that day. He'd done nothing to discourage Denny from following him.

Denny had always followed him. Born eleven months after Hick, Denny and he had grown up more like twins than just brothers. They even seemed to know what the other was thinking. And they always had each other's backs.

Until that day.

Susannah touched his arm, and he jumped.

"What is it?" she whispered.

Miss Bonnie was asleep against her. Cooter was wrapped in his blankets, back turned to them. How long had Hick been lost in his thoughts?

"Memories." His voice was gruff, and he tried to smile. "Nothing to worry about."

She shifted Miss Bonnie onto her blankets and covered the child, then returned to his side.

"Tell me." Her voice was low and musical, not unlike the piano. "I want to know. I want to understand."

"You couldn't understand." He didn't want her to. Didn't want to see the condemnation or, even worse, the pity in her eyes.

"Does it have to do with Denny?"

If she'd punched him in the gut, she couldn't have surprised him more. He had to force himself to draw in a breath. Force himself to remain seated. Force himself to look at her and not hide his face.

"What do you know about Denny?"

"You called out for him when you were ill." Compassion filled her voice. "You said you couldn't save him. You worried about your mother as well." She cocked her head. "Was Denny your brother?"

He closed his eyes and forced in another breath, managing to nod in response.

Her arms came around him, but he couldn't move, couldn't put his arms around her in return. Couldn't face her. "I got him killed." The words escaped before he could stop them.

"He died in the war, Samuel."

"He went to war because of me."

She touched his cheek, hand smooth and gentle yet also strong and sure. "My brothers all went to war. Two of them died, one of them went missing. That's the way with war."

"But my brother came with *me*, left because of *me*."

"That's what brothers do. All three of mine saddled their horses and rode away together. Daddy and Mama and I watched and waved as they left. We never saw any of them again." Sadness laced her voice, but it didn't seem to crush her as it did him. After all, she hadn't sent her brothers into battle.

"I volunteered for a scouting assignment. I knew it was risky. Denny volunteered beside me. I should have told him to stay behind."

"Would he have, if you'd told him?" Distant lightning illuminated the tent for a moment, her face turned toward him. "Was he so biddable?"

Hick snorted. "Denny was many things, but not biddable."

"Were you his senior officer?"

"Nope, we were both cavalry troopers. I wasn't promoted until after."

"Then you couldn't have stopped him from volunteering, even if you'd wanted to."

"But..."

She was right. But she didn't know everything. "I'd promised Ma I'd take care of him. She said it was my responsibility since I'd talked him into joining."

"That wasn't fair of her, Samuel." She traced his chin with the tips of her fingers. "I imagine she spoke out of grief, having two of her boys heading to war, but it still wasn't fair to make you promise that. No one has the power to protect another when the bullets start flying. Everyone just... does their best."

His best hadn't been good enough, but Susannah's words comforted him. He wanted them to be true.

Bonnie's music and the voices around Susannah filled the tent church and soothed her heart. It still ached for Samuel and his scars from the war, scars he carried inside on his soul. He fidgeted next to her on the bench. It didn't take divine intervention to know that he'd rather be anywhere else. She was proud of him. In spite of his obvious discomfort, he was staying for Bonnie.

Her husband truly was a kind man.

The door on the church's wooden false front had been left open. Pastor Mark said he wanted the music to pour into the street. It must have worked on someone, because a man entered as the small congregation finished the second hymn. He dragged off a battered hat, exposing dark wavy hair badly in need of a barber, as did the tangled bush of a beard that hid the lower half of his face. His clothing hung on him like sheets on a line. He was beyond lean and approaching emaciated.

He reminded Susannah of Abel when she'd first seen him in the temporary prison at Blackshear.

Pastor Mark invited them all to be seated, then started his sermon. It was a simple one, easy to follow, but Susannah kept glancing at the man who had taken a seat on the bench across the aisle. He kept his head bowed the entire time, elbows on his knees, hat dangling above his worn boots.

"What is it?" Samuel's breath grazed her ear.

"That man." She tipped her head slightly. "He reminds me of someone." Abel, but not exactly. It was something else. Something familiar in a different way.

Pastor Mark wrapped up his sermon and encouraged them all to stand and join him in another hymn, explaining that they should enjoy Bonnie's playing as she was only passing through. He asked her to play "Amazing Grace."

The sweet notes filled the tent structure again, but when the voices lifted the words, Susannah grasped Samuel's arm for support.

She knew that voice.

Letting go of Samuel's arm and ignoring the bafflement on his face, she stepped into the aisle. The man on the other side saw her then, recognition clear in his dark blue eyes. Eyes so like hers.

"Jesse?" She breathed the name more than said it, and he couldn't have heard her above the singing, but he dropped his chin and stared at the dirt floor.

Samuel was so close behind her the heat of his body soaked through her clothing. "Who is this man?"

She fumbled for Samuel's hand, holding tightly, anchoring herself in case this was all a cruel mistake. "Jesse? Is it really you?"

He didn't raise his face. "It's good to see you, Susannah."

With a soft cry, she dropped Samuel's hand and threw her arms around her brother.

CHAPTER 31

H E REEKED OF ALCOHOL, tobacco, sweat, and other things Hick's wife shouldn't be hugging. But Hick could only stand and watch as she did, tears flowing, sobbing into the nasty mess of a man.

She'd called him Jesse, the name of her missing brother.

So they weren't all dead, but this one didn't look too much alive. His grubby hands finally raised and patted Susannah on the back.

Hick fought the urge to tear them away from her.

Pastor Mark appeared at his side, and Hick looked around. Everyone was staring at them. At Susannah and her brother, at least.

Cooter wore his ear-to-ear grin.

Miss Bonnie had a shy smile but hung behind Cooter.

When had the music stopped?

"Seems we have a family reunion here." The pastor held up his hands. "What a glorious day."

That was one way to look at it.

Cooter's elbow connected with his ribs. "Ain't that somethin'? Her brother done showin' up right here in the Lord's house." He shook his head. "I'd call that a miracle."

A miracle? The bedraggled and smelly man in front of Susannah couldn't resemble something supernatural any less if he tried. Nope, that man was going to be trouble. He looked like he could barely stand on his own two feet.

The weight of another person added to those Hick was responsible for smacked against the back of his knees. He retreated and sank to the bench they'd shared during the service. Miss Bonnie came to his side, pressing close. She wasn't sure of the person across the aisle either.

Smart girl.

The clamor settled down, and the congregation left for places un-known. Even Pastor Mark had disappeared. Susannah came to Hick and took his hand. "Come meet my brother." Her eyes were awash in a stormy blue of emotions.

He stood, towering over the brother, who wasn't much taller than Susannah.

"This is Jesse, my middle brother." To him, she said, "And this is Samuel, my husband."

Was it just wishful thinking on his part, or did her voice carry a note of pride in that last statement? Hick offered his hand. "Most folks call me Hick."

Jesse's grip was surprisingly firm as he met Hick's eyes. "Pleasure to meet you. My sister is obviously well cared for."

She was beautiful in the dress she'd bought for their wedding, and she did look the picture of health. None of that had anything to do with Hick, but he nodded at the compliment anyway.

"Are you working on the railroad?" Hick might as well get to the heart of the matter. He had a feeling there were secrets—most likely unpleasant—to be uncovered.

Jesse glanced toward the door as if looking for an escape. "No. Just drifted in."

"But you're here. You're alive." Susannah flashed a brilliant smile. "I can't tell you how much that means to me."

If it meant that much to his wife, it meant Hick was going to have to get involved. Did she have any idea what Jesse's condition and his words meant? Probably not. But Hick did.

And he didn't like it.

Jesse scratched at his beard. "How are Mama and Daddy? And Philip?"

Susannah's face fell. The joy drained from her like water from a tipped barrel. "You don't know?"

Her brother shook his head. "After John fell at Manassas, I..." An-other glance toward the door.

The hair along the back of Hick's neck stood at attention.

"They are all gone, Jesse."

He bowed his head, one hand covering his eyes, shoulders slumped. "Even Mama?"

"She never recovered from John's death. Daddy stayed with us until she passed, then he joined the war."

Jesse's head whipped up. "He was a doctor. How could he have been killed?" Anger laced the words.

"Not in battle. It was dysentery." She shrugged. "Maybe with the work and the grief and all, he just didn't have enough left to fight it off."

"Philip?"

"Died in battle, we were told."

Jesse dropped to the bench behind him then, grabbed both sides of his hair and rocked front to back, not making a sound.

For the first time, Hick was moved. He'd seen the same in others who had fought in the war. A mental struggle to accept the unacceptable that turned physical. He'd been there himself a few times.

He knew a broken man when he saw one.

The question remained, however. What had caused Jesse to break? How far down into that pit had he slid? And was it Hick's responsibility to try and pull him out?

One look at his wife's face told him the answer to the last question.

Susannah knelt by the fire and stirred the pot of beans and salt pork. Samuel had gone with Jesse and Cooter to the river to bathe. Jesse certainly needed it. Her brother's condition was not good, though at least cleanliness was easy enough to come by with the river just a brisk walk away.

But the rest of it?

She stopped stirring when beans splashed over onto the coals. The stench of burning beans filling the air behind the church tent. Pastor Mark had given his blessing for them to stay another night. But come morning, they would leave Hell on Wheels, the last bastion of civilization before the mountains.

Would Jesse ride with them?

Did he even own a horse?

He'd wolfed down the leftover biscuits and bacon she'd set aside for their lunch like he hadn't seen food in days. As skinny as he was, that might be closer to the mark than was comfortable.

She hadn't known what to do when he'd started rocking back and forth, but Samuel had stepped in and taken over, as if he'd done it before. He'd ordered her to make coffee—strong coffee—and put something together to eat. Then he'd gotten Jesse back on his feet and had taken him outside. She had no idea what passed between them, but both seemed ill at ease during their sparse meal. They'd left for the river shortly after.

"Mrs. Hick?" Bonnie had wiped the last of the plates and cups dry. "Yes?"

"Is your brother a nice man?"

Susannah had to force herself not to respond harshly. After all, Bonnie was just a child, and Jesse was... not the brother Susannah remembered. He'd been barely grown when he and the others had ridden away to war, just turned nineteen. He'd been the prankster of the trio, the witty one, the brother who could always make her laugh.

"He was. He has obviously been through some difficult times. I barely recognized him." She hadn't really, not until he sang. He was the only one of the bunch of them who could carry a tune. Mama had loved to hear Jesse sing. "I'm sure he's still nice, but it may take a while before he feels like himself again." She held out her arms and hugged the girl when she pressed close. "He just learned that his daddy and mama and brother are dead."

Bonnie nodded against her shoulder. "I remember what that feels like." Then she lifted her head and gazed at Susannah with sad eyes. "Does this mean you aren't an orphan like me anymore?"

Oh, the poor dear. She took the little girl by the shoulders and looked her square in the eye. "I don't think either of us is an orphan anymore."

"You don't?"

"I don't. After all, we have both Mr. Hickman and Mr. Cooter, don't we?"

She nodded, her curls bouncing with the motion.

"Well, then. We aren't alone. We might be a collection of strangers who met along the trail, but if we want, we can be a family."

That earned Susannah a grin wide enough to expose the fresh gap where a tooth had fallen out the night before.

The scuff of boots against the ground gave warning someone was coming around the church. Susannah rose and tucked Bonnie behind her until the person came into view.

She almost didn't recognize Jesse. Clean-shaven and wearing a new suit of clothes, her brother still didn't much resemble the young man who'd ridden away from Blackshear. There were lines on his face too deep for his age, and a jagged scar traced from in front of his right ear to his jaw below the corner of his mouth.

"Jesse." Her heart pinched at the hesitancy on his face. "Oh, Jesse." She rushed to him and hugged him tight.

This time, his arms came around her. This time, he spoke against her hair. "Sorry for the face, but I can't do anything about that."

She pushed back and cupped his cheeks with her palms. "You're alive, brother, and that's all I care about."

He coughed, looked toward Bonnie, who'd stayed by the fire, then back at her. "Your husband says I should tell you some things."

The lack of emotion in his voice left a sinking feeling inside her. "Bonnie." Susannah turned and force a smile for the child. "Why don't you play the piano for a little while? It may be your last chance."

The girl nodded and slipped through the open back corner of the church tent. In moments, the music reached them. She'd chosen to play a somber tune, an old hymn Susannah couldn't remember the words to, but it fit the mood there beside her brother.

Susannah took a deep breath and waited, braced for whatever he had to say.

"I'm a deserter, Susannah." His words were low, his face turned aside.

"Oh, Jesse." She touched his arm. He flinched, but she didn't let go. "The war was a mistake. A terrible, wasteful mistake. I'm glad you're alive and here with me." He didn't respond, so she gave his arm a shake. "Do you hear me? I don't care why you're here. I'm just glad you are."

"It's not that easy, sister." He finally dragged his eyes back to her. "I watched John fall. He was a long way down the line from me, but I saw it." He shook his head. "I couldn't get to him. I couldn't break the line. I couldn't do... anything." He looked skyward, blinking furiously, then back at her. "I couldn't even fire my gun." Failure was written across his face. "I was useless."

"I don't care." She raised her chin. "I don't. You're here, and that's all that matters to me."

"Maybe. Now. But I snuck away in the night after that battle. I stole a set of clothes off a wash line several days later. I headed west and changed my name. Jesse Jessup no longer exists."

"I'll call you whatever you want me to, just..." She bit back a sob. "Just don't disappear again."

"There's more."

She wasn't sure she could take more.

He wiped the back of a shaking hand across his mouth. "I'm a drunk, Susannah. A worthless drunk." He held his hands out. "I need a drink. I need it, or I can't stop the shakes."

Her world tilted for a moment, then she planted her feet and wagged her finger under his nose. "You may not use the name Jessup anymore, Jesse, but you're still a Jessup at heart. It's a battle to win over liquor, but you can do it." She let her hand fall to her side. "If you want to."

He shook his head again.

"Then why were you in church this morning?"

"I'll trade you two horses, your choice from the bunch, for that blue roan stallion you rode in on." The livery stable owner leaned to one side and spit.

No surprise that a horseman would have noted Cobalt. Hick gritted his teeth. It wasn't that he wouldn't give up the horse for Susannah. If it meant her life, he'd do it in a heartbeat. But they needed the stallion to set up a horse ranch. Cobalt was more than just a horse—he was their future.

Susannah's brother, on the other hand, was a liability. A huge liability. A deserter. Hick had no illusions that the man could get himself straightened out. He'd known more than one drunk in the army. Men who turned to a bottle for their courage.

Jesse hadn't even managed that. He'd turned coward and run. The wretch had flat out said he'd been a drunken bum ever since, working when he needed money, hopping rides on the trains, and sleeping off hangovers in local jails.

Still, he hadn't tried to sugarcoat things when Hick had asked him straight out for his story. Hick got the impression it was the first time he'd dumped his guts about his past since the battle at Bull Run—Manassas as the Southerners called it. But at least he'd come clean.

Now Jesse needed a horse if he was going to leave with them in the morning, and Susannah wasn't likely to leave without him.

Deep down, Hick understood. He'd give anything—do anything—to have Denny back. His wife had her brother again. Maybe a small part of Hick was jealous. It wasn't easy to admit it to himself, but there it was.

"How much for the gray?" Hick pointed to a mare with a silver-gray coat and almost white mane and tail, its head hanging to its knees. She wasn't very big, but neither was Jesse. The mare was a well-built little mustang. If she had half the heart of Cooter's Rumpus, she'd be a nice start to his herd.

The man rubbed his chin and named an overinflated price. Hick offered him half. They haggled a bit, but the truth was, he had the only horses for sale in Hell on Wheels, and they both knew it. Hick passed over more money than he wanted to and got a sorry excuse for a saddle, a blanket, and bridle added to the deal.

Hick led the gray around the church.

"Well, lookee there." Cooter popped to his feet. "Ain't that a sweet little mustang."

"She might be." He handed the reins to Cooter. "You want to see how she moves? She's a bit short for me." He feared his boot toes would knock into the backs of her knees.

Cooter snugged the saddle's cinch and swung aboard. The mustang squealed, pitched a couple of times, and then leveled out. She knew what to do when Cooter asked, but it was obvious she hadn't been ridden much.

Hick shot a glance at Jesse. "You can ride, can't you?" Maybe he should have asked that before he bought the horse, but what was done was done.

"I can ride." Resentment colored the words.

"Jesse was always a fine rider." Susannah was quick to come to his defense.

Hick would have to tread carefully. The last thing he wanted was to get his wife's back up. When he looked at Jesse, he needed to think of Denny. It galled him, of course, but Susannah saw him the same way Hick would have seen Denny. He needed to remember that. He jerked his head toward the mustang. "Get acquainted with her. She'll be your mount for the next few weeks."

Jesse rose and took the animal from Cooter, but he didn't mount.

Susannah touched Hick's arm. "Thank you." Respect, appreciation, or whatever it was shining in her eyes fired up Hick's insides.

"There wasn't much to choose from, but I think the mare will do."

"She's a sweet-looking mare." Susannah cast a glance at the horse and her brother.

"Sweet?" He grinned at her. "Don't be saddling her with any silly names. She's the start of our herd. She and Cobalt are our future."

Susannah plopped her hands on her hips and cocked her head. "This is about Peaches, isn't it? What do you have against my mule and her name?"

He snorted. "That mule hates me."

Susannah giggled. "She knows you don't like her. If you'd say her name and treat her like a lady, she'd act like one." Then she turned back to the gray mare. "She's the color of cloudy sky. Let's name her Sky."

That was a fitting name, much better than Peaches. "Sky she is."

"Dinner is nearly finished. Why don't you see to the animals while I get the dumplings made?"

He walked to where Jesse still stroked the mare's face, speaking in a low voice. The mare's ears twitched at the sounds, but she stood relaxed, one hip sagged. "Susannah says her name is Sky."

"It suits her."

"Bring her around with the others. We'll get them fed and then have dinner."

They led the horses to the water trough near the church two at a time, then moved the picket line to where they could reach more grass. The mule pinned her ears at the mare, and they had to make room at the other end of the line for Sky, tying her next to old Trooper. He didn't much care who stood beside him. His years in the cavalry had seen to that.

"Let's get our dinner," Hick said.

"Hick?" Jesse stopped before they reached the back of the church.

"Yeah?"

"I won't let you down." He rubbed shaking hands against his trousers. "I'll make her proud of me."

"It'll be rough for a few days—a couple of weeks—but then it'll get better."

"I know."

Hick turned to face him fully. "Do you? Have you seen anyone go through it?"

Jesse turned his face away. "Once. He didn't make it, though."

"Went back to drinking?"

"Shot himself in the head."

Anger seeped into Hick's voice, but he couldn't stop it. "Don't do that. Don't even think about doing that." He poked Jesse in the chest with his finger—hard enough to move the man back a step. "It'd kill her if you did."

Eyes far too much like Susannah's met his, understanding clear in their depths. "I know. I think that's what will get me through." He raised shaking hands. "I want a drink so bad I can barely think, but as long as I can see her..."

Hick took a step closer. "If you need more than that, remember this. If you hurt my wife in any way, any way at all, you'll have me to answer to."

Jesse nodded, still looking Hick square in the eyes. "Even if you are a Yankee, I'm glad my sister married a man like you."

That sucked the wind from Hick's lungs. After all...

Who was he to be held up as some sort of virtuous man?

CHAPTER 32

S USANNAH YAWNED THEN CAUGHT her balance when Peaches took an awkward step.

"Are you all right, Mrs. Hick?"

"I am." She patted Bonnie's hand, holding tightly to the back of the saddle. "I'm just tired."

The little girl rested her head between Susannah's shoulders. "Me too."

They'd been on the trail for six days. They were truly alone. Even the train hadn't reached this far west. Jesse and Cooter stayed one on each side of Peaches most of the time, while Samuel scouted ahead on Cobalt, leaving Jesse to lead Trooper, who carried the bulk of their worldly possessions.

But not the two bottles of whiskey Samuel had insisted they bring along. She'd argued with him over that, a moment she didn't like to remember. Until then, they'd had no harsh words between them since the wedding. She thought the whiskey too great a risk to Jesse, of course. Samuel had remained steadfast that they—or the horses—might require it to prevent infection from wounds.

He was right, of course. And he never let those bottles out of his reach, even sleeping with his saddlebag as his pillow.

Jesse, for his part, was beginning to improve. He was able to keep down his food. In the early days of withdrawal, she had feared he might starve before he could overcome the alcohol. He rode easily in the saddle, no longer hunched over. He glanced at her and nodded, as if he'd read her thoughts. They hadn't spoken of his addiction again, there wasn't any need to, but that didn't stop her from worrying.

While assisting Daddy all those years, she'd seen more than one drunk die a horrible death. Daddy said their livers gave out, poisoned by the alcohol. She'd been distressed when the patients would drink right in front of Daddy almost while drawing their last breaths. But he'd explained that stopping wouldn't save them at that point, and it dulled the pain.

Watching Jesse's pain the past week had illustrated what he'd meant.

Pride in her brother filled her with hope. He may have deserted, but that was years ago, while he was still so young. He had a whole new life ahead of him. A sober life in a new place, far away from those who would condemn him. He was Jesse Jessup once again. Not the carefree, fun-loving youth from Blackshear, but at least he was owning his real name.

It was a good start.

And just that morning, Samuel had handed him a pistol. Susannah wasn't sure what had passed between the two men, but the significance of the moment hadn't been lost on her. Perhaps it was acknowledging the progress Jesse had made that Samuel trusted him with the gun.

Perhaps it had more to do with the tracks they'd crossed shortly after breaking camp that morning. Unshod horse prints. Wild horses? Or Indians?

Cooter was riding easy in his saddle, too, but with his rifle out of its scabbard and resting across his thighs, eyes scanning the countryside.

A puff of dust approached them from the northwest. Not enough dust for more than one rider. Susannah had learned to spot Samuel's return by those puffs of dust.

Cooter straightened. "Whoa." He pulled Rumpus to a halt.

Susannah stopped Peaches.

"He's coming in fast." Jesse tied Trooper's lead rope to the horn of his saddle, then slipped the pistol from his belt.

Susannah twisted to see Bonnie. "Hold on tight if we have to gallop. Hold onto me, not the saddle."

The little girl nodded, eyes round and mouth tight.

Susannah took the reins in both hands and waited.

Cobalt came to a sliding stop in front of them, gave a head-tossing snort, and then wheeled in a tight circle.

"Indians, maybe a dozen of them, heading our way." Samuel pointed north. "There's a shallow ravine that way with a handful of trees. I think we can make it, but they'll see our dust." His eyes met Susannah's, a fire of hazel determination in their depths.

Samuel continued, "Jesse, take my rifle and give me the Colt. Cooter, hand Susannah your rifle and draw your pistol." They exchanged weapons. "Jesse, Susannah, run north and you'll see the trees—they'll look like bushes—slightly to the west. Go as fast as that molly will run." He paused a heartbeat. "Better ride astride for this, Susannah. Cooter and I will cover your backs. Once you're in the ravine, cover us with those long guns."

Susannah managed to hike her skirts and get her right leg over the saddle horn, fumbling her foot into the stirrup.

Samuel looked them over one last time. "Everyone ready?" At their nods, he said, "Then ride!"

"Hold on, Bonnie." Susannah thumped her heels into Peaches's sides as Jesse did the same with Sky. The mustang sprang forward, Trooper on its heels, and Peaches responded to the challenge.

Bonnie clung like a cocklebur, her hands knotted together in front of Susannah's waist.

Peaches was a steady and comfortable ride at a walk and trot, even at a canter, but at a full gallop, Susannah had to concentrate to keep her seat centered and balanced while holding the rifle in one hand. That concentration served her well until shouts and screeches from behind reached them. She didn't have to urge any more speed from Peaches. The mule found a bit more on her own.

Where were Samuel and Cooter?

Susannah couldn't look back. Keeping her balance was challenging enough, but to twist might dislodge Bonnie. "Why aren't they shooting?" she yelled at Jesse who stayed at her side even though the mustang could have outpaced her mule.

"They won't waste bullets. They won't shoot until they know they can hit something."

Bullets—their supply was in the packs carried by Trooper.

"This way." Jesse veered the mustang to the left.

Susannah saw it then, the tops of trees that looked like bushes growing from the flat prairie. She urged Peaches on. The mule had her long ears pinned flat against her neck and was giving it all she had. Hopefully it would be enough.

A pistol shot rang out. Was it Samuel? Cooter? Or one of those chasing them?

The rim of the ravine was in sight, a few large rocks marking its border. Jesse pointed to the right and took the lead. Susannah followed, trusting him to find a way down that the horses and mule could handle.

Another pistol shot rang out, then a third, a fourth. Did the men have any bullets to reload? Fear—already clogging her throat—spiked all the way to her toes. And then Jesse disappeared over the edge of the ravine. He hadn't slowed down, so she didn't either.

"Lean back, Bonnie. Hang on."

Peaches's front end dropped out from under her. Susannah squeezed her knees as tightly as she could and took the rest of her body's weight on the stirrups, glad she'd tossed modesty aside for safety's sake.

Bonnie shrieked but held fast. Stones and dirt slipped and slid beneath the mule's hooves and rump as she skidded to the bottom of the ravine.

Jesse was already out of his saddle and scrambling to the top with his rifle. "Stay below with the horses," he yelled, "but have your rifle ready."

"Stay on Peaches." Susannah managed to get her leg over the molly's neck, then slid awkwardly off the animal, ignoring the tearing of her skirt in the process.

Bonnie hopped into the saddle and took the reins.

"Good girl." Susannah propped the rifle against a tree and tied the horses. It wouldn't do to have them spook and run off. She grabbed the rifle again just as Rumpus came sliding down the same path they'd taken into the ravine.

The fear clogging Susannah's throat threatened to choke her.

Where was Samuel?

The Indians weren't shooting their guns, which told Hick that they were short on ammunition, but as they charged closer, an arrow winged past his shoulder. He'd hung back, giving the others time to make it to the ravine. Once they were there, he was fairly certain they could hold off the attack. High ground was always his choice over a ravine, but on the prairie, high ground was hard to come by.

Another arrow cut the air far too close to Hick's elbow, but Cooter was already over the rim of the ravine, so Hick gave Cobalt one last kick. The mustang leveled out and sprang over the edge. Hick had a moment to adjust his weight, and then the horse's hooves were scrambling for purchase among the loose stones. They slipped and slid until they slammed into the ravine floor.

Susannah was beside him before the horse came to a full stop, thrusting Cooter's rifle into his hands. "Take it. I have my pistol." She grabbed the stallion's reins.

Hick sprinted to Trooper and grabbed a box of rifle cartridges and a box of pistol bullets from the pack, thankful that he always stored them within easy reach.

Susannah clutched the Colt Dragoon from her saddlebag and stood next to Bonnie, who was astride on the mule.

Yells and screams from above were peppered with shots. Rifle shots. The Indians were firing. Cooter's pistol spit back at them. Where was the report from Jesse's rifle? What was the man doing?

Anger flared as Hick scrambled to the rim of the ravine. Cooter was scrunched behind one of the largest rocks, picking his target.

The Indians parted into two groups and circled back.

Cooter fired off another shot. An Indian hunched forward on his horse, grabbed his arm, and sped away. Cooter grinned at Hick.

Hick tossed him a box of bullets for the pistol. "Where's Jesse?" So help him, if that man had deserted again...

Cooter pointed to the right, where Jesse was positioned behind the thickest tree trunk, waiting.

Waiting for what?

Another round of yells signaled the Indians' return.

Hick thumbed bullets into his Colt .45 and jammed it into his holster then crouched behind a rock not nearly big enough to hide all of him. He dropped his legs back into the ravine, his hips on the rim. It wasn't ideal, he'd have to shoot up at an angle, but at least he was covered. He rested the Spencer's barrel on the rock.

The Indians charged at a full gallop, some of them lying sideways along their horses, making them almost impossible targets. Hick ground his teeth together and aimed, waiting for them to get close enough that he couldn't miss.

Boom!

The rifle report caught Hick by surprise. One of the Indians who'd been draped over the side of his mount slid to the ground. From where he was, Jesse'd had the angle for a clean shot.

And he'd taken it.

Another Indian did an amazing mounted dive to pick up the fallen warrior and sling him over his horse. Hick fired a shot, but the Indian was high-tailing it south. Several other warriors raised their bows, lances, and rifles, yelling some sort of threats before they also disappeared to the south, raising a thick trail of dust into the air to mark their retreat.

"Ya thinkin' they'll be back?" Cooter asked.

"I don't know." Hick glanced into the ravine. Susannah hadn't moved. She stared at him, Colt Dragoon cradled in her arms.

Jesse picked his way across the rim to Hick's side. "That should be the end of them."

Hick whipped his head around. "What do you know about it?"

Jesse pulled back a half step. "I've learned a few things out here." He handed the rifle to Hick.

Taking a deep breath, Hick settled his anger and gave Cooter back his rifle. After all, Jesse had made a good shot—once he made one. "What have you learned?"

"Learned to pick out the leader and drop him if possible. The Indians don't like it when their leader falls. They won't be back today or tonight, but it'd be a good idea to keep traveling until dark."

There was nothing in his face or voice to make Hick doubt him, so he pushed away from the rim and slid to the bottom of the ravine.

"You two okay?" he asked Susannah.

"We're fine. Will they return?"

"Jesse says not. Not soon, anyway." He gave her brother a quick nod. "Says he dropped the leader, and so they'll stay away for a while, but we need to ride on."

"That sure were some shootin'," Cooter said. "Jesse here done slicked that Injun offen his horse easy as pluckin' a leech offen yer leg."

That was one way to put it. Hick turned to Jesse and worked to keep his voice even. "How did you know which one was the leader?"

"Last year I was down in Texas. I hired on with Nelson Story. We drove six hundred head of Texas longhorn cattle all the way from Texas to past Fort Laramie." He pointed northwest. "Maybe a week's ride from here. I learned plenty about Indians along the way."

"Had a lotta run ins with 'em?" Cooter asked.

"Some, but our scout was experienced. He taught me a lot." Jesse looked away, something like regret on his face.

Hick didn't ask any questions. If Jesse wanted them to know more, he'd tell them. But for the first time, Hick had a good feeling about having the ex-Confederate riding with them.

They'd been on the trail for more than two weeks—closer to three—and everything in Susannah ached. Hick was pushing them hard, but after the Indian attack, nobody complained. The horses were tired and so was Peaches. The mule had even protested being saddled that morning. Jesse had jumped on and ridden her through a little crow-hopping before she settled down. She'd been good as gold for Susannah since. Likely too tired to fuss.

The mountains were so close they could smell them now. The wind came down their heights carrying the tang of pine trees and hardwoods, scents she'd missed since reaching the prairie. Scents reminiscent of Georgia.

She shook her head. It was no time to be homesick for a place she could never return to. And didn't want to, truly. There was nothing left there but heartache and loss. Wyoming, on the other hand, held her husband, her brother, Bonnie, and Cooter.

Covering as much as thirty-five miles a day, according to Samuel, Susannah finally realized what an unrealistic goal finding Bonnie's aunt and uncle was. They'd seen no one since the Indian attack more than a week past. Not so much as an abandoned cabin, much less a trading post.

When Samuel had said they'd be isolated, she'd thought she'd understood what he meant, but she hadn't. Not really. The truth was settling in, even though she hadn't found a way to talk to the little girl about it yet.

The Indians worried her—more than a little. Jesse was sure they wouldn't follow so far, something about the size of the band and it more likely being a hunting party than a raiding or war party.

She lifted her chin and let the scented breeze bathe her face. There was still danger, of course. No place on earth was without its dangers. At least out here, there was no one to look down at her for her Southern tongue. No one to point fingers and whisper behind her back. And most of all...

Samuel was here.

They'd had few scattered minutes alone since they'd left the fort, but whenever they did, she couldn't deny the spark kindling between them. She welcomed it. She relished seeing it reflected in his eyes.

Soon, they'd be a real married couple with a cabin and the start of a ranch. They'd have a couple of ranch hands in Jesse and Cooter. And if Susannah couldn't bear a child of her own, they'd have Bonnie to complete their family. In all, Susannah was almost as satisfied as she was exhausted.

CHAPTER 33

H ICK RUBBED HIS EYES and looked again. He hadn't imagined it. A long, low cabin with a stone chimney at one end was nestled in the prettiest valley he'd seen in the foothills yet. An almost vertical wall of stone rose from behind it. Two large outbuildings, likely a barn and what looked like another cabin, squatted nearby, plus a few small buildings. A river flowed through the valley, parting grass that rippled in the breeze. A trio of horses and a pair of oxen grazed in a pasture.

Smoke rose from the chimney, making lazy swirls against the endless blue of the sky. Someone was home. Hick'd probably been spotted already, so he sat on Cobalt and waited for the others to crest the hill behind him. Cooter appeared first, pulling Rumpus to a halt beside Hick.

"Lookee there." The young man pushed his hat to the back of his head and scrubbed his brow. "I sure enough didn't plan on seein' that."

"Neither did I."

"Reckon they knows we're here?"

Hick shot a look around the open valley. "We'd be pretty hard to miss."

Susannah appeared with Jesse close behind. Her eyes rounded at the sight, and she stopped on Hick's other side. "People."

What must it look like to her? A tiny pocket of civilization, no doubt. She'd said nothing about the vastness of these lands, not a whisper of complaint. But he'd seen the tightness around her eyes since the Indian attack. He'd even felt an answering tightness more than once. If anything happened to her...

"I didn't expect that," Jesse said. "Hadn't heard of anyone homesteading this far out."

They'd learned that Jesse had been living hand-to-mouth in the area since leaving the cattle drive. Twice since they'd skirted around bands of Indians thanks to his knowledge and experience. He'd proved himself to be useful.

More importantly, he seemed to have come through the worst of the shakes and sickness brought on by abstaining from alcohol. A battle he seemed determined to win.

One of the cabin's two doors opened. A large man filled the opening, rifle held across his chest, ready to swing into action if need be.

"Looks like an invitation to approach to me." Hick nudged Cobalt with his heels.

"That there fella don't appear overly friendly," Cooter said.

"Keep your hands away from your guns, and we'll be fine." Hick kept the horse at a steady walk. The stallion tossed its head, nostrils flared, picking up Hick's unease.

They splashed across the river which came almost to Hick's stirrups, a river deep enough to last even in a dry summer. The set-up was as close to perfect as he'd ever hoped to find.

Too bad he hadn't gotten there first.

Hick stopped about ten yards from the man in the doorway. There was something almost familiar...

"Hick? Sam Hickman?" The man pointed beyond Hick toward Jesse. "And that can't be Trooper?"

He knew that voice, a rustic touch of Scottish burr thickening it.

"Will McKinnon?"

The man leaned his rifle against the cabin's wall and strode forward. "I can't believe it. How on earth did you find me out here?"

Hick dismounted and grasped the man's hand a moment before he was pulled into a bear hug by one of the few men as tall as himself.

"And who are these folks with..." His voice trailed off, eyes on Miss Bonnie.

A long moment stretched there in the beautiful valley.

"Uncle Willie?"

A gasp came from the doorway of the cabin, and then a woman streaked out. Red hair and calico were all Hick could grasp until she pulled Miss Bonnie from behind Susannah. Then it was a tangle of calico and matching red hair. Will joined them, wrapping his arms around both but staring over their heads at Hick.

"Her folks?" Will's voice was lower and rougher, if that were possible, the lines on his face saying he already knew the answer.

"Cooter and I buried them about halfway across Nebraska."

The woman sobbed but kept her hold on Miss Bonnie.

"Indians?" Will asked.

"Cholera," Susannah said. "It's a miracle Bonnie didn't succumb to it."

Will snapped his attention to Susannah, probably at her Southern drawl, but the woman said, "Thank you for bringing her to us."

Will cleared his throat. "You men put your animals in the corral on the other side of the barn, then we can make proper introductions." He held his hands out, offering to assist Susannah down, and she allowed it. "Come with us into the cabin, ma'am."

Hick stifled the flare of jealousy—which was ridiculous—at Will's hands on Susannah's waist. But he wasted no time stripping the horses and mule of their gear and stowing it in the barn before turning the animals into the grassy corral.

"How'd ya know him, Hick?" Cooter asked.

"We rode together in the war."

Jesse stiffened on the other side of Hick.

Hick cuffed him on the shoulder. "The war's over. We're in Wyoming to make a new start. Time to let the past be the past."

Strangely enough, he meant it. And not just for Jesse. It was time for Hick to let the past be the past too. The war had taken enough from him. It was time to let go and move forward.

Susannah had to clench her fingers together to keep from pulling Bonnie away from her aunt. What was wrong with her? She'd wanted to find Bonnie's family. She was elated for the little girl. So why did she have to fight back tears?

Sadie McKinnon was everything Susannah could have hoped Bonnie's aunt would be. She obviously loved Bonnie, refusing to release her. Although she'd lowered the girl to the ground, she kept Bonnie pressed against her side. And then in the cabin—part of which was a trading post—she introduced a young boy near Bonnie's age and a baby girl. Bonnie's eyes sparkled as she greeted her cousins.

Her real family.

Susannah's arms had never felt more empty.

She managed to smile and nod and make all the right responses until the men arrived. Introductions were made. Samuel and Will had fought together in the war. There was a brief pause when Jesse spoke, his words unmistakably Southern, although not as thickly accented as her own. But the awkwardness passed naturally and the conversation flowed. Sadie stood to make supper, and Susannah joined her in the side of the cabin that was taken up by the huge stone fireplace. There was no cast iron stove to cook on, but then, Susannah had been cooking over open fires for months. She poked at the glowing embers in the fireplace and added a split log from the stack nearby.

"I can't tell you what it means to me." Sadie filled a pot with water from a bucket and swung it over the rekindled fire. "My sister and her family were due here weeks ago. I knew something terrible had happened." She sniffed and dabbed at her eyes with the edge of her apron. "I hoped and prayed they'd still arrive, but every day the hope dwindled and the prayers seemed more hollow."

Susannah looked across the room at Bonnie, who was entertaining the baby. "She's a wonderful little girl." She glanced back at Sadie. "She'll be a good helper for you with baby Martha. And getting to know Liam will be good for her after losing her brothers." Her throat ached as the words left her.

Sadie gripped her arm. "Thank-you isn't enough. Not for what you've done."

"It was Cooter who never wavered in finding you." And Cooter would no doubt say it was a miracle that they'd discovered Bonnie's family. Perhaps he was right. It made little sense otherwise. "I had given up hope once we reached this territory. It's so…"

"Big?" Sadie smiled. "I know what you mean." She nodded toward the men. "I hope they are discussing a way for you to stay here, or at least close by. I can't tell you how good it is to see another white woman."

"You must trade with the Indians."

"We've had no problems with them." Sadie pulled a bowl from a shelf and sifted flour into it. "Will is cautious, even though they respect him. He trades fairly, of course, but they are a suspicious lot. I'm sure with good reason."

"How do you get supplies here?" There'd been no road, no hint of a trail, leading here.

"Will's partners, more men he knew in the war, arrange for mule trains to bring in shipments. They stay in the small cabin when they're here, but that's not often." She shook the nearly empty flour barrel. "We run out of things sometimes."

Sadie paused, bowl pressed to her middle. "Where will you go, now that you've delivered Bonnie to us?"

That was the question Susannah had been avoiding. She glanced at Samuel, and he met her eyes from across the room. To her surprise—and delight—he grinned at her. An unguarded grin that stripped years from his face and did delicious things to her middle.

"It was quite a risk, bringing your family out here." Hick pointed to the baby Miss Bonnie was tending. "What made you decide to do it?"

"It was just Sadie and Liam. Little Martha was born here, of course." Will ran his hands down his thighs. "I needed to get away. After the war..." His voice trailed off before he shot a sharp look at Hick. "Don't you remember me talking about it those last months? Seems it was all I did. I dreamed of getting out of the cavalry, into civilian clothes, and moving to these mountains. You probably got sick of hearing me talk about them."

Hick searched his memories—sliding past the most painful ones—and remembered. Had that been what pulled Hick west all along? Had it fueled his desire to see the mountains? Had he, somewhere deep inside, followed Will's dream to this very place?

Will leaned close and whispered, "Bonnie's folks were supposed to join us and help run the place. That's who the other cabin was for, just until we could get a larger one built." Will sat up straight and blinked. "Say, Hick, why don't you and your wife stay? The cabin's empty. You can come into business with me and—"

Hick raised his hand, cutting Will off. "I'm not a business person. I came here looking for a place to start a horse ranch, to raise fine horses for the cavalry."

"Always was about the horses for you." Will clouted him on the shoulder. "I should have known." He turned to Jesse and Cooter. "What about you two?"

"Oh, I figger Hick here will need a top hand with horses, and I'm thinkin' that's me," Cooter said.

"I'm not a businessman either," Jesse said. "Working horses is good for me."

Will slapped his palms on his knees. "Then why not set up for horses here? I doubt you could find better grazing or fresher water than we have. Plenty of grass to cut and dry for the winter too." He turned back to Hick. "What do you say? You can have the little cabin while we build something larger. The men can sleep in the barn until the weather turns. We should have another cabin up by then."

Hick glanced at Susannah, who couldn't have heard what they'd been saying, but who was looking straight at him anyway. Her lovely dark blue eyes were serious and maybe hopeful. He grinned and only barely suppressed the urge to yell across the long building that they were staying.

They'd made it.

They'd have good neighbors and added protection should the Indians prove hostile at some point. The land around them was made for raising horses. It was the perfect place to make their new start.

His wife returned his grin, and for the first time in years, everything felt right.

Susannah slipped her hand into her husband's. Samuel had asked her to walk with him after their supper of biscuits and gravy. For the first time in weeks, they didn't have to do anything to prepare to move in the morning. They were staying.

They were home.

Bonnie would be across the yard from her. Not hers to raise, as she'd secretly hoped, but not lost to her either. And Sadie had taken to Susannah as if they'd been best friends for years. The other woman hadn't said a word about her Georgia accent.

It was like a dream come true, but Cooter would no doubt give the credit to a higher source. Susannah sure would not argue with him.

Samuel tightened his grip on her fingers, then stopped and faced her, the width of his shoulders blocking the last of the sun's rays before it dove behind the mountains, crowning him in orange and gold. He took her other hand and gripped them both.

"Susannah." He glanced at the small cabin set back against the wall of stone. His Adam's apple bobbed in that endearing way she'd come to understand was Samuel at his most vulnerable before he turned back to her. "This is acceptable to you?"

He wasn't talking about the cabin or the valley or the McKinnons.

"More than acceptable."

"I believe we can make a good life here."

"I believe you're right. I like your friends. They're very nice."

Samuel rubbed his thumbs across the backs of her hands. "I owe Will a lot. More than I can tell you."

"Then don't. Don't speak of the war until and unless you wish to. If and when that happens, I will listen, and I won't cast judgment."

He shook his head. "It would be hard not to."

"As someone once said to me, 'You can't possibly understand.'"

He groaned. "I'm sorry for that."

"Don't be. You were correct, as you so often and irritatingly are." She smiled to remove any sting from her words. "I couldn't see past my own pain from the war back then." Was it truly just months ago? So much had happened.

"We were a couple of the walking wounded, weren't we." It wasn't a question, so it didn't need an answer.

"The key is that we *were*. Now we *are.*" Susannah dropped his hands and cupped his rough cheeks in her palms. "Now, we will raise our horses. We will build our future." She moved her hands behind his neck."

She looked away from the raw emotion in his eyes to the darkening landscape around them, fighting a sudden onset of shyness. "Our ranch will need a name."

"Something majestic sounding, I think." The pride of ownership was strong in his voice.

"To reflect the land and the horses we'll raise."

They both angled slightly to watch Cobalt and Sky in the corral, the stallion tossing its head. "We have a great start with those two. Cooter, Jesse, and I will round up wild mares once we get more corrals built and another barn."

"They are our beginning, Cobalt and Sky." She sucked in a quick breath. "That's it."

"What?" His brow crinkled.

"Cobalt Skies. The majestic name for our ranch."

His smile flamed the slow burn that had started inside her when they'd left the McKinnons' cabin.

"Are you content to stay here and build Cobalt Skies with me? No more dreams of Oregon?"

"I don't need Oregon when I have you."

He pulled her closer, his chin resting on the top of her head. "We'll raise more than just horses here. We'll raise a family."

Susannah pulled back and looked at him, hating to ruin the moment, but he needed to know.

"What is it?" he asked.

"Abel and I were married for three years. In that time, there were no children." She blinked back the threatening tears. "He never fully regained his health after prison, but what if it was me? What if I can't—?"

He pressed a finger to her lips. "If there's one thing you and I are good at, Mrs. Hickman, it's attracting strays. If we don't make a family the old-fashioned way, I have no doubt we'll find our family." He chuckled. "Or more likely, it'll find us."

She had married an exceptional man.

"But if you don't mind." He pulled her close again. "I wouldn't mind trying the old-fashioned way first."

His arms came around her then, his lips meeting hers for a long, satisfying moment before he slipped one arm behind her knees and lifted her against his chest, striding toward the little cabin.

Toward their future—together.

Author's Historical Notes

During Sherman's march to the sea, the Confederacy moved many Union prisoners from Andersonville and other prisons to temporary camps. The one at Blackshear, Georgia, was nothing more than an open camp with guards around it. No fence, no walls, and no real shelters, yet it housed at least 5,000 prisoners, most of them near starvation. The townspeople, having little food of their own at that point in November, 1864, nevertheless shared what they had with the prisoners. A number of prisoners were able to escape, despite the perimeters being heavily guarded.

Quantrill's Raiders were a band of guerrilla fighters—what we'd call terrorists today—not connected to the Confederate Army. William Clarke Quantrill joined the Missouri Confederate troops early in the war but served with them for only a short time before gathering his own army. It was the skirmishes between Quantrill and the Union that prompted Brigadier General Thomas Ewing, Union Army, to issue Order Number 11 on August 25, 1863, which exiled everyone in Bates, Jackson, Cass, and Vernon Counties from their homes. They were not allowed to return until after the war was over, although many never did.

The wagon trains were starting to wind down after the Civil War as the railroad expanded and finally connected the two coasts, but there were still wagon trains heading west into the 1870s.

There was a cholera outbreak in Omaha in 1867, but it actually happened in the fall of that year. I moved it to the spring to work with the storyline. Dr. James H. Peabody and Dr. J.R. Conkling are true historical figures who helped prevent the disease from getting out of control, saving the young town from certain disaster. John M. Bury was the first victim, and he was a tenant of the Thomas Finan boarding house. Dr. Peabody contracted cholera during the outbreak but survived.

Colonel Gibbon was in charge of Fort Kearny, Nebraska, in 1867. The prairie having little lumber, the forts were open without a stockade of any sort at the time of this story. The objective of the prairie forts was to keep the peace and allow westward expansion. One can argue if those objectives were within the rights of the growing nation of the United States, but it is history as it happened.

Hell on Wheels was the name given to the towns that sprang up when the railroad reached a new end as it spread across the country. The first was set up north of Fort Kearny, Nebraska, in 1866. The towns - consisting largely of tents and prefabricated panels that could be disassembled and reset easily - would remain until the tracks were far enough along that it was worth packing everything up and moving again. Besides saloon keepers, gamblers, and prostitutes, there were also speculators who moved in with the hopes that the towns would survive once the railroad moved on.

The first recorded cattle drive into Wyoming was accomplished by Nelson Story in 1866. He and his cowboys moved a herd of six hundred longhorns from Texas past Fort Laramie, Wyoming, and up along the Bozeman Trail.

Like the fictional Sam Hickman, many ex-Civil War soldiers made their way west to start a new life. Some turned outlaw, but many made a positive mark on the expansion of the Union.

Reviews are Golden

Reviews are the lifeblood of authors. Leaving a review on **Amazon**, **Goodreads**, and/or **BookBub** means that more readers will find our books! Reviews can be long or short - your honest opinion of the book. Shout-outs on any social media platforms also help!

ABOUT PEGG THOMAS

Pegg Thomas lives in Michigan's Upper Peninsula with Michael, her husband of *mumble* years. She creates American stories with real history and fictional characters inspired by her ancestors who immigrated here in the early 1600s.

Pegg won the 2019 FHL Readers' Choice Award for novellas, was a double-finalist for the 2019 ACFW Carol Award for novellas, and a finalist for the 2019 ACFW Editor of the Year. She was a finalist in the 2021 FHL Readers' Choice Award for novellas. Pegg won the 2022 Selah Award for historical romance and placed 2nd with her second entry. She was a finalist for the 2023 FHL Selah Award, placed 2nd in the 2024 Selah Award, and won the 2024 Will Rogers Silver AND Bronze Medallion Awards. Pegg spent 3 ½ years as the managing editor of Smitten Historical Romance.

PeggThomas.com
Facebook
Goodreads
BookBub
Amazon
Newsletter signup